RICKY FLEET
HELLSPAWN SENTINEL

HELLSPAWN SERIES - BOOK 3

BRICK, NEW JERSEY

2016

HELLSPAWN: SENTINEL – Book Three in the Hellspawn Series
©2016 Ricky Fleet
First Edition
Edited by Christina Hargis Smith
Cover art by Jeffrey Kosh Graphics
Published by Optimus Maximus Publishing, LLC
www.optimusmaximuspublishing.com

ISBN-10: 1-944732-15-2
ISBN-13: 978-1-944732-15-8

DEDICATED TO

I am dedicating Hellspawn Sentinel, book 3 in the series to my magnificent beta readers: Denise, Joan, Stephanie, and Maura. You are the glue that holds indie authors together, the last bastion of defence against a typo or plot error. I truly value your time in helping me and I am honoured to call you all my friends.

Acknowledgements

As always, my wife and children have been fantastic through the whole process. Words of encouragement and steaming mugs of tea have kept my engine burning as I tried to guide my flawed family across the devastation of southern England.

My sister Donna who has supported me at every step. Or should I say bullying me to hurry up so she can see what happens next to my plucky band.

My editor and publisher Christina, without whom none of this would be possible.

All the amazing social media groups who have helped to support me: All Things Zombie with Jeffrey, Zombie Book of the Month Club with Christy and Shaun, and, of course, the wonder that is The Living Army. A group of amazing people led by Mr R.R. Haywood. They've welcomed me into the pack and made me feel like part of the family.

Lastly to my readers. Never in my wildest dreams could I imagine that you would like my story enough to want more. Your friendship and messages of support mean the world to me.

Thank you.

HELLSPAWN

SENTINEL

BOOK THREE IN THE HELLSPAWN SERIES

A Novel by
Ricky Fleet

OPTIMUS MAXIMUS PUBLISHING
Brick, New Jersey
2016

PROLOGUE

The group of survivors had suffered their first loss and the heartache was overwhelming. Paige had died to save the lives of those she had come to love. It was a sacrifice as old as time. To some extent, they were all unprepared for the death of one of their own. The battles and adversity they had faced had given them a sense of destiny, a subconscious belief that they would make it unharmed and thrive in the world as everything else crumbled to dust.

The poison that had been introduced with the rescue of Debbie and the discovery of Mike had been removed like a tumor by the cowardly attack that had cost Paige her life. The wound of the removal would be with them forever, only healing with the divine retribution that would come as the two would-be murderers drew their final breath and descended to the darkest corners of Hell.

Each member sat in silence as the burning devastation receded from view; crying, hugging, lacking the words to comfort each other as they all tried to make sense of the loss and the fact that her smile would never again brighten their days. The soldiers knew the feeling all too well from their fallen brethren on the killing fields of the Middle-East. Despite their acquaintance only lasting a single day, they both wrestled with inner turmoil. As the trained professionals, they analyzed their every action for mistakes

3

that could have caused the death. No amount of self-reproach could erase the truth; it was just a cruel twist of fate that caused the shell casing to lodge in the assault rifle at the wrong moment.

The outskirts of Chichester burned, ignited by the explosion of the huge gas container that fed the cities heating fuel. In one fell stroke, the group had destroyed tens of thousands of the Hellspawn. Knowledge of the remaining population of sixty million and their new propensity to eat anything living marred the sense of achievement. The path ahead was clear, reach the sanctuary of the sprawling, impenetrable castle or die trying. Nothing less would be acceptable. Their perilous journey was only going to get harder.

CHAPTER ONE

"**W**e got the bitch, she is really dead!" exclaimed Debbie, barely able to suppress a gleeful cheer.

"Shut your fucking mouth!" Mike hissed and pulled her further behind the small hospital radio building. In the day it had broadcast from morning until night, soothing tunes and talk that aided in the recuperation of the hospital patients.

The chaos of the escape had given them a window of opportunity. From the dark shadows of the shrubbery they watched the vehicles exit in convoy. The forlorn faces in the seats gave Debbie a strange sexual thrill and she found her hand rubbing between her legs, teasing the orgasm that was close to taking her. Mike looked over and grabbed her hand, pulling it away roughly.

"This isn't the time!" he growled quietly. He felt the same rush, the sense of power that had accompanied the assault and death. There would be time to celebrate later, if they ever made it to safety.

"Sorry," she replied, pulling a pouting face that Mike ignored.

The line of dead stretched out for what seemed like an eternity. Men, women, and children all shuffled past for nearly fifteen minutes, until the whole city had practically emptied in pursuit of the last remaining living flesh.

"We give it another five minutes, just in case," Mike said to Debbie who nodded.

"How many do you think there were?" she asked with wonder in her voice.

"Tens of thousands," Mike answered. He had to admit it had been quite the spectacle, and this was only one small city in a country of huge metropolises. They stopped talking in whispers and stood up, still concealed but feeling more confident.

"I would love to see Peter's face right now," she said, wringing her hands with the delicious thought.

"Are you a complete idiot?" Mike demanded and grabbed her by her top, shaking her.

"What do you mean? Why are you being so horrible to me?" Debbie complained and started crying.

"We didn't achieve anything, other than pissing off the very people that would have happily left us for dead. Who gives a shit if we managed to kill your ex's new bit of pussy?" he almost shouted in her face.

"I..." she hesitated, unable to argue with his assessment. She had been so lost in the euphoria of striking back at Peter that she had forgotten the main point of the attack was to kill Braiden and Kurt, the two people who had insulted and physically assaulted them both. Now that they were off and running, with a score to settle that would only be sated with blood, she felt a pang of nerves in the pit of her stomach.

"See, we are worse off than if we had just waited for a better opportunity," he complained, furious at how it had all gone so wrong. Now they were abandoned and on foot in the middle of the city. Only the mass exodus of the zombie occupants would give them a chance of survival.

"You were the one who missed Kurt, I knocked Braiden out cold." She scowled and Mike backhanded her, sending her sprawling out from the bushes and into the daylight.

"You watch your mouth. If you had been watching me, you would have known when to hit them!" he said and held out a hand for her to take.

"Fuck off!" she cursed and struggled to rise through her swimming vision.

"Don't be like that, I'm sorry. You just mouth off and make me angry sometimes," he apologized and helped her up. The irony of her new relationship was completely lost on Debbie, who was unable to see the similarities to how she had treated Peter for years. Even if she had the empathy to understand, it was unlikely she could ever feel guilty about it anyway.

"Mike, we have to go," gasped Debbie as she wiped the blood from her lips.

Around the side of the building came the slower zombies; the ones that were unable to keep up with the main horde who surged out of the city. Each and every one was in pieces, missing arms and legs, or a combination of the two. Some were merely hollowed out trunks with arms, viscera trailing in place of legs. They advanced by dragging themselves over the tarmac like a slab of cheese on a grater, leaving a smeared trail on the rough surface. Others stood on their one good leg, then flopped forwards with a slap, breaking their bones in a repeated maneuver to move toward their prey. Pulped faces groaned and eventually they would crack their skull open and kill themselves, but at the moment they were still deadly. Mike and Debbie hastily retreated.

It couldn't have worked out better for the two outcasts; the city was deserted apart from the occasional cadaver who they just rushed around with a fair amount of ease. Their weapons would keep them safe if they needed to fight, but they decided that there was no point in endangering themselves unnecessarily.

"This is so eerie," Debbie whispered unnecessarily, in awe of the vacant streets and total absence of sound.

"I'm a little spooked myself if I'm honest," Mike replied quietly. It was not the time for false bravado. The loneliness they both felt was infectious and they longed to be back with the family, however bizarre that may have seemed to them. Even the presence of groups of zombies was a type of company, regardless of the threat. The abandoned streets were littered with the remains of the zombie outbreak. Cars ploughed into buildings with sections collapsed from the spreading fire. Windows and doors were smashed on nearly every abode or shop where people had sought a hiding place, without success. The ground was awash with the once living remnants of the population, flesh, blood, limbs, and bodies were scattered everywhere. Travelling through the more rural areas with the others had left them ill prepared for the visual assault they were facing. It was as if they were walking down the main shopping precinct in Hell. Where once people had hustled and bustled with frenetic energy to satisfy their consumer urges, now the shops lay unattended. Filled with goods that would never be sold in currency that was now worthless, they called out to them from their old life. Jewelry shops with millions of pounds' worth of gold and diamonds on display were untouched, the shiny baubles worth less than a tin of beans or bottle of water.

"We need to find some better gear, there is a camping shop just east of the center of town," Debbie informed Mike. The cold was biting into them and though they wore thick layers, the material was not ideal for cross country travel.

"Ok, lead the way," he urged and followed, casting wary glances back in case their mortal enemies had decided to follow. All was quiet except for the lone walkers that had not heeded the call of the hospital and now trailed the pair.

They reached the shop and the door opened with a jangle of an overhead bell mounted on the door frame.

They winced and listened for any signs of movement for a few seconds, before deciding the way was clear.

"We won't have time to get our stuff before those three are on us," Debbie cautioned.

"Don't worry, the others showed us how to handle them. I hide behind this clothes rack and you act as bait. Simple," he explained and she wrinkled her nose at being termed 'bait' for undead freaks.

They stripped out of their outer clothing and selected lighter, but much better insulated thermal clothing. Debbie fitted her life preserver again, knowing that it had already saved her life once in the farm's garden.

"They are here," she said and Mike ducked into cover as the trio of festering flesh lumbered into view. She let out a quiet whistle, only wishing to ensure she had the attention of the closest zombies, not any that may be lurking hidden in the vicinity. Their milky, dripping eyes turned to her and they lurched through the shop doorway, smashing the pane of glass and slashing themselves deeply. The noise would attract anything close and Debbie's fear jumped ten notches as the bell rung, announcing their new guests. Mike was fast as lightning and hacked at the three undead before they could attack Debbie. The last one sprayed her with dark green, stinking blood and she wiped madly at her face to get the liquid off.

"Why did you do that?" she spluttered, spitting on the floor in case any had entered her mouth.

"Did what? Saved your ass?" He smirked at her discomfort.

"Ugh, now I have to change again. Just keep your eye out for any more that heard the glass breaking. Why you didn't just open the door before they get here I don't know," she complained and started undressing.

"Well fuck me, I'm sorry. I didn't realize I was your fucking butler," he grunted, flipping her turned back the bird. If they had been in a safer spot she would have received a second slap.

They were left undisturbed for the rest of their looting spree. Footwear was swapped for more solid hiking boots, their trainers topping the pile of disposed clothes. They gathered tents, sleeping bags, ground rolls for padding, and two heavy duty rucksacks. Looking at the darkening sky, Mike took two waterproof ponchos from the rack and pushed them into the bags as well. In the glass display case there were assorted flint sticks, multi tools, knives, and other useful equipment that they crammed into their pockets, just in case. Their journey would be overland, though nothing further than a mile from what was once called civilization. The chances of them needing the maps and compasses was remote, but why take the chance. They left the shop, kitted like they were headed to the top of Mount Everest.

"You look so goofy," Mike joked, laughing at her ensemble.

"You are dressed in exactly the same clothes!" she answered, slapping him on the shoulder.

"Hey, would you look at that!" Mike pointed to a couple of bikes that had been dropped in the middle of the street.

"I'd rather cycle than be on foot. I want to get out of here," she agreed and they climbed onto the machines.

"It didn't do the two losers who dropped them any good, though," Mike added, considering the benefits of a quiet and stealthy escape as opposed to bombing down the street on the bikes.

"The place would have been crawling with them. We may as well be the last people on Earth, it will be fine," Debbie reasoned.

"We need some food and drink too," he said and they set off, the rubber singing on the tarmac as they sped along.

"There is a small convenience store about half a mile away, we could try there. It's either that or we have to raid the supermarket, and I don't think that will be empty..." She shivered, imagining the aisles and their new decaying shoppers, wandering the rows forever, unable to buy what they sought.

Debbie slowed to a stop and laid her bike down outside the shop. The entrance was open and they approached the dark interior carefully. Mike picked up a jar of raspberry jam that had rolled outside.

"Let's see if anyone's home," he said and threw it as hard as he could through the doorway. The glass smashed, but the sticky contents dulled the noise so that it would only disturb anything lurking within.

"I don't hear anything," Debbie whispered as she strained to catch the smallest shuffle or groan.

"Ok, just grab water and dry stuff, biscuits and crackers," Mike directed and they filled a separate travelling bag with the goods.

"I would give anything for some meat," Debbie complained, longingly. She rifled through packets of pre-packed chicken and ham, tossing them onto the floor as her frustration grew into anger. Foil sealed green and brown mold had replaced the moist and tender contents since the refrigerators had stopped working.

"I bet you would," Mike joked lewdly, squeezing her bum.

"Fuck off!" Debbie said and pushed him away, "You said it wasn't the time, remember?"

"Don't you get smart with me, you whore," Mike sneered through clenched teeth, "I say when it's time, do you understand?"

"Yeah ok, Mike, whatever you say," she husked, turning to sit on the edge of the nearest shelf. She pulled at the waistband of her jeans and knickers, dropping them to the floor. Biting her lip seductively, one hand roamed

11

downwards, parting the moist lips with her fingers. Although she feared Mike, she was drawn to his power like a moth to a flame. She needed him, craved his attention, whether it was positive or negative. They were bonded by the blood of others.

"It's time," Mike said, stepping forward with a leer on his face.

CHAPTER TWO

The Foxhounds pulled up and stopped at the train station in Boxgrove. Jonesy climbed out and shouldered his rifle, aiming and firing at the small group of zombies that had left the gardens of the trackside homes. DB jumped down and covered the rear, picking off targets with quietened reports.

"All clear," said Jonesy, scanning the area and seeing nothing more that posed an immediate danger.

The survivors stepped down from the vehicles and Jonesy and DB could only give them pats on the back, a hollow platitude that couldn't assuage their pain. Kurt smiled weakly at the gesture and walked over to the others in the lead Foxhound. Braiden didn't follow and, instead, walked off a short way and stood waiting for a zombie in the distance to arrive. The hatred and grief was unlike any he had felt before, greater even than the leaving of his mother. His feelings of abandonment were diminishing with each passing day as his environment matured him beyond his scant years. He had been with Debbie a matter of days and would now kill her if he had the chance. His poor mother had suffered at the hands of a similar individual for thirteen years before escaping.

In a way, by nurturing Paige through her mental break, he had gained an appreciation of the love that people can have in life. It had served to cement the bond with his new family and pull him back from the brink of self-destruction. Left unfettered, he would have likely experienced a mad descent into the pit of anger and spontaneous violence just like his true kin; Lennie Sullivan.

The corpse was reaching for Braiden, but he felt no fear. All he saw were the images of Mike and Debbie superimposed on the rotting face, fueling his anger. He swung a kick and swept the legs sideways from under the zombie. It hit the ground hard and Braiden gave it no chance to recover, stamping repeatedly and breaking all four limbs to incapacitate the monster. It squirmed on the ground, unable to right itself. Like a toppled beetle, it thrashed the flopping extremities and chomped on nothing. Standing over it, Braiden's blazing heat receded a little and the zombie was just that again; a poor victim of the plague of dead. It wasn't his enemy in the truest sense of the word; it felt no joy or victory in the conquests of the living. It was primal, an instinct that any remaining scientists the world over were trying to understand. Instead of attacking it in a frenzy, he calmly knelt and pushed its skull down by the forehead, stilling it. The screwdriver entered its right ear and pierced the brain. Its eyes rolled, now truly dead.

Braiden stood and turned back to the other survivors, jumping in shock when he saw John only a few paces away.

"You alright, lad?" John asked with genuine concern, "I was just making sure you didn't get hurt."

Braiden shrugged, struggling to find any words that would articulate the conflicting emotions that battled in his mind. John took another step forward and placed a hand on Braiden's shoulder, trying to get him to meet his gaze.

"I know how much you loved her, Son. We all loved her," John said, voice breaking with sorrow.

"Yeah," Braiden whispered, looking directly at him with tears brimming.

"She will always live on in our hearts, her warmth and kindness made us better people, myself included," John stated, his own tears threatening to break the dam of his inner will, "You too, I think."

"She was my friend..." Braiden managed, before a heavy sob silenced his words.

"I know she was, nothing will ever change that," John commiserated, squeezing the young boy's shoulder in support.

"You don't understand," Braiden whispered, looking at his dirty shoes.

"I think I do. Do you think I didn't notice how you cared for her, how you fed her while your food went cold? How you cleaned her and made sure she was warm and comfortable. Who was it that came out in darkest night, through the dead in the garden and woods to come and guide us in? You did. You saved her life just as surely as I did that night." John was crying now, his strong façade dropping away and revealing a tenderness that Braiden didn't realize existed.

"I'm really going to miss her," Braiden said, wiping at the flowing tears.

"Me too, Son. She became like a daughter to me," John explained.

"And a sister to me," Braiden added, looking at John once more.

"She loved you especially, she told me that," John said with sincerity.

"Really?" Braiden smiled through his tears.

"Absolutely. Not only because you are brave and loving, but because you saved that damned mutt too!" John pointed over to Honey, who was sat watching the others.

"Her name's Honey," Braiden laughed at John's good natured jibe.

"She picked a lovely name," John declared, his mind playing the first moments of her return from her catatonia. "It's my fault."

"What? Her choosing the name Honey?" Braiden asked, confused at the look of misery that was washing over Johns face.

"No... her dying," John placed a hand over his eyes and shuddered with the force of his sobbing, "I should have come with you, protected you all from those fucking animals!"

"It's ok, Grandad. You couldn't have known, we were all just desperate to get away from there and they took their chance." Braiden was now the one providing comfort. He waited for the rebuke for not calling him John, but it didn't come.

John caught the wary look and said, "You call me Grandad as much as you like, lad, you are my grandson and I am as proud of you as anyone could ever be. I'm so sorry I have been so mean to you and the way I have spoken to you at times, I failed you..." The sobbing returned and Braiden was amazed to find himself taking John in his embrace. They wept for their shared loss, supporting each other through the grief.

"Never. You have saved our lives over and over. You hold us all together, like an elder," Braiden said and then realized that he had just insulted John's age, "I meant..."

John chuckled and pulled away, "I take it as a compliment, don't worry."

They wiped away the moisture from their damp cheeks and composed themselves. There would be more upset, they could be sure of that. But at least they had taken the first tentative steps towards acceptance.

"Grandad?" Braiden inquired.

"What's up?" John replied as they made their way back to the rest of the survivors.

"If we ever find them, you won't try and stop me will you?" Braiden asked, concerned about the response.

"Son, if we ever find them, I promise I will be first in line to help you!" John uttered with conviction. He had made a mistake in trying to maintain morality in the new world. Those ways were gone. Retribution would satisfy justice and, as had been proven with Phil and HB's gang, protect the lives of the weak and innocent.

"Dad. Braiden. You guys ok?" Kurt asked them.

"We will be, not yet a while. Give us time," John said quietly and Kurt gave them each a quick hug.

Honey was confused and bewildered. She wandered between Peter and Braiden, sniffing Paige's scent, but unable to find her mistress. She jumped into the first Foxhound, nose smelling every corner and searched within, then jumped down and ran to the rear door of the second. She climbed aboard and repeated the search. She leapt down and ran a complete circle around both vehicles, her whines growing in intensity as her anxiety grew.

"Here, girl," Braiden called and the yellow furred member of the group came over and started nuzzling at his outstretched hand, "Mummy's gone, but I will look after you now. We all will, ok?"

Braiden stroked and talked to her, calming her down. Her eyes still searched the distance and her ears pricked at the slightest noise in case it was her lost friend returning.

"Where's Peter?" asked Kurt, seeing that he was not with them.

"He's still out. Christina is looking him over, but I think it's just been too much for him," Sarah sympathized. Kurt took her in his arms and pulled Sam in who was looking lost. They stood there for long seconds, enjoying the contact and the warmth of the hug.

Gloria was talking to Jodi who longed to help the group.

17

"I wish there was something I could do," Jodi said to the old teacher.

"There is, my dear. You have to be strong in their place while they come to terms with what has happened. They will not be thinking clearly and that can be dangerous. Would you do that for me?" Gloria offered, knowing that Jodi would feel guilty until the day she died because of the actions of her ex-partner.

"I will watch over them all, you can count on me," Jodi proclaimed and Gloria smiled.

"Thank you," Gloria took her hand and gave it a squeeze. Jodi's mouth moved but nothing came out, she wanted to say something and Gloria waited patiently while she got the words straight in her mind.

"Why would he do something like this?" Jodi whispered, finally able to ask the question that was eating her up inside.

"I don't know, sweetheart," Gloria answered honestly, "This horror has given everyone the opportunity to become what they have always yearned to be. With no consequences, evil has taken hold in people hearts."

"I can't believe I never saw it. I am such a fool," Jodi bowed her head in shame.

"Nonsense. People are adept at hiding their inner desires from those closest to them. You can't blame yourself," Gloria tried to placate Jodi, knowing it was probably hopeless.

"But I do, and always will," Jodi said and started to cry. Gloria passed the gun to DB who was feeling awkward at the strong emotions that were on display. She gently held his massive hand and he felt a glow spread into his heart. His family was almost undoubtedly gone, but helping these strangers gave him a purpose. It was the only thing that would stop him putting a gun in his mouth and ending it all.

"Come here," Gloria embraced her, "I think God has a plan for us all. I know that seems a bizarre thing to say, but the events I have witnessed and the trials we have overcome have given me hope."

"If that's the case, then I hope God gives me a chance at paying him back for the pain he has caused. My feelings blinded me to what he was, I see it now," Jodi admitted. Her guilt and sense of responsibility convinced Gloria that she would prove to be a valuable member of the family.

"Your feelings and loyalty will be what gets us through this mess. We are lucky to have you with us," Gloria said with heartfelt honesty.

"So lucky that one of you is dead," Jodi said with self-derision, "I wish it could have been me out there. It would have been right that I was the one to fall for Mike's betrayal."

"Paige laid down her life to save Kurt, Braiden, and yourself. Her love gave us all strength. Now you have to honor that sacrifice by making sure this group survives, do you understand?" Gloria asked.

"Yes. Sorry for the self-pity," Jodi apologized and wiped away her tears. She clenched her bat tight and laid it on her shoulder, ready to swing for the bleachers if anything came close to her new friends.

"You have a way with people," DB said, smiling broadly.

"I try to make them see their true qualities. Like you, brave and selfless, risking your life for total strangers," Gloria replied, stroking his cheek in a motherly gesture.

"I'm sorry I couldn't save your friend," he said, unable to shake the sense of responsibility. His massive frame dwarfed the kindly teacher, but he felt small in her presence; like a child, wanting to hear her words of reassurance and love.

"You saved us, darling, don't forget that. We will always be there for you, no matter what the future brings," Gloria stated with conviction.

"Thank you, ma'am," DB replied and handed the shotgun back to her.

Jonesy and Kurt had walked onto the train crossing, looking up and down the tracks. The station was deserted and the sign saying 'Boxgrove' swayed on the chains in the afternoon breeze. Scattered across the floor was hundreds of pounds in coins, spilled from the broken ticket machine, glinting in the hazy sunlight. Whoever had taken the chance to break into the machine would have quickly discovered that money was useless. They couldn't bribe the zombies to spare them, only lament their worship of the altar of wealth as they were eaten.

"What do you think? The tracks are the most direct route to Ford, and then the castle," Kurt asked the soldier who was analyzing as many angles as he could think of.

"I like the protection the fenced off railway line gives us, I admit. I just don't like the fact we will be on a course with little chance to deviate," Jonesy answered, scratching his chin; a gesture that Kurt thought only existed in fiction.

"What do you mean, deviate?" Kurt wondered.

"Those ditches by the side fences may be too much for the Foxhounds. If we come across a group of them on the track, we will have to backtrack for miles," Jonesy replied.

Kurt gave it some thought. They would be unlikely to find a route to take any roads to where they were going that weren't solid with cars and monsters. Overland would be safer for the group, but he would regret losing the mobility and firepower of the armored troop carriers.

"I think we should take the chance. Slow and steady is the way forward. If we encounter resistance, we head back and find a place to lay low while we plan another route," Kurt suggested. "What do you think?"

"Ok, let's do it. If you drive the lead vehicle, I will ride the gun in case we encounter resistance," Jonesy said and they walked back to the others to explain the plan. They all felt relieved that, for now, they wouldn't be on foot. Kurt started the engine and familiarized himself with the clunky controls; the machines were built for combat, not comfort.

"Everyone ready?" Kurt asked his passengers.

They all answered except Peter who was still stretched out in the back. Kurt reached out of the window and stuck his thumb up in a 'ready to go' gesture and Jodi flashed him, signaling she was ready. He accelerated and mounted the rail with a lurching jolt, straddling the metal runners. The tires crunched onwards, rolling over the ballast that supported the weight of the train carriages. The setting sun was in front of them, guiding them down the line like a spotlight. It stretched on for long miles, a strange road that could be their salvation, or their doom. Kurt knew that they needed a base that would be difficult to breach; it would buy them time to adjust and plan for the future. The one thought that worried him every second of the day was that the castle had been built to survive sieges by thousands of soldiers in bygone years. It was designed to be impenetrable, so how they would get inside with the dead on their heels was a huge obstacle to be overcome.

"Kurt, we need to think about stopping soon. The sun will be down and we need to organize a watch during the night," Jonesy called down from the gunnery turret.

"I was thinking the same thing," Kurt called back. The sun was dropping slowly but surely into the horizon, and the darkness was nowhere to be cruising around in. They had made good progress of several miles unencumbered, which would mean they would arrive at Ford in less than an hour at their carefully slow pace.

"Are we going to sleep in here tonight, Dad?" Sam asked. It would be cramped but safe, so he wasn't concerned.

Kurt was about to answer, until rounding a bend, he saw the first train on the tracks. Across the country there would be thousands of unmoving carriages, stranded with the lack of electricity. Kurt stopped the vehicle and let the engine idle, looking around for any signs of life.

"What's up, Kurt?" Jonesy asked, looking for a threat that would cause the pause.

"I'm thinking we might be better off spending the night inside the train. The seats would make passable beds and we are high enough from the ground to be safe," he replied over his shoulder.

"Why have we stopped?" DB shouted over the engine noise from the second Foxhound.

"Bedding down in there! Thoughts?" Jonesy yelled back, pointing at the train.

"Sounds good to me, high ground advantage if anything comes for us," DB called back, seeing the same tactical benefits as Kurt had done.

"Ok, Kurt, roll up alongside and we will see what's inside," Jonesy banged on the top of the vehicle for him to advance.

Kurt moved slowly, guided the Foxhound over onto the other tracks to skirt the waiting carriages. The darkened windows captured the reflected light of the sun, blinding them to the danger. The noise was their confirmation, the hammering on the glass a dead giveaway to what lurked within.

"I didn't expect to see anyone," Jonesy mused to himself, "Why would they stay inside?"

Kurt had heard him talking and assumed he was asking him, "We didn't lose electricity for a couple of days, maybe the driver saw the shit that was going down and backed it out here between stations to wait it out?"

"Maybe… but why would you just stay in there and die of dehydration rather than climbing down and trying to escape?" Jonesy asked.

Kurt squinted and managed to see past the reflected glare. The stones of the track had been disturbed and there were slimy smears up and down the carriages, like green snail trails. The dead had been here, hoping to feed on the trapped commuters, until they succumbed and the food went bad.

"Look, blood on the side. We had walkers here," Kurt explained and Jonesy nodded to himself without answering.

Jonesy was weighing their options and Kurt waited patiently for the plan. The standard carriages were now filled with mobile corpses and there would be no telling if there would be anywhere clean enough to sleep.

"Right, we will clear the first class section if they haven't worked out how to use door handles. Most of the time it's empty because it was so damned expensive. DB!" Jonesy called to his friend.

"Whassup?"

"Jump down and uncouple the front carriage. Pull the pin and we will pull that carriage forward a few feet. Kurt get to the front and back it up," Jonesy instructed and the Foxhound grumbled forward.

DB ran down the side of the train, cautious of the blood stains. The underside of the train was totally exposed and nothing could be seen underneath or on the other side. They were alone, except the ones trapped inside. Jonesy was securing a chain to the front end of the driver's carriage that also housed the three first class cabins, comprising eight seats in each with a privacy curtain to keep out unwanted attention. DB wrestled the steel pin from the train coupling and climbed back into the second vehicle, covering Jonesy where he was exposed. Jonesy whistled and Kurt slowly crept forward until the chain pulled taut. The wheels juddered and the rubber spun on the loose stone of the track. With a grinding protest from rusting axles, the train was separated and DB was the center of attention from those inside, eager for fresh meat. Some of the undead causing a commotion were unharmed, but others had been horrifically mauled. They must have fallen prey to the first to die, running around in horror.

Trapped with monsters pursuing them and prevented from escape by more of the wailing dead. DB crossed himself in sympathy at the poor people.

"Look alive!" Jonesy called and DB looked away, leaving the damned passengers and their eternal journey.

"What's the plan for the ones in there?" Kurt asked as he climbed out of the driver's seat.

"DB is going to open the door from the roof of the Foxhound. They will come pouring out and fall onto the tracks. From that height they will probably break something but we kill them quick before they can recover. Sound good?" Jonesy explained and Kurt laughed.

"Good? No. Necessary? Yes," he answered.

"Everyone get ready. Choppers only, but I will cover you. DB, when I say, pull that door open. Tell her to get you close and then back away when you give the signal!" Jonesy called and through the rear doors the survivors piled out, arming themselves and standing at a safe distance from the carriage.

Jodi pulled forward as instructed and DB climbed on the roof. He reached out, pulled the door and the first zombie tumbled out, surprised by the suddenly missing barrier. DB grabbed it by the hair and smashed it repeatedly into the roof of the vehicle until the skull spilled its contents. Jodi had backed up and the rest of the dead reached the open doorway. They fell the seven feet and landed hard on the other rail, breaking spines and bones. The others used the opportunity to vent some rage after the events of the morning, and the dead were butchered without mercy. The pile of bodies lay leaking their fluids on the graveled ground and the looks of enjoyment on her family's faces made Gloria's heart ache with sorrow.

"During all the horror, the dead have lost their dignity. Could we please use the stones and give them a proper burial?" she asked the group. It was a way to honor the lives of the unknown dead, and attempt to regain a little of their waning humanity.

"They don't care anymore, why waste the energy?" Braiden said, meaning no disrespect. He was just speaking logically.

"The lady is right," said DB stepping forward. "It won't take long and it shows we can still care. If God is watching, he may just save our ass in the future."

Gloria laughed at his motives, "It shows we are still decent human beings. If He is watching, we aren't doing it for brownie points. Although a favor wouldn't go amiss," Gloria admitted with a quick glance skyward.

"I'll get the shovels," Jonesy offered and collected the two Army issue tools from inside the Foxhounds.

Peter had woken from his healing slumber and stood to the side, face expressionless. Christina had spoken to him briefly and had assured them that the time would come when he would let his grief out. Kurt wasn't so sure. Peter had the look of a man lost, with nothing left to live for. His previous love had caused the death of his new love, a strange tangle of emotion and ultimate betrayal. Kurt walked over and took out the crumpled picture of Paige with her baby, holding it out to him.

"Get that thing away from me," Peter said, a look of dismay twisting his features.

"She wanted you to have it," Kurt replied calmly, trying to hand the picture over again.

"I said get it the fuck away from me!" Peter screamed and pushed Kurt as hard as he could.

Kurt's heel caught on the rail and he fell backwards, sprawling on the tracks. Landing awkwardly on his ass, the pain shot up his spine, causing him to cry out. Peters face went from furious to distraught in a split second and he rushed forward to help Kurt up.

"I'm sorry, Kurt. Are you ok? I didn't hurt you did I?" Peter flapped around like an old maid, taking Kurt's hand and helping him to his feet.

"Only my pride, Pete. Don't worry," Kurt smiled with a grimace of pain as a twinge swept up his back.

"I don't know what came over me, I just don't think I'm ready to look at the picture yet," Peter explained and Kurt understood all too well.

"I'll keep hold of it until you are, ok?" Kurt said and Peter breathed a sigh of relief.

"I know she is gone, don't worry about me freaking out again. It's just every time I close my eyes all I see is Debbie's poisonous face, gloating that she has hurt me more than it was ever possible with her fists," Peter lowered his head and started to weep. Kurt placed a comforting arm around his shoulders and stood there quietly, commiserating with his friend.

The others had pulled the bodies into a line and the loose stone chippings of the track bed proved a decent material to give a worthy burial. The ground was frozen, so digging a hole would have been out of the question. They all stood in a circle around the fallen strangers, people they had never known, but now paid their respects. Gloria stepped forward with head bowed.

"The Lord is my shepherd; I shall not want. He makes me lie down in green pastures.

He leads me beside still waters. He restores my soul. He leads me in paths of righteousness

for his name's sake. Even though I walk through the valley of the shadow of death, I will fear no evil, for you are with me; your rod and your staff, they comfort me. You prepare a table before me in the presence of my enemies; you anoint my head with oil; my cup overflows. Surely goodness and mercy shall follow me all the days of my life, and I shall dwell in the house of the Lord forever. Amen," she finished.

"That was lovely, thank you," DB said and Gloria nodded. Jonesy got back to business and the group moved away from the final resting place of the train passengers.

"The plan is; we back the two vehicles up to the door. That way we can climb out through the gunnery position and then back down inside if we need to. If any of those dead fucks shows up, we can pick them off with ease," Jonesy explained.

The Foxhounds were moved against the train carriage and, one by one, they climbed through the open door. Of the three private booths, one was beyond redemption. Blood and gore covered every surface, including the ceiling. The stench of decomposition was overpowering so they pulled opened the inner window and sealed it by closing and sealing the door with tape, praying that the smell wouldn't spread. The two remaining rooms were untouched as Jonesy had surmised. They prepared their food and laid the bedding out. It was decided that the women would have the long, padded seats to lay on and the men would take the floor. The sun set and the twilight was a mixture of subtle blues, oranges, and purples in the dying light. It was decided that there would be no light after dark because of their position; the tracks were raised and the open fields meant they could be seen for a mile in all directions. The curtains had been ripped off by vandals, and only the last strip of fabric was attached to the steel rings.

"Tomorrow we push for Ford town. Then we take the road north to Arundel and the castle," DB laid out their next move, but they all knew what had to be done. Their fear grew as the darkness took hold; they knew that Ford had a population of over ten thousand and there was no telling how many they would face.

"Would you mind telling us what happened at the barracks?" Sam asked innocently, still infatuated with the bravery and skill of the trained soldiers.

"We weren't on guard duty at the time, our twelve-hour stint was up and we had gone for a bite of late breakfast," DB's voice was deep and melodic, taking them all back to that fateful morning.

CHAPTER THREE

DB and Jonesy handed their rifles back to Corporal Hague who was manning the weapons storage desk and signed them back in. They always made fun of the desk jockey, not classing him as a real soldier despite the fact that he was their superior and had undergone the same training. Anyone that sought the safety of an office was fair game for the real men within the Army.

"Long night?" the corporal asked, trying to make conversation.

"Too long," replied DB, ignoring the temptation to ridicule the thin, wiry man in thick glasses. He had already received a reprimand from command about the banter. The 'new' Army was becoming pussy whipped and scared of its own shadow since several reports of systematic bullying and intimidation had been revealed by the government.

"Can you believe that shit? A warning for a bit of a joke with Corporal Spectacles," Jonesy shook his head in bewilderment.

"You made the mistake of thinking that we joined the Army to become trained killers and defend our nation. You only have to look at the new breed of officer with their sociology degrees to see how low we have fallen," DB replied with anger.

"Give me a CO that screams in my face and makes me do a thousand press ups, instead of one who invites me into his office for a latte and a chat," Jonesy replied.

"Amen, brother" answered DB.

They walked into the mess hall and the smells of bacon and eggs hit them like an olfactory orgasm. There was nothing in the world like that aroma after a hard night's work, pacing to and fro in the dark. The chef piled their plates high and they seated themselves with several of the others in their platoon.

"I am getting royally drunk tonight!" declared Private Harkiss, much to the glee of his peers who whooped and hollered.

"Lucky bastard!" said DB grinning. It would be a week or more before he was rotated to leave the base.

"Not as lucky as the girls in Emsworth will be!" Harkiss laughed, thrusting his pelvis back and forth. The others roared with laughter and slapped him on the back.

"Shut up, Harkiss, the best you can hope for will be lubricant and a sock," joked Jonesy and Harkiss playfully punched him on the arm, knocking his fork of eggs onto the table.

"Wanker!" Harkiss called back as he made his way to the recreation room.

"No, you tit. You will be the wanker later; didn't you just hear me?" Jonesy shouted over his shoulder and was rewarded with the middle finger of his friend.

The table quietened down and the only noises in the mostly abandoned hall were the kitchen staff cooking and cleaning, and the slurping and chewing of hungry soldiers. The peace was broken by the shrill cacophony of the claxon in the corner of the room. The tannoy crackled into life and the sound of Major Albright's voice rebounded from the walls.

"We are now at critical threat level. Our response has been changed to exceptional. All teams mobilise and await

further instruction, out." The voice faded and every soldier jumped up, leaving their food and running to their quarters. The rhythmic sounds of heavy boots on the floor rung out from every corridor as the men and women geared up and waited for orders.

"Training drill?" DB asked the others as they waited by their bunks.

"Probably. You know how they love fucking with our meals," complained Jonesy, the taste of crispy bacon still on his tongue.

"With any luck we can be back at our plate before it gets cold," DB offered hopefully. He was still starving.

Shouts and movement greeted them from around the corner and Sergeant Crown strode into their room.

"You ready to rock and roll?" Crown said as he reached them.

"Yes, sir. What's going on?" Jonesy asked.

"No idea, we had the call come down from top brass to go on high alert. Now we stand here with our dicks in our hands until we get the call," their superior explained.

The radio beeped in his hand and the voices of the guards on the gatehouse came through, "We can see civilians, two dozen at least approaching on foot. Request orders, over."

"Hold your fire, keep them at a distance in case they are wired with suicide vests. We haven't been briefed on the exact nature of the imminent attack, out," Major Albright responded.

"Good to see the brass are keeping us appraised as normal," Jonesy said sarcastically.

"You watch your mouth, soldier. Our only purpose in life is to follow orders, and kill who they tell us to. Decisions are above our pay grade," Crown replied with disapproval.

The faint cracks of gunfire reached them through the windows. They rushed over, but their side of the building

31

only gave them a view of the tumultuous ocean, driven by the high winds that churned the water.

"It's coming from the gate, what the fuck is going on?" Private Pelman asked, looking around the group. His inquiry was met with confused shrugs.

"What do you think, Sarge? Shall we head to the weapons lockup?" Jonesy inquired.

"Better to be safe than sorry, let's go," he answered and ran out of the room. The rest followed and as they passed the other sleeping quarters, his whole platoon fell into position and jogged behind him. They reached the weapon store and the bespectacled soldier was flustered at the sudden interruption of the warning and now the gathered troops.

"Sir, I'm afraid I can't just issue you all with weapons without the proper paperwork. I haven't received any orders to the contrary," whined Corporal Hague. The eyes of the troops were on him and their derisive grins caused him to flush with embarrassment.

"I know you have orders, but you can hear the fucking gunfire! We are under attack!" Crown shouted straight in his face and no one would have been surprised to see him start bawling or wet himself.

"I... I..." he blustered.

The radio came to life again and the screams that ripped from the speakers made them all cringe. "They are attacking us! Oh God, they are eating Mackenzie! There are more coming. Request backup, over." More gunfire followed and the clerk was struggling to swallow, his throat bobbing with the lump of fear that paralyzed him.

"Sergeant Crown, get your men to the gate immediately. Sergeant Holbeck, your platoon will provide cover. Artillery teams to your positions and await instruction. Prepare for close cover, out," the Major barked from the radio.

"You heard the man, load up!" Crown shouted and the soldiers pushed past the Corporal who had gone as white as a ghost. Goodness knows how he would cope when he was assigned to Afghanistan. Little did they know that they would never again see an overseas deployment against a human enemy.

"Hustle! Hustle!" yelled their CO and they filed out, fully kitted with assault rifles and magazines.

They raced across the parade ground and the sounds of screams carried over the autumn wind. Sporadic gunfire cracked and the closest guard towers had been occupied by snipers who fired off single rounds into the growing crowd. Sergeant Crown's platoon shouldered their weapons and crouched low, training their sights on the advancing civilians. The last woman soldier standing ran over from her firing position behind the small gate building. The others were on the floor, flailing around, screaming in pain.

"Get those bastards off!" ordered Crown. DB and Jonesy, along with eight others, ran forward and grabbed at the figures who were on top of their comrades. They threw them aside and the full horror of the situation was revealed. The fallen troops had been partly eaten, large chunks of flesh were missing and blood spurted from torn arteries in necks and arms.

"Medic!" screamed DB as he single-handedly pulled a hideously injured soldier to cover. He had no idea who it was, because most of the face was missing, revealing patches of red skull.

Jonesy took up position and went to one knee, aiming his gun centre mass of the first body to rise. It was a woman and she was rotten. The flesh was mottled with purple and black patches where she had been buried only a few weeks ago. A second passed while he processed the information, then he fired. The bullets ripped through the chest and sent the woman cartwheeling backwards. It was

33

pointless to dwell on how the hell it was happening, the evidence was right in front of his eyes and he believed his own senses. The wind switched direction and the smell of death and excrement filled his nostrils. It was an old, familiar companion this fragrance. He had encountered it on numerous occasions on the dusty streets of the Middle-East, discovering a local who had been executed and left to decay as a deterrent to others. They had never got up and walked though.

"Holy shit, they aren't staying down!" cried out Private Carrol as another assailant regained his footing, ignoring three large wounds in his chest.

Jonesy couldn't believe the words that were about to pour from his mouth, but he shouted them anyway, "Shoot them in the head!"

He retreated to the bridge entrance and provided cover fire for the rest of the soldiers as they carried the other two wounded back to safety. Sure enough, with the skulls exploding and the brain splattering the road, the dead stayed dead. In the distance, he could see cars speeding down the road, swerving in and out of the walking menace like some macabre slalom.

"Get the floor barriers raised, we don't know who is in those vehicles. They could be as crazy as those bastards," shouted Crown while DB sprinted for the hut. He reached inside and entered the security code. The solid steel bars rose from the ground, ready to prevent any would-be suicide bomber from driving an explosive laden truck or car into the compound.

The sergeant held the radio to his mouth, "Major, we have casualties at the gate. Civilians of unknown origin have tried to eat the guards. I repeat the last, they have taken bites from the troops. We have civilian vehicles approaching, so we have raised the barrier. Do we allow entry to any survivors? Over."

The major's voice came back to him, calm and collected. He didn't seem perturbed at the reports of cannibalism. "No. Civilians are to be held at the gate until we get control of the situation. Maintain position. Lieutenant Baxter, bring four Vikings to the main entrance and provide heavy machine gun cover, over"

"They are on the way, sir, over," Baxter replied.

How they all hated the sadistic bastard. He seemed to take pleasure in catching soldiers out, meting out harsh punishments for any infraction to the Army code of conduct.

"We can't just leave them out there, sir. They will be sitting ducks!" Harkiss yelled over the sounds of gunfire.

"We have our orders, soldier!" Crown replied, although he totally agreed.

If all of those on foot coming down the road were infected with whatever disease caused the psychotic behaviour, the cars wouldn't stand a chance. Using binoculars, he could see there were at least another seventy snaking down towards them. It was a moot point in the end anyway; a car tried to pass a small school bus and swerved in at the wrong time, catching it on the front wing. The bus hit the kerb and flipped onto its side, skidding down the road in a blaze of sparks. Three of the horrors were pulled underneath the sliding hulk and ended up as long, wet streaks on the road. The desperate driver that had caused the accident had spun out and the car lay steaming in the ditch. The stricken bus came to rest blocking most of the road, with only a small gap for the long trail of cars to squeeze through. Whether it was the British sense of politeness, or the fear of hurting someone, the lead car stopped when a zombie blocked the gap. It was quickly surrounded and the occupants pulled out and devoured. The roadblock was complete and the sergeant watched the dead move back up the street, flensing the flesh from every living being.

35

"Major, request permission to engage the enemy. We have innocent civilians on the approach road being killed, over," Crown begged.

"Negative, Sergeant, pull your men back to the south side of the bridge. You are to control the situation until Lieutenant Baxter arrives to block the entrance, over," replied the major.

"But, sir, there are women and children out there!" shouted the sergeant.

"Careful, Sergeant. I understand your frustration, but we have been given orders to secure the base and await further instructions. Now pull your men back and hold position, over," answered the major, ending the discussion.

"FUCK!" screamed Crown and he threw his radio against the bridge wall, shattering it into fragments.

"Sarge, let's just go out there. He can't court martial all of us," DB suggested.

Crown lifted the binoculars to get a fresh view and his heart sank. An aching void opened in his soul as he saw a converging wave of dead coming from Emsworth town. The people were trapped between the group moving northwards and the new horde heading south. By the time they reached them on foot, it would be too late. The soldiers looked to him for guidance, eager to get some payback. He could only shake his head and walk back towards the base, the binoculars falling to the ground. Jonesy looked at DB with confusion, they had never seen their superior like this. Picking up the lenses, DB looked and he lowered them too, his face bearing the same sense of hopelessness.

"What the fuck is happening?" DB asked quietly, looking up and seeing the Vikings rumble around the side hangar.

"I don't know, partner, but we are sure as hell going to find out. Zombies? They only exist in horror movies," Jonesy tried to convince himself, and failed. He had seen

the hearts shredded with splinters of his bullets and they still got up, wanting to feed.

Screams from inside the base brought them running and the medic was being helped after losing part of his hand to the faceless soldier who was chewing greedily. Two of his team were trying to hold the figure down, mistaking the attack as some sort of accident or madness brought on by pain. They both paid for their efforts with chunks taken from their arms and they too, were led away, blood pouring.

"Get them to the infirmary, now!" DB yelled.

The flayed man on the ground stood up, seeking his next victim. Jonesy stepped forward and shot a hole through its bloody skull from only six feet away.

"What the hell are you doing, soldier?" cried out the sergeant.

"Sir, they are zombies. You have seen the punishment they can take. Only head shots keep them down," Jonesy held his superior by the arm.

He reluctantly nodded and it was then that Lieutenant Baxter arrived, brakes shrieking.

"What is the situation, Sergeant? Are all your men clear?" Baxter asked, surveying the blood and bodies.

"Zombies, sir," responded Crown, meeting the icy blue, cold stare.

"Very funny. I am not in the mood for games, do you understand me?" Baxter stood only inches from the sergeant, a favoured tactic to intimidate the men.

"Take a look for yourself, sir," said DB, offering the binoculars. Baxter snatched them away and raised them to his face, seeing the unfolding events on the access road.

"Let's get that bridge sealed. You four, manoeuvre the rear of the vehicles to block the road, keep them tight. Now!" he barked at the drivers and they revved the engines, expertly sealing the entrance with tonnes of solid steel, leaving only an inch between them.

"Do you believe me now?" Crown chided, pointing at the first cadavers as they stumbled across the bridge. Their wounds and trailing guts were enough to convince any sane mind.

"I don't believe in made up stories," sneered the lieutenant, walking away to talk on the radio in private.

"Cunt," muttered Jonesy and spat on the floor.

"I would punish you, except I agree. I don't blame him for trying to hold onto his sanity, though. I don't think I will ever sleep again," the sergeant replied with a shudder. The binoculars had revealed things he would give anything to forget.

"Sir, we should go and keep an eye on those that were bitten. You know what is meant to happen…" DB said to Crown and distant shouts of terror and pain confirmed his worst fears.

"We lost fourteen more soldiers trying to contain the infected. People just didn't believe what was happening," Jonesy said quietly, remembering the friends he had lost.

"Jesus Christ. I am sorry," consoled John.

"We knew the risks when we signed up. None of us expected it to come from the zombie apocalypse though," DB said with regret.

"How many troops are left at the barracks?" Kurt asked.

"We were part of two battalions, around twelve hundred men and machines. After it all went to hell, some of us were deployed to Porton Down to protect the facility. You may have seen the choppers moving artillery and armoured vehicles. What a waste," Jonesy replied.

DB remembered the radio transmission and continued, "While we had the opportunity, we should have relocated the scientists to the Daresford Institute and their underground facility. Why the fuck did the brass try and hold the centre? Jesus Christ, it's always the grunts who pay for their mistakes."

"They're idiots," John agreed, shaking his head.

"It's always the best and bravest who suffer while those at the top hide and survive. When this is all over, if we make it, we will ensure it is the other way 'round," DB vowed.

"By the time we left the barracks, there were just over three hundred and twenty left. Baxter has a personal guard of about thirty loyalists who would follow him to hell if he ordered it. I pray we get the chance to send them there!" Jonesy growled.

CHAPTER FOUR

The soldiers stood to attention on the parade ground, shivering from the cold that penetrated their uniforms. For over an hour they had waited patiently, afraid to break formation and draw the attention of their crazed superior and his compliant henchmen.

"We have to do something!" whispered Corporal Derby.

"What do you suggest? We try and take their guns and we end up shot too, is that what you want?" replied Private Heath.

"Of course not, but Bennett is our friend," said the Corporal, hoping to get some support from the others.

"Baxter is still our commanding officer; you are talking about insubordination. Hell, maybe treason if you try and kill him," whispered another voice from behind.

"How do we know he is following orders himself? This isn't the Army I signed up for," complained Derby.

"The world has changed. The Army has to change too," said Heath with resignation.

"Shut your mouths!" yelled a sergeant from the sidelines.

Major Albright had allegedly been recalled because of his value to the chain of command. Rumors were rampant that he had simply fled to try and find his family, an option he had denied to his own troops. The dissatisfaction had grown over the following weeks until the base was nearly in open mutiny. Soldiers would abscond in the night to try and reach their own loved ones, weakening the base defenses further. Only the iron fist of Lieutenant Baxter had reigned in the trouble and punishments were swift and severe, without exception.

"Here they come," said another voice from the crowd.

Bennett was handcuffed and being pushed forward by two burly soldiers who had been recently promoted for their unflinching loyalty to Baxter. Bullies before, now they had the rank to act carte blanche. Beatings and forty-eight-hour guard postings were common. Three soldiers had died from exhaustion and exposure from the extended duty on the perimeter. Day by day, the remaining troops had fallen into line and order was restored. It was gradually becoming apparent to the new commander that an undercurrent of hostility and hatred was blossoming in the hearts of his charges. They spoke in hushed tones in the dark of night, plotting another way. The secret radio transmission to DB had been intercepted, but others took their place. They hadn't abandoned their brothers out in the world; they would still try and help where they could.

"Ladies and gentlemen, in times of war, the importance of discipline is even more paramount to the survival of your fellow soldier. Without discipline, we have anarchy and chaos!" Baxter shouted. He looked around the blank faces in the crowd, his cold stare adding to the chill. "I have always prided myself on being firm, but fair. I didn't volunteer for this position; it was entrusted to me by Major Albright. He saw in me the strength and resilience to lead you all beyond this hell. With me, you have a chance at survival, of making something magnificent in this world. All I ask is for your obedience and loyalty!"

"We're not dogs, you fucking lunatic!" yelled a soldier who had heard enough of the sanctimonious lecture. The enforcers rushed over and cracked him around the head with their rifles, splitting the man's scalp. Blood poured from the wound and they ignored it while kicking him mercilessly. When he was still, they dragged him away and through the doors to the cells. He would not be seen again until he was brought in front of them for punishment.

"Why do you insist on testing me? Are you hungry? No, because you eat my food. Are you thirsty? No, because you drink my water. I can't understand your need to bite the hand that feeds you," Baxter said with a face that spoke of genuine disappointment. It was as if he was addressing errant children.

"Sir, prisoner is in position. Shall we form up the line?" Sergeant Strickland asked, meaning the firing squad.

"No, I don't think so. I shall deal with it personally this time," Baxter answered, pulling his pistol from its holder.

"Remember what you signed up for; to protect people, to fight our enemies, whoever they are. Not hide behind the fences and watch the whole world die!" Bennett shouted from his position; tied to a post that had been installed at the behest of Baxter for these occasions.

"You signed up to follow orders!" screamed Baxter an inch from his face, "Sergeant, gag the prisoner!"

A rag was duly tied around his mouth, silencing the protests that threatened the stability of the base. Baxter could feel the anger radiating from the crowd, they just didn't have the ability to understand why he was doing this. It was for their own good. The temptation to appeal to their sense of responsibility, their military honor, was nearly overwhelming. Instead, he sighed and lowered his head in resignation, then turned and shot Bennett straight through the heart at point blank range. Yells of denial and anger were swiftly silenced by the barrels of the rifles that covered them. Bennett coughed up a huge gout of blood, then slumped forward. Eyes had narrowed with contempt and rage, but it would not spill over today. He still had enough firepower to ensure control. The armory was fully locked and heavily guarded around the clock by Baxter loyalists to prevent any temptation.

"Bennett was a traitor to us all. He supported deserters and wasted ammunition that could have saved lives." Baxter tried to justify himself, ignoring the irony that they had actually used the shells to save lives. Just not those chosen by the madman.

"You all know the punishment for dissent. Justice has been served here today," barked one of the sergeants. The heads turned in his direction and their glares caused him to fall quiet and avert his gaze. He knew that if the tables were ever turned, he would be shown no mercy by his fellow troops.

Bennett started to tremble in his bindings, his body going into spasms as the reanimation was taking hold. Suddenly he fell still, before his head rose and the dead eyes took in the gathered crowds. The all too familiar groan of desire issued forth from his mouth, coupled with a torrent of blood that covered the ground around his feet.

"And now he pays the price for his betrayal once more," Baxter fired a single round through Bennett's forehead, blowing the brains all over the frosty ground to his rear.

The body would be left as a warning to others who would pass it on the way to guard duty. The barbarity that a supposed 'gentleman officer' was capable of was no better than the enemies they had faced in the Middle-East. A supposed civilized country had devolved in a matter of weeks, leaving their humanity behind.

"Everyone fall out, you are dismissed!" shouted Baxter, walking off.

He turned after a few paces, and saw that only his chosen few were following. The others were unmoving, looking at their dead comrade. With no prompting, every soldier, male and female, saluted. Lowering their arms, they remained standing in mourning, resolute. Baxter was apoplectic with rage and he took out his pistol, ready to start shooting indiscriminately into the crowd. How dare they ignore his order.

"Sir, I don't think that will help," warned Strickland, gently easing the gun hand down, "Begging your pardon, sir, but we shouldn't shake the hornet's nest." The sergeant was all too aware how far the soldiers had been pushed, and anyone has their breaking point where self-preservation is no longer the ascendant tendency.

"So be it!" growled Baxter and strode back into the command building.

The other troops hadn't flinched at their near shooting. They stared at the bleeding form of the artillery commander with introspection, minds plotting.

CHAPTER FIVE

"I didn't think I would sleep a wink after yesterday," said Peter, rubbing his eyes. "I was gone as soon as my head hit the pillow."

"It's a healing sleep, you needed it," explained Christina, kneeling beside him.

"Is everyone else awake?" Peter asked. The darkness had started to recede, but it would be a while before the sun rose from the horizon.

"No, not yet. You were feverish and muttering in your sleep so I've been keeping an eye on you. It is not unheard of for an emotional trauma to manifest physically," replied the doctor.

Jodi walked up to the door and smiled, though Peter could only make out the faint outlines from the meagre light. He lifted a hand and she replied in kind, before putting the baseball bat back on her shoulder and walking off down the carriage.

"She has been keeping watch all night. Everything has been quiet though," Christina explained.

"I will take over, you get back to bed for an hour," Peter said to the doctor and she climbed back into her makeshift bunk. Jodi averted her eyes when Peter offered to finish out the night, ducking through the door to her compartment.

"Thanks," she said quietly, before starting to close the door.

"Hey, wait. Come here," Peter whispered and she hesitated for a few seconds before sighing and walking back out into the narrow corridor.

"I know what you are going to say. You can't make me feel any worse than I already do," she still looked down and Peter could see the first tears running down her cheeks. He took her by the chin and raised her face so they were looking at each other.

"That's not what I wanted to talk to you about. I wanted to say I don't hold you responsible. No one knows better than me what can be lurking within someone's mind, the things they can be capable of. Mike made his choice and I hope to have the chance to even the score one day," Peter explained to her solemnly.

"But you were in love and he's robbed you of that. It was my fault he was at the bar, my poor life choices that led to me keeping him around. If I had kicked him out when I suspected he was dealing drugs, he would never have been able to hurt you," she replied and Peter took her in his arms to show he felt no animosity towards their new friend.

"And if you hadn't gone into business and bought the pub, you would probably be dead now too. There are so many what ifs. Life is just one big cosmic fuckup," he spat the words with derision.

"So you really forgive me?" Jodi looked hopeful.

"No," Peter replied, "Because there is nothing forgive. Get some rest and I will wake you at dawn."

Jodi broke contact, paused, and then gave him a kiss on the cheek. A gesture of love and gratitude.

Peter watched her get comfortable and then started to prowl back and forth, staring out of the windows. The dead world was still hard to become accustomed to. The glow of streetlights rising into the night, the passage of cars along the roads used to be like fireflies floating in the distance. It was just the moonlight now, the cold indifference of the rotating barren rock striking the land, giving it an eerie luminosity. His mind returned to the image of Paige, her radiant smile, her innocent ways, and a lump formed in his throat that wouldn't disappear. His heart physically ached with the pain of the loss and a swift cardiac arrest would be a welcome relief. He would happily sacrifice his plans of revenge if he could stop the pain. He lacked the courage to end his own life though. The thought of taking the gun and swallowing the barrel filled him with irrational fear that the heart attack didn't. He shook his head in the darkness at his bizarre, grief driven thoughts. When his body refused to heed his yearning for the sweet release of death, he continued on to the next window. The moisture in the air had formed into ice crystals that reflected the light on the cold pane. It never failed to amaze him how the beautiful patterns were created and he leaned in closer to get a better look. The cold emanated from the glass and he closed his eyes, pressing his forehead to the frozen surface. It numbed his skin, but the anesthetic quality could not penetrate to his brain and the sorrow contained within.

"Why did you have to leave me? You should have saved yourself," he whispered and the glass fogged inches from his face.

He felt guilty for harboring the wish that one of the others had sacrificed themselves, instead of Paige. His selfish desire for a true love that would fill the void that Debbie's vindictive abuse had left in him wasn't unusual, but he still felt rotten anyway. Every single one of them had risked their life for his in some form or other and he forced the self-pity down deep inside. If he couldn't get past it, it would consume him and alienate him from the group.

"Sort it out, you pathetic bastard," he muttered to his vague reflection.

Movement from behind caused him to jump like a teenager caught masturbating and his cheeks flushed with embarrassment at his inner thoughts. Kurt had woken and heard his friend's faint whispers, thinking that he wasn't alone.

"Hey, Pete, are you ok?" Kurt asked.

"Yeah, fine. I was just thinking out loud, sorry if I woke you. Get back to sleep and I will wake you up in a while," he babbled, the words pouring out.

"No, it's fine. I will keep you company," Kurt replied. He didn't want to leave Peter alone in the dark with all the emotions he would be facing. They fell silent and Kurt's presence was enough to give some new strength to Peter. His resolve returned and the shame turned to burning hatred. Kurt watched him surreptitiously and saw the changes in his face; from forlorn, to an angry scowl. Peter caught Kurt in his peripheral vision and saw he was smiling.

"Are you ready now?" Kurt asked, holding out the glossy square picture.

Peter looked at it and was shocked to see his hand reach out and take it. He wasn't ready to look just yet, and instead held it against his chest. A calm spread through his body and he imagined he could feel Paige behind him, her arms encircling him with love.

"Thank you for keeping it safe," Peter said and Kurt nodded, reaching out and squeezing his shoulder.

"Anytime, mate," Kurt said and looked back out of the window. The glow on the horizon grew in intensity as if someone was slowly turning a dimmer switch up. The first rays of sunshine reached them and they felt the warmth, sighing as the cold was driven away slightly. In the distance a rooster crowed, announcing both the morning's arrival and its presence to anything that may be listening.

"What I wouldn't give for some roast chicken," Peter said, licking his lips.

"We have some tinned chicken. The awful jelly doesn't help though," Kurt smiled and wrinkled his nose. It felt like eating meaty phlegm.

"I vote we go and find that bird before we do anything else," Peter joked. The rest of the group were rousing themselves from slumber, with yawns and stretches coming from the two compartments.

"When we are safe, we are definitely going to get some chickens. Just think of all those eggs," Kurt said, his mouth watering at the thought.

"I'll hold you to that. Looks like everyone's up," Peter commented and they rejoined the others.

"Morning, all," DB said, stretching. Because of his size he couldn't stretch properly and had to bow down to get the numbness out of his arms. His cramped sleeping space hadn't been conducive to a good night's sleep.

"It was better than sleeping under the stars, but I'd kill for a soft mattress," Jonesy said to the gathered survivors which brought weary chuckles.

"What's next?" Braiden asked.

"We arm up and push on for Ford. I highly doubt the roads will be clear of cars so we will have to think on our feet. The railway track drops off towards Angmering so we can't follow it any further," John explained.

"Give us twenty minutes to do a quick field clean of the guns and we will roll out. Gloria, let me have the shotgun and we will spruce it up for you." DB held out his hand and Gloria passed the gun.

The boys watched in fascination as the two soldiers stripped their guns on the bonnets of the two military vehicles. Components were unclipped and placed carefully on the blanket that had been unfurled to keep the parts dry. They sprayed each piece and wiped away any dust or residue that had gathered in the mechanisms. Oil was applied to the sections after they had been cleaned and they were expertly reassembled within minutes.

49

"That was so cool," Braiden exclaimed.

"I tell you what. When we get to the castle, I will show you how it all works and teach you how to use one. How does that sound?" Jonesy offered and the boy's eyes went wide with excitement.

"That would be great, I think your guns do more damage than this," Sam said, raising the slingshot.

"I don't know. I've seen you use that thing and you are lethal." DB grinned and patted him on the back. The praise from the soldier made him look like the cat that got the cream, Braiden was sure he could hear him purr.

Peter handed out small plastic bowls of canned fruit, a light breakfast high in energy for what they may face. He was happy to keep busy, as it kept his mind from dwelling on the truth. Lost in the task, he had accidentally filled an extra bowl, throwing it away in anger when he remembered its contents would not be needed any more. This brought renewed tears that dripped onto his waterproof life preserver.

All preparations had been made and the two vehicles moved off from their overnight shelter. The trapped zombies in the detached carriages hammered on the toughened glass, saying farewell to the breakfast they would never eat. The tires rumbled over the sleepers as they progressed down the track and John pulled up when Jonesy slapped on the roof. They were half a mile away from the station and the binoculars revealed a crowd of zombies gathered on the tracks as well as waiting on the platforms. Jonesy shuddered and looked behind him, imagining a rusted, burning train was going to speed past to pick up the passengers on their final journey to hell. He shook the macabre thought out of his mind and indicated for Jodi to pull alongside. DB looked over, waiting for an update.

"The station is dead city, mate. There are cars abandoned over the gates too, so we would need to push though," Jonesy explained. "Let's head back."

"I may have a solution," John called up from the driver's seat.

"I'm all ears," said DB.

John climbed out of the Foxhound so he could better detail his plan. "Before I even tell you, how much power have those beasts got?" he asked, pointing at the camouflaged vehicles.

"They have three-point-two-liter turbo diesel engines, enough to haul that weight about on the battlefield," Jonesy replied, slapping the Foxhound.

John stared thoughtfully for a few moments while he mulled over his idea. Kurt had climbed out and interrupted his thinking.

"What's up?" he said, looking at the trio. DB and Jonesy just pointed at John who had come to a conclusion.

"I think we can push our train carriage along the tracks and let it clear a path for us. It's nearly fifty tons and if we can get it rolling there is a slight downhill gradient past the one-mile signal," he talked aloud even though he was still working out the logistics of the move.

"So a fifty-ton battering ram?" Kurt laughed and John clapped his hands together.

"Exactly! I think we can use it as bait as well, to lure them away from the station. If we set it on fire, they should want to follow it if our previous experience is anything to go by," John surmised after their home and the block of flats they had burned. The matter was settled.

"Fuck it, let's give it a try!" DB nodded his agreement and they mounted up and drove back to the disconnected train carriage.

"I haven't done math since high school so my opinion may not count for much. How will that," Jodi inquired, pointing at the armored carrier, "Push that?" she pointed at the heavy carriage.

It was true. The vehicle, despite its protective capabilities, was dwarfed by the train.

"It could burn the clutch out. Getting it rolling with sufficient speed is a whole different ballgame to dragging it a few feet," John was deliberating to himself again.

"Can't we pull and push it at the same time?" added Christina.

"That's a brilliant idea. Jonesy, do they have anything to tie to the coupler at the front?" John smiled at the doctor and they gathered a tow chain from the storage compartment.

"The trains are designed to be fire resistant, the seats don't burn well," Braiden revealed and his face darkened with embarrassment. The group ignored another glimpse into his colorful past and just accepted the information.

"We need to gather some stuff to burn then," stated Gloria, giving the boy a quick hug.

They foraged in the fence line, ripping bushes and thin branches free and piling them by the train. Within fifteen minutes they had a huge pile of tinder and Sam hopped up into the carriage. They passed the material up and he crammed it into the private compartments, scratching himself on a thorn bush that Braiden had pulled free.

"Cheers, Braiden!" Sam called down, shooting his brother the pricked finger. He picked up a thin branch and launched it down at his giggling sibling.

"Missed!" Braiden called out, laughing after dodging to the side.

Honey didn't miss a trick and claimed the stick, wagging her tail and dropping it at Braiden's feet.

"Throw it for her a few times. She hasn't had a chance to have much fun," Sarah said and Braiden launched the stick down the track. The dog raced off in hot pursuit, causing the group to laugh at the innocent escapades.

Seeing the hound rushing to and fro was therapeutic after the vile horror they had all witnessed. All activity ceased while they watched. Birds sung from the closest trees and took flight in a wild flock, moving synchronously towards another perch when Honey got too close in her mad rush.

"I think we are ready!" called down Sam.

"We are ready down here, light it up and hop on down," answered Jonesy.

Sam set light to a couple of soiled blankets they no longer used and the fire quickly took hold, consuming the bushes and rotten branches. He jumped down and the soldier softened the fall by catching him under the armpits.

"All we need is to get it up to a brisk walk, four or five miles an hour should do. On the decline it might reach ten or fifteen and that should be enough clear our path. With any luck most of the locals will be tempted away from the station by the flames," John instructed.

"If it won't shift easily, or the clutches look like they may burn out, we give up and just go back," Jonesy ordered. The plan wasn't worth wrecking two perfectly good transports.

"Agreed. Let's do this," DB finished.

Everybody climbed aboard except Kurt who was the communication between the cars, standing to the side to shout information. Once the strange convoy got moving, he would hop in the open passenger door for the rest of the short journey. Sarah had been tasked with unlooping the chain from the rear of the Foxhound when they had reached the correct speed.

"Ok, slowly!" called Kurt and the engines roared with the effort.

The chain at the front pulled taut and the tires spun on the track. Jonesy eased off and opted to pull away slowly, allowing the clutch to do the work. He revved carefully, but the train seemed to be rooted to the spot. The smell of the overheating clutch rose through the floor and Jonesy was on the verge of giving up. With a shriek, whatever corrosion had seized the train overnight was freed and the huge wheels started to rotate, inch by agonizing inch. With the reduction in power needed, Jonesy was able to ease back and give the clutch a rest. The stench was being blown away by the open door and the slow passage of air through to the open rear doors.

"We are good!" Kurt shouted to DB in the rear who filled the growing gap and added his own vehicle's power to the maneuver. DB gave him a thumbs up and Kurt hopped into the waiting seat.

"What speed are we at?" called Sarah from the back.

"We are at five... now. Pull the chain," Jonesy shouted over his shoulder.

"For the love of God, mind your hands!" Kurt warned and looked at Jonesy. The soldier eased off the accelerator and dropped the clutch, slowing the lead vehicle by a fraction, allowing the chain to slacken enough for Sarah to quickly pull it loose and drop it.

The train carriage was trundling along slowly and Jonesy dropped to the side, mounting the rails and braking as it passed. He dropped into position behind DB and slowly pushed up from behind with a crump as his bumper met the back of the other. DB eased off and they split the load between the two Foxhounds to try and protect the engines from damage. Some of the carriage windows popped from the heat and glass shards scattered across the ground as they passed. The smoke was getting thicker and it was lucky that they reached the decline at that point or they would have had to back off and abandon the attempt.

"Fingers crossed everybody!" John shouted, wafting the smoke away. They quickly climbed out and lined up, watching the passage of the blazing train as it moved away.

Jonesy had a horrible feeling of déjà-vu as the fiery, hell bound train from his imagination gathered speed. He passed the binoculars to Kurt who got the full view of the destruction. The zombies on the track saw the harbinger as it came for them. It belched fire from the sides, the flames rising and taking on the shape of wings like a metallic phoenix. The fifty tons would never take flight, but the force of the slow moving behemoth churned every single zombie in its path without slowing by any fraction. The patiently waiting, rotting commuters were aghast to see their ride passing without stopping and flopped down onto the tracks like a group of lemmings. Instead of falling to their deaths like the suicidal creatures, they stood and gave chase. The hulk reached the cars and vans that had crashed or been abandoned on the crossing. It tossed them aside like matchbox toys, with some exploding as the petrol tanks were shattered and spilled their flammable liquid near the inferno that used to be a train carriage. One of the destroyed cars was trapped under the front and showered sparks as the chassis was dragged along the track, gradually forcing itself further beneath the undercarriage. The train came to a stop in the middle of the bridge that spanned the River Arun, dripping the melting bodywork with hissing splashes into the water below.

"They are taking the bait," Kurt whispered, willing the groups still in the station to follow their brethren. He was intent upon the scene and the first dead reached the bridge. It was solely for trains and the bridge had no deck, only side alleys in case of emergency for the passengers to evacuate. Most of the zombies toppled through the gaps in the steel floor beams, dropping into the waiting water.

"There are only a handful left, it worked perfectly!" Kurt congratulated his father and they all celebrated quietly at the success.

"Our next dilemma is where we go when we reach the other side of the tracks. I know the roads will be jammed and I doubt the Hounds will take more of the damage we sustained while pushing the cars out of the way in

Chichester," Jonesy said, looking at the crumpled bodywork.

"We have more pressing problems," DB warned, "Those aren't rain clouds, I think we are going to be getting some heavy snow."

In the distance the delicate wisps of white in the sky were gathering themselves into mighty cumulonimbus clouds, towering into the high atmosphere like the puffy battlements of a sky fortress.

"A storm? Un-fucking-believable!" hissed Kurt as their shelter burned on the bridge.

"We have an hour or so, then we will be in the thick of it," DB continued.

"We need shelter, so we have two options I feel," Gloria explained, "We go back and clear another carriage, which would keep us dry and warm. The danger is that the station will refill with the dead and we will be back to square one. Would the engines cope with another tug of war with the train carriages?" she looked to Jonesy.

"Not a chance," he replied.

"Then it seems we must push on," stated Gloria with a firm nod.

"I think you are right, love," John backed her up and nobody complained. The thought of fighting through another carriage of zombies wasn't a problem as such, they were all just desperate to keep moving. The goal would, quite literally, be in sight within a few miles. The huge towers and crenellations of the castle would loom large in the distance. A heartening sight for the survivors, but a terrifying visage for the soldiers of medieval times who would be marching to do battle at the base of the structure.

"When we reach the road we will need to think quickly. If the roads are blocked, do we try and go over the fields and gardens?" Jonesy pondered.

"There is a small mooring about a hundred yards up the river. If we can find a boat, we could load it up and get within throwing distance of the main guardhouse of the castle," said Christina, pointing just to the right of the rising smoke of the train.

"We have tried that before at Emsworth when we tried to seek sanctuary at the barracks," Kurt explained and DB and Jonesy looked away with shame, "There is no telling if there will be keys or the ability to get it started, if we get trapped on one we will just float out to sea."

Seeing the sadness in the faces of the soldiers, Sarah gave them both a quick hug, "Kurt wasn't trying to criticize you, you were only following orders."

Kurt nodded his agreement, "Absolutely. We are forever in your debt, guys. I was just explaining what happened for those of you who weren't with us."

"I know. I just can't shake the feeling we should have done something about Baxter. None of this shit would have happened if we had ended him when he went crazy." DB shook his head with sorrow at the loss of Paige and knowledge of Bennett's likely execution.

"At some point we will try and communicate with the others on the next frequency. We will see what is going on there," Jonesy said, patting his comrade on the back. The small, but rapidly growing, insurrection on the barracks had organized more than one emergency channel. It was only the length of broadcast required during the artillery fire that had given away their secret. They couldn't know that every single radio had been collected under penalty of death.

"Ok," DB replied, "As for the boat, I will swim and drag the bastard to the castle if I need to!"

The group laughed in an attempt to hide their fear at the unknown events in front of them and climbed aboard the vehicles. Jodi and John took the driving to allow the soldiers to man the mounted heavy machine guns. They reached the station and the number of zombies had been reduced to a handful. That didn't include the churned mess that the train had carved through the waiting horde. Parts of what were once people reached out in their dismembered state, no longer able to move without arms or legs. The appendages were strewn along the line, giving them a wet, green route through the more complete dead. Jodi reached the station gates and even though the train had punched through, the roads on either side leading to the crossing were choked with abandoned cars. Small fires raged in the debris and this had further dispersed the threat, giving them a few seconds to discuss their options.

"The boats are down there," Christina called out, indicating a small access track further down the road that couldn't be reached. The cheerfully colored 'Welcome to Ford Marina' sign mocked them with its proximity; a tempting, but dangerous lure.

"What about that one?" Jodi shouted over the engine, pointing to a dirty, rutted track.

"I think it's an old builder's compound. When we were travelling the river, all I could see were bricks and lumber." Christina answered.

"Take it. It's our only option at the moment!" DB called out from the gun turret and Jodi floored it, wheels spinning on a pile of severed limbs.

They bounced over the rails and reached the entrance. A sign stating "All Trespassers Will Be Prosecuted" was ignored; laws designed by man were obsolete. The dead world only had one rule; survival of the fittest. A chain link gate stood wide open and they reached the main yard. Storage buildings lined the compound, filled with huge piles of bricks, varying timber lengths and other material. The longest building had sections of rail laid on racks, ready to be lifted onto transport trucks.

"It's a railway supply depot," DB said to the others as it finally clicked.

He climbed out of the turret to survey the surroundings and the rest of the group joined him. A couple of cadavers walked out from behind the main office and Sam dispatched them with skilled silence. The bearings whistled through the air and shattered bone and brain as they penetrated the skulls. Sam nonchalantly put the slingshot back into his jacket and turned around to find the group grinning. His family were all so proud of how he had grown into a man in the past few weeks. Where he would have once trembled with fear at the sight of an approaching corpse, he now stood stoic and brave.

"Way to go, killer!" DB chuckled and squeezed his shoulder, reinforcing the earlier sentiment of his deadly skill.

"Thanks," said Sam, blushing.

"Stay sharp, there may be more," whispered Jonesy, looking around. The only noise they could hear was the burning train and the groans of the dead who were investigating.

John walked over to the fence that separated the compound from the river bank. The land dropped off at an angle before it reached the muddied riverside and the vehicles would suffer a bumpy ride if they chose to take that route. Jonesy joined the pair and looked at the steep gradient, deep in thought.

"I don't like it, but I am not leaving the Foxhounds here while we go on foot," he confirmed.

"If we get stuck, we could be in real trouble. What if they topple and roll?" Christina asked.

"They have a low center of gravity. We have a better than a fifty-fifty chance of making it down in one piece," Jonesy added.

Christina showed Jonesy the small dock that waited for them down river. The boats were small and only meant for sightseeing; they were not suitable for the task of transporting the survivors and their equipment to Arundel. A smile formed on John's lips as he caught sight of a long canal boat bobbing on the flowing water further down the moorings.

"If we can get that hulk moving, we will have shelter and enough space to stow all of our food and guns," John declared.

"I've been on one of those before, they are slow but we aren't in any rush," Christina explained and a howling gust of frigid wind encircled them, causing synchronous shivers. Their attention had been so rapt on the shambling danger, they had almost forgotten the shifting clouds as they moved overhead, ready to unleash a white hell.

"It's time to go!" yelled DB as the first flakes descended.

Honey leapt around, biting the frozen treats out of the air until Braiden whistled and she came to his side obediently. The group made to climb in the Foxhounds but Jonesy cautioned and they paused.

"I think we need to be careful. If it rolls, I only want one of us in the vehicle," he explained. Handing his gun to DB, he slowly accelerated to the fence, finally pushing through with the sound of splintering wood as the posts yielded to the uneven battle.

They all watched and held their breath without realizing as the front end tipped forward. For a moment it looked as if the weight would carry the rear up and over, crashing the vehicle and Jonesy down in a rending jumble of metal and flesh. The center of gravity stabilized and the back settled down on the suspension without cartwheeling down the bank. Jonesy took it slowly, the bumps and divots in the ground bucked him around in the seat and at the final ten feet he threw caution to the wind and gunned it. The front bumper hit the flat ground and churned up a huge mound of moist earth before skidding to a stop on the river bank.

They sighed audibly with relief as Jonesy's grinning face appeared over the top of the vehicle and raise a thumb. DB passed over the two rifles to John and Kurt and they handled them with comical care, barely daring to hold them tight.

"Don't worry, they won't go off unless you want them to. I've switched the safeties on," DB laughed and squeezed his huge bulk into the driver's seat of the second vehicle.

He straightened the Foxhound and aimed for the hole in the fence, assuming that by following the same line Jonesy had taken he would be safe. Only at the last minute did he realize everything was wrong. The lead vehicle had compressed the wet ground deeply in its passing, meaning that DB's Hound tilted further forward. Coupled with his extra weight and fewer supplies in the rear, it toppled forward. In a split second of fear, he touched the brake and the maneuver was doomed. In a wild crashing tumult, the armored people carrier spun end over end before crashing down on its roof only feet from where Jonesy stood.

"Oh God, no!" cried Gloria as she watched the second soldier rush to the aid of his friend.

"Quickly, we have to see if he is ok," Kurt called out and they started their own descent on foot. Honey raced down, loving the speed she could build up before falling in a tangled heap when momentum met the reality of the bottom of the slope. She stood up and shook herself, before running to the mangled wreckage. The humans fared no better and all of them had a muddy bottom from skidding down the bank when they lost their footing. Christina rounded the smoking vehicle and found Jonesy pulling the unconscious figure of DB through the twisted door.

"No, don't move him!" she called out and Jonesy lowered him carefully to the ground.

"Sorry," he replied. His face was granite, but he was tearing himself up inside. He knew not to move someone who was injured, that it could cause irreparable injury to the spine. The sight of his friend covered in blood and slumped half in and half out of the vehicle was enough to throw his instincts off.

"Hold his head straight!" the doctor ordered him and he knelt on the wet earth, clasping the cold cheeks of DB and holding him perfectly still. They were face to face, although upside down, and Jonesy was surprised how serene his friend looked. Being oblivious to the living hell they endured, even for a few hours, filled Jonesy with a baffling jealousy. After witnessing the horror of the past few weeks, he supposed it wasn't unusual to desire a surcease from the pain and fear.

"I can't feel any broken bones. As for spinal injuries we will have to wait and see," said Christina, the note of chastisement not lost on the group.

"There's a lot of blood up here, Doc," Jonesy informed Christina, watching the spreading trail between his knees soak into the earth.

The doctor felt around the skull, searching for injury and behind his ear was a rising lump of split scalp. The blood was trickling through her fingers so she reached into one of the scattered bags and took out a clean t-shirt.

"Press this to the wound," she ordered Braiden and he positioned himself by the side of the soldier, reaching through and pressing firmly.

"How are we going to move him? We need something flat," Gloria stated and was about to climb back up the slope to collect some timber until Jonesy called out.

"There is a folding field stretcher in the back," Jonesy tried nodding, unable to remove his hands and Kurt followed, but went to the wrong section, "No, to the left. That's it."

Kurt and Gloria slotted the pieces together with the soldier's instruction and laid it to the side of the unconscious body. With much grunting, they managed to heave DB into place, before covering him with several thick blankets. The snow was falling heavily by the time they had secured his head with a neck brace.

"We need to get him to the boat as quickly as possible, this cold could finish him off," Christina explained.

"What about the supplies?" John looked around. While DB was being checked they had gathered all of the food and weaponry that had been thrown clear of the crashing vehicle. The mounted gun on the turret seat was smashed beyond repair, but the smaller machine guns and pistols had survived. Some of the food containers had been ruptured and Honey gratefully fed on the spilled contents.

"DB goes in the back of the Hound, we go on foot," John said and looked at Jonesy for confirmation.

"Agreed. We can carry as much as we are able, and come back for the rest. Load up!"

The stretcher was carried to the surviving vehicle and they slid DB inside after moving some of the supplies. Christina seated herself to keep the pressure on and she watched as the first trickle of blood ran from his right ear. Her heart sank at the possibility the skull was fractured; it would have meant possible surgery in a sterile environment by highly trained surgeons. On the road, fleeing millions of walking dead, with sparse equipment and no way of maintaining safe conditions? She may as well smother him in his sleep.

"I'll drive him!" offered Jodi.

She climbed aboard and started moving slowly, watching intently for as many ruts and depressions in the ground as she could avoid. The riverbank was not a clear road and despite her best efforts, it lurched around more than she would have liked. The windscreen wipers cleared the screen of settled snowflakes which were immediately replaced by more. Behind, the rest of the group followed, bearing the burden of the food and some of the guns and ammunition.

"Whoa, look at that!" Sam whispered. To their left, the flowing river was filled with the fallen zombies from the railway bridge. They bobbed past on the current, reaching for the survivors before going under the water, only to surface again with water pouring from their chomping mouths.

"Thank God they can't get their footing and come ashore," said Gloria with a small prayer.

They reached the dock and it had seen better days. A lack of interest and funding left it in a poor state, with water rotten boards a constant danger to the few remaining river folks.

"We will need to watch our footing and move slowly," Jonesy explained as he scanned along the walkway.

The canal boat itself was a beautifully crafted specimen, eleven-foot-wide and over sixty-foot long. The sides and top had been intricately painted with roses and castle motifs, for reasons the group could never know without the owner's explanation. The roof was in the process of being covered by snow, hiding the artwork until the temperature rose to melt it. The women stood guard and the men each took a corner of the stretcher, straining as the weight was lifted. Step by slow step, they walked up the gangplank and reached the flat dock. Their combined weight made the wood creak and groan in protest and Kurt was convinced that all five would plunge headlong into the murk of the river to join the passing dead. By placing each foot with care on the sturdier boards, they made it to the barge and climbed aboard unscathed.

"Get the door!" Jonesy said with a grimace and took the full weight of the second corner to free Kurt for the task.

Pulling out his hammer, Kurt smashed at the lock until the mechanism split apart. He lifted the door panel and they entered the rear of the vessel which led to a well-furnished bedroom. They gently laid DB's stretcher inside on the double bed where he was finally out of the falling snow. Christina resumed her duties and tended to the fallen soldier as the men returned to the females at the riverbank who had stood guard. Three corpses lay slain at their feet who had ventured too close, the work of baseball bat and small hatchets. The women were formidable; sprayed with splashes of undead blood and ferocious in their determination to protect their new family.

"Stay here, we will be able to manage the last bits. Make sure nothing gets up that ramp," Kurt hugged Sarah close and kissed her.

"I love you, be quick," she said as he pulled away. Kurt nodded and brushed away some snow that was gathering on her exposed hair.

Jonesy led the gathering party back up the river, holding his arm up to shield his streaming eyes from the biting wind. The flakes whirled around his arm and hit his face anyway, the storm was growing in intensity by the minute. Visibility had been reduced to about thirty feet and small tornadoes of air twisted the falling ice particles in hypnotic patterns. The remaining boxes of ammunition and food were picked up and the wail of the banshee wind was broken by another, familiar outcry. Looking up, Kurt saw the gathered dead who must have followed them from the station. They lined the top of the incline, deep into the builder's yard. As if a dam had been breached, the tide of flesh washed downwards. Unable to maintain their footing in their new condition, they just threw themselves down the slope, bouncing and crunching as unfeeling limbs shattered. The piled corpses started to rise as more joined the heap. Those that had suffered broken legs dragged themselves through the snow, leaving a green trail on the pristine white ground.

"Run!" Jonesy yelled and they fled from the pursuing monsters. The snow crunched underfoot as it was compacted and Braiden slipped over on the icy ground, the box of ammunition he carried spilling the shiny shells all about. He scrambled onto his knees and started to gather handfuls of mud, snow and casings. Jonesy grabbed him under the arm, pulling him away from the task.

"Leave it, we have to get on the boat!" Jonesy shouted, trying to be heard over the hammering wind. Braiden reluctantly left the contents and they were gladdened when the women appeared through the snow fog.

"We have company. Get on the boat!" Kurt called out and they ran up the ramp without hesitation.

"Kurt, we need to blow the ramp, open that box and take out one of the grenades while I cover you!" Jonesy called out and took the rifle from his shoulder. The uninjured zombies came striding out of the snowstorm and Jonesy picked them off with precision while Kurt lifted the small, egg shaped death dealer from the foam padding.

"What do I do with it?" Kurt questioned, thinking they were going to be using it against the dead. Against living beings, the slivers of metal would be deadly. Against the dead who felt no pain and only fell with a destroyed brain, they would be useless.

"Pull the pin. As soon as you release the handle it is live, for fuck sake don't keep hold of it. Roll it down the ramp and get yourself laid flat on the dock, ok?" Jonesy instructed Kurt.

Finally understanding, he nodded his agreement and pulled the pin. Jonesy took one last shot, spraying the snow with a final gout of blood and then ducked away, ready to take cover when Kurt tossed the metal ball of explosives. The grenade was lobbed gently underhand and it bounced on the timber, meeting the first zombie to reach the access ramp. Kurt had already thrown himself down and his weight crashed him through the rotten wood as the grenade exploded. The cadaver was sent flying into the air in pieces and the concussive blast had shattered the fragile dock into splinters. The ramp was no more, and the dead could only moan their angst at the meat that was so close, but still so far. Kurt's feet dangled in the frozen water, his grip on the icy wood slipping. Jonesy grabbed his arm and started to lift, unable to comprehend how the man weighed so much. Kurt was trying to say something as John joined them and, taking his other arm, they roared and slumped backwards with his weight. The zombie that had clutched onto his legs from the water was pulled up with them and lifted its head. Their awkward position meant Kurt struggled to push himself up, and John and Jonesy were pinned underneath. The zombie opened its mouth in triumph and struck downwards, attempting to bite Kurt's shoulder. The crack of Gloria's shotgun pulverized the head before it could take its fatal bite and the decapitated body toppled into the water.

"Thank you, Gloria, oh thank you," cried Sarah who had seen the whole thing.

She embraced the teacher and then ran to her struggling husband. By helping him climb off, the others were able to get their footing and their celebration was brief. The driving snow was a cloying blanket that robbed them of heat and breath. If they had been out in the open, they might have wandered aimlessly, blinded by the total whiteness, before succumbing to the freezing temperatures. The jetty led them straight to the long boat and they climbed aboard, sheltering inside and closing the hatch. The wind took on an unnatural life, shrieking around the boat as if it was a hunter whose prey had eluded it.

CHAPTER SIX

Lieutenant Baxter paced in the darkened room, lost in thought. The dull glow of the computer screens shed an eerie light on the scowling face and the only other man in the room felt sure he was alone with the Devil. The deteriorating mental state of their superior and his homicidal rages was the subject of hushed conversations across the whole barracks. Since the execution of Bennett and the soldier who had dared to criticize the lieutenant on the parade ground, the mood was close to breaking point. The fear of the gun was diminishing and it wouldn't take much for the ill-treated troops to finally snap. Baxter could sense the hair trigger hostility as he prowled the corridors with his henchmen. Salutes were still given, but with a carefully disguised contempt. No longer delivered with speed, they almost saluted in a fashion akin to a slow clap of derision.

"There! What was that?" Baxter shouted and loomed over the young soldier's shoulder pointing at the screen.

Such was the suddenness of the gesture, Private Morrow dropped the handheld controller he was using to direct the images on the monitors. Baxter glared and Morrow felt around in the darkness of the floor, until his fingers brushed the plastic casing and he was able to retrieve it.

"Sorry, sir. I've got it now, no need to worry," babbled Morrow under the scrutiny of the lieutenant's cold gaze.

"Do you think you might like to regain control before the multi-million-pound piece of equipment crashes?" asked Baxter, snidely.

"Yes, sir. Sorry, sir," Morrow replied and was terrified to see the unmanned aerial drone in freefall. The ground was rushing up to meet the plummeting machine at a staggering pace. His shaking hands were nearly his undoing and it was only luck that allowed him to regain control and bring it horizontal before it impacted. He let out a shaky, pent up breath and smiled weakly at the officer who was still scowling.

"I asked you before you had a fit of hysterics, to check over there." Baxter pointed to the north of Chichester. They had found the pile of smoldering remains of the apartment at the hospital and the zombie filled artillery craters on the outskirts of the city. The powerful camera followed the road until they discovered the blackened radius of the gas explosion.

"What the hell happened here, sir?" asked the private with awe.

"Zoom in, there." Baxter pointed to the obvious epicenter of the blast and the metal walls of the huge cylinder were visible on the high definition images.

"Was that one of our shells?" questioned Morrow with a confused frown.

"Clever bastards," growled the lieutenant with grudging respect. "They blew the Lavant gas supply, it's how they got away."

Among the blackened, matchstick like stumps of burnt trees milled thousands of the dead. The heat had been sufficient to burn them but not to kill them. The zoomed image came across the multiple screens and the zombies skin was cracking and leaking green fluids onto the ground. They could no longer distinguish between male and female as the hair had been burned away, leaving the scalp split and skull showing, a contrast of blackened flesh against white bone.

"Dear God in Heaven," whispered Morrow at the macabre sight.

"There is only one God you need to worry about. *Me*," smiled Baxter. It was an awful rictus that looked demonic in the awkward lighting of the UAV control booth. His eyes seemed to glow with a faint red hue, but it could have been Morrows overactive imagination at the inhuman atrocities that Baxter had carried out.

"Of course, sir," the young soldier nodded and Baxter was placated.

"Follow the road," Baxter ordered and the pilot corrected the course and zoomed back out, glad that the hideous images were gone.

The drone circled at ten thousand feet, observing the abandoned vehicles that looked like miniature child's toys with the distance.

"Look, see how they have pushed the cars out of the way to get past," Baxter pointed out the trail and then his mood soured, "With my fucking Foxhounds!"

"Sir, that must be the way they went. The roads into Lavant town are blocked solid and the only clear route is towards Boxgrove," said Morrow, groveling with the information and praying the growing anger wouldn't spill over.

Baxter sighed and the tension went out of him in an instant, "Good work, Private. I will be checking on the guards at the main entrance now, keep me appraised of when you find more information."

"You can count on me, sir," proclaimed Morrow.

As the door closed quietly, the private set the drone to autopilot and placed the controller down on the console. He placed his head in his hands and let loose the terrified shivers that had been threatening to overwhelm him during his time with Baxter.

"You coward, you are helping him to find your friends so he can kill them!" Morrow said to himself. Tears of fear and shame coated his cheeks. If he had half the bravery of DB, Jonesy, or Bennett he would crash the drone and to hell with the consequences. He regarded the small plastic device as if it was a viper ready to strike, filling him with venom. With a glum reluctance, he picked it up and resumed the search. It wasn't a snake, but the mere act of holding it filled him with a poisonous self-loathing that was infinitely worse than a death by snake bite.

The images rolled of the dead land.

***

"Sir, any news?" Sergeant Filton asked as he followed his commanding officer.

"Not yet, but it is only a matter of time," replied Baxter.

Sergeant Moseby looked across and frowned at his companion. They were nearly having to jog to keep up the pace with their superior as he headed for the parade ground to check on the guard posting at the front gate. They had discussed the rising tension and the insubordination of the troops when ordered to dismiss after Bennett's execution. They were increasingly worried about the hateful looks they caught out of the corner of their eye and no longer heavily punished the culprits, hoping to garner some mercy for what was bubbling just beneath the surface. It wouldn't work though; they had hurt too many people when the initial power had been given to them by Baxter. They had firmly nailed their flag to his mast and, for good or ill, they had made their decision.

"Request permission to speak freely, sir," asked Moseby, cautiously. His question could wind up with him tied to the post and shot.

"Please do, sergeant, you know I value your council on the undead threat." Baxter stopped and turned to face him, the stern gaze almost enough to still his tongue. Filton looked worried and was trying to get him to be quiet with surreptitious facial movements and shakes of the head.

"Erm, it wasn't about the dead, sir. I was just wondering if maybe we should try and build bridges with the troops, sir," Moseby started, his mouth suddenly dry as Baxter cocked his head, studying him as a cat would study a tasty mouse.

"What do you suggest, Sergeant?" Baxter asked, smiling coldly.

"Well, sir… I was thinking we could postpone the coming executions," Moseby said and swallowed hard.

"And why on earth would I countenance delaying a just punishment for soldiers who have tried to commit desertion?" Baxter took a pace forward, crowding the subordinate.

"I thought it may show your, um, leadership and compassion, sir," Moseby offered. Filton closed his eyes and shook his head, sure that his friend has just doomed himself by questioning the officers command and motives.

Baxter stared and time seemed to drag on into infinity, Moseby felt his stomach clench and bladder weaken, but eventually he answered, "I think I understand your motives. You fear your fellow soldiers, yes?"

"They hate us more than the dead, sir," whispered Moseby, confirming the fact. He waited for the shot or the order to be detained, awaiting his own turn at the post.

"You know I didn't ask for this, don't you?" Baxter asked the men and they nodded enthusiastically at the change in the conversation. "To be a good leader is to make the hard calls, the unpopular decisions. That can sometimes mean punishing the few for the deeds of the many. The executions are a way of controlling the masses, protecting them from themselves you could say."

"I understand, sir," Filton agreed, although he wasn't sure killing several soldiers a week was protecting anyone. He just wanted to put the conversation to bed and beat the shit out of his friend later for being such a moron.

"I hope you do, because one day you may be put in a position where you have to be hated to get the job done. The executions will go ahead as planned. I will hear no more about the matter," Baxter finished and strode off, leaving the men to count their blessings before swiftly catching up.

They reached the new 'gatehouse'; four heavily armored Viking vehicles that blocked the barracks side of the island access bridge. A makeshift staircase had been erected to allow easy access to the tops for patrol. Two soldiers paced back and forth on the armored roof while two more were always sat in the rotating gun turrets. Not a shot had been fired at the gathered crowd since the initial battle. It had been decided that the ammunition would be wasted and the fallen dead could have provided their own rotting staircase for the remaining horde of fifty thousand cadavers if the bodies piled.

"Any change?" called up Baxter to a young, female recruit. She turned slowly and the response was delayed by a fraction of a second, a typical trait of one of his soldiers who hated the new regime.

"No, sir. More arrive daily, I expect it's the growing volume of their moans acting as a beacon to the others," she replied. Her stare was too forthright and Baxter made a mental note to keep a close eye on this one. The other three guards were watching the exchange with interest.

"What is your name, soldier?" he inquired.

"Eldridge, sir. Private Beth Eldridge," she replied. The way she uttered the words was almost challenging and Baxter was certain she would be trouble in the future.

"Keep up the good work," Baxter called to the four-person team, nodding.

"Yes, sir," she replied, holding his gaze until he turned and walked away.

"Filton, are they still staring?" Baxter asked as they marched away and the sergeant looked back over his shoulder.

"Only Private Eldridge, sir. The others have resumed their lookout positions," explained Filton, watching the young female look away slowly.

"I want her watched from now on. There is trouble in her eyes and I want it nipped in the bud if she ever tries to make a move against us," ordered the lieutenant.

"As you wish, sir," complied Filton and he ran off, seeking a couple of trusted eyes to start the watch.

"Sergeant Mosely," started Baxter, coming to a halt and looking directly at the soldier, "If you ever question my decisions again, you will join those awaiting the post. Do I make myself clear?"

Mosely couldn't speak. He had been so relieved that Baxter hadn't exploded in a rage, that he assumed his question had been taken well. Nothing could be further from the truth and he merely nodded in terror.

"Good." Baxter traced a finger across the sergeant's brow and it came away wet with nervous perspiration. He licked the wet tip and smiled. "Fear is a powerful force is it not? I hope my point is made."

Mosely stood frozen and the lieutenant walked away towards the communication building. As soon as the officer was out of sight, he vomited all over the icy ground.

***

Two guards came to attention upon seeing Baxter and they offered crisp salutes which he returned.

"How have they been?" he asked his men.

"Quiet as mice. I think the last beating was enough to convince them that trying to get out was a bad idea," the largest replied. He had a face that had seen many street fights before realizing in the Army he would have the opportunity to kill for money and not run the risk of imprisonment for his compulsions. A true thug, he was among the most trusted of Baxter's coterie. The information contained within the communications room was too important for wider circulation among the troops, which was why it was kept under armed guard around the clock.

"Good. It's reassuring to know I can count on you," Baxter said with sincerity to the man and then looked at his partner, "On both of you."

"Always, sir!" they said in unison and returned to their original position.

The keypad bleeped as the code was entered and he pushed inside. The smell that wafted over him was awful; with only two of the communications experts left, they were confined to the twelve-foot square room at all times. This meant a lack of washing, and a toilet consisting of a bucket in the corner which was emptied every eight hours. The two prisoners stood up and saluted weakly. Working around the clock with only brief periods of sleep was talking its toll and Baxter would have to consider letting them get some air soon or they would break under the strain. A third and fourth recruit were being sought for training but no one had come forward. More drastic measures would need to be taken to find 'volunteers'.

"Good morning, gentlemen, how are you?" Baxter asked cheerfully, hoping to instill some positivity in the men.

"Fine, sir," answered Corporal Graff wearily. He had heavy dark patches under his eyes and he slumped back into the chair with exhaustion. The other private just about managed a salute, but the arm fell to his side as if it was made of lead. Something must be done soon, Baxter decided, or he would be deaf to the comings and goings of the command structure.

"Update," ordered Baxter, trying to ignore the rising stench of the morning excrement from the bucket.

"We are being constantly hailed by HMS Dauntless. They know we are here from satellite reconnaissance and want to know why we are refusing to answer," laid out the corporal nervously.

"Maintain radio silence and continue scanning the frequencies to see if anyone has hidden a radio since the Bennett incident," said Baxter, ignoring the communication request from his superiors. When the dead had overrun key facilities, the top brass had been evacuated to the floating fortress. They now directed the sparse remnants of the British Armed Forces from the safety of the destroyer.

"But, sir, they are threatening to send a chopper to investigate. They are currently just off the coast of the Isle of Wight," complained the second soldier.

"It makes no difference. Dauntless can only hold one helicopter, they won't risk it on the unknown. If they surprise me and they send it, we will just shoot it out of the sky," replied the commander without concern. They were disgusted at how he casually described committing mass murder to protect his fiefdom, and looked at each other with shock.

"And if they send one from another base?" questioned Graff, looking around at his superior.

"The rest of the armed forces are in full retreat. Even if they could muster more than one, we will just say that the communications were damaged and we had no qualified engineers alive to repair it," Baxter said menacingly. The threat that they would be killed to cover Baxter's mutiny ensured their compliance.

"Ok, sir," whispered Graff.

"So, there has been no chatter on any other frequency?" the Lieutenant got back on track.

"Only some local pockets of survivors trying to connect with each other. They are gradually falling silent though, sir," said the Private with sadness.

Their silence meant they had probably fallen to the dead, or they were out of battery power for their CB radios and totally alone, which meant much the same thing. Baxter couldn't have been less interested in the remaining survivors and he waved his hand dismissively for them to move on.

"We have heard some sporadic communication that is allegedly from the government bunker under Whitehall, but it is gone now so we can't confirm," Graff added and Baxter was taken aback.

"The government has survived?" he said quietly, pondering the ramifications. It would scupper his plans if the command and control structure was reinstated. He would be tried for treason and hanged for his supposed crimes, when all he had wanted was to see England rise from the ashes of the apocalypse. They wouldn't understand his motives or devotion to the greater good of humanity. The zombies were a gift from God, a cleansing plague to remove the weakest from society. Only the strong would survive, led by Baxter into a new age.

"Are you ok, sir?" asked the private when Baxter became lost in the reverie of his vision.

"Yes," the lieutenant answered, momentarily confused at where he was, "Carry on. And if you hear anything else from the bunker, let me know immediately!"

"Yes, sir."

Baxter left them and was glad for the cleaner air of the corridor. Why did the ministers have to live? They weren't the chosen! They were weak and deceptive, always lying to further their own selfish ends. Why wouldn't they just lay down and die?

CHAPTER SEVEN

"**W**ow," uttered Debbie at the devastation she bore witness to.

Mike stood at the corner of the building they were hiding behind and observed it too, whistling at the spectacle. The sprawling train station was a larger hub that diverted services towards London and the northerly cities from the south of England. During the panic, several trains had been involved in a collision and the resulting crash had sent the fifty ton carriages barreling through the main pedestrian sky bridge supports that spanned aerially over the tracks. Any commuter who had been unfortunate enough to be switching platforms in the overhead tunnel had plunged fifty feet down. It had fallen lopsidedly, with one end settling onto the roof of the southern station building and the other crushing through the brickwork and hitting the ground. It reminded Debbie of an old hamster cage she had owned, with angled tunnels to provide amusement for the loveable rodent. As if the collapse hadn't been deadly enough for the victims, the next train had sheared cleanly through the bottom of the glass and steel structure before derailing and ploughing through the main entrance and ticket offices. Fire had destroyed the northern station building and they could see the charred husks of people in the burned out carriages which had jumped the rails. Blackened skeletons of victims sat welded to the charred seats, their arms raised as if clawing at the consuming fire. Mike was thinking the poor bastards were lucky to avoid what came after.

"Can you see any zombies?" Debbie whispered over his shoulder.

Mike was so rapt on the scene that he didn't hear her. The silence of the day was replaced in his mind by the catastrophic shrieks and explosions of concrete meeting high velocity, steel trains and the screams of the dying and the groans of the recently deceased as they rose from the accident to finish the job.

"Mike?" Debbie asked, putting a hand on his shoulder.

"Huh?" Mike said, "Sorry. I was just imagining what happened here. Jesus Christ."

"It's like something out of a movie," she agreed, "I just wondered if you could see any of… them."

Mike looked around. The area was mostly clear but movement in the still day caught his eye on the tracks and roads.

"We need to get around and the only way is through that," Mike pointed at the burned rubble of the entrance building.

"Why not just go over the crossing?" Debbie asked, until she saw that the wreckage was still crowded with zombies who hadn't been able to reach the fiery column of the burning flats at the hospital.

"Too many of them. And the fences are topped with razor wire to stop trespassing. We would be cut to ribbons if we tried to climb them," he answered.

If the bladed wire wasn't enough of a deterrent, the tracks had a gathering of the crash victims too, milling around and trapped on the line forever. Some had been thrown clear upon impact and they were shredded and broken. Others were people who had gone to try and help; policemen, ambulance paramedics, and members of the public. They were mostly eaten and little more than wandering skeletons, with exposed ligaments and tendons stretching and pulling their torn frames around. Their abandoned emergency response vehicles sat silent, the flashing lights and sirens long ago draining the battery as horror unfolded all around.

"We move car to car, staying low," Mike explained and Debbie nodded.

She didn't want to go through the abandoned station as it looked dangerous and unstable, but Mike pulled her onwards. As they scrambled over the road between the cars, she found herself wondering what Peter was doing right now and how hard he had taken the loss of Paige. The bitter jealously at her, now dead, love rival was partly due to the speed at which Peter had given up on their years together for the slut. But more than that, it was the sure knowledge that he had never felt as strongly for her as he did for Paige. The two had known each other for a few short days, and in that time their new love had eclipsed his old feelings for Debbie as if they had never existed. Did she still love him, she thought, was that what it was? Impossible, Peter was a puling specimen and she had bagged Mike Arater; a strong and powerful alpha male. Still, she couldn't fathom the bitter longing she harbored for him. How did the old saying go? Absence makes the heart grow fonder?

"Bullshit," she whispered from behind a stationary Lexus.

"What did you say to me?" demanded Mike, staring at her.

"I wasn't saying it to you," she said, thinking quickly, "I was just thinking about those fuckers."

"With any luck, they have been killed by the horde that was following them," he growled and Debbie felt a pang of fear at the thought of Peter being dead.

She ground her teeth so hard that the muscles started to ache in her jaw, anything to expel the silly feeling of regret that was growing inside her heart. Mike saw an opening and took her by the hand, crouching low and running for the shattered wall on the nearest side of the building. They reached the pile of debris and paused, looking into the partly concealed station hall. The roof had collapsed inwards and added wood to the inferno that had raged here weeks ago. The asbestos roof sheets were fire scorched, yet undamaged. They lay on piles of ash that had been their timber supports until the train smashed through the main ticket office and several walls, destroying the structural integrity of the building. All was still in the large space, and Debbie took a single step onto the mound of smashed bricks, before leaping back with a shriek as something brushed her ankle.

"You fucking idiot!" Mike hissed as he pushed her away. From the pile, several hands that were camouflaged by dust began moving. They were attempting to reach for the survivors which they could hear, but it was impossible from their entombment in the collapsed walls. Debbie stamped wildly at the hand that had scared her and it cracked, the wrist bones breaking through the dried flesh.

"They are under there!" Debbie cried out, thinking Mike hadn't understood why she jumped backwards. Knowing that just inches below the surface, people had died and reanimated appalled her.

"I know, and now your noise will have brought more of them. Move your ass!" snarled Mike in anger. From the corner, a solitary zombie was approaching, then another and another.

"Sorry, I didn't mean to," Debbie whined like a child.

Mike pushed past her, holding his arms out for balance on the unstable pile of station wall which shifted dangerously underneath him. The seismic sensation was most likely due to the softer, fleshier parts of the mound that were moving and the hands grasped with increased desperation. Debbie was sobbing and followed, stepping carefully to avoid the skeletal fingers.

"Which way?" she asked as they stepped down into the station hall with no roof.

Mike looked around and the only way that was clear was the tunnel that had fallen, spanning both sides of the station. It had crashed down and settled several feet above the dead on the lower portion of the tracks due to the awkward angle.

"Through the sky bridge!" Mike pointed.

They hurried over, breaking the sheets of corrugated roofing and causing choking clouds of dust. Any asbestos fibers they inhaled would possibly cause health issues in their later life, but the immediate risk of being eaten alive was more pressing. Among the ashes were skeletons which also crunched sickly underfoot as they passed. They reached the tunnel which rose upwards at an angle towards the other platform. It had hit the roof, but the weight had not been sufficient at the time to crash through to ground level on the other side. Looking left, the concrete staircase that had climbed to the walkway was still intact, though now it led to the open sky and a sheer drop of forty feet.

"Watch your step and careful what you hold onto," Mike explained, no longer furious. They had a difficult enough job ahead of them, without the added risk heightened emotions would bring. Every window pane had shattered along the entire length and only pointed shards remained, lining the open frames that they would need to hold onto if they wished to navigate the steeply climbing tunnel. The rubble underfoot crunched and shifted with their weight. If they slipped, it would slide them straight down into the waiting pile of glass at the bottom, cutting them to shreds.

"Use the hatchet to break it out," Debbie advised and Mike chipped away at the glinting slivers. Thankfully, the putty holding the fragments was old and it crumbled easily, leaving a safer metal edge to hold onto in place of the jagged remnants.

They slowly shuffled up the ramp, kicking glass out of the way to leave clean patches to stand on during their ascent. Moving sideways like crabs, they made slow progress and the zombies had reached the foot of the slope when they were only twenty feet through the hundred-foot tunnel.

"Shit!" Mike complained, starting to feel claustrophobic. It wasn't because of confinement, just being caught in such a predicament with no other way of escape. Now if they fell, they would provide a nice meal. Sliced like ham for the waiting teeth of the dead.

"It's fine. We just take it slowly," Debbie soothed, trying to stop him from going into a meltdown.

Mike took several deep breaths, just like Sarah had shown him. His heartrate stopped racing and he stared out of the wide window, looking up at the sky. The colossal expanse of open air calmed him and he didn't feel as confined. The dead were having no luck, falling after a couple of steps and rolling to the bottom. They stood and were embedded with great daggers of clear glass, a fate that would await the living survivors should they lose their footing.

"Why did I have to look? Fucking hell!" Mike cursed himself, closing his eyes. There was a reason people said don't look down.

"Mike?" Debbie asked with fear at his apparent freeze.

With one final shaky breath, he started to sidestep again, moving towards their next obstacle. The train had ripped the floor away and the open hole looked down upon the zombies that had gathered underneath from the tracks.

"There's no way across, we are trapped!" Debbie started to sob.

"There's a way. You won't like it though," Mike said and looked upwards. The roof was intact and if they reached out they could clasp the steel girders that held the roof in place.

"You have got to be fucking joking! You want us to swing across like monkeys?" she laughed, but it was a mixture of fear and disbelief.

"Didn't you ever go on the raised bars at the park when you were younger?" Mike asked. He was scared too, though their options were limited to either proceed, or get eaten by going back.

"Of course, but it didn't involve hanging over a crowd of ravening fucking monsters!" she shouted at Mike.

Ignoring the temptation to shout back and hit her, he pulled her close and cuddled her instead. The contact was enough to calm her for the moment and buy them time to plan the crossing. Mike felt confident that he would have the strength to swing across, even with the added weight of his backpack. He was in extremely good shape, but the same couldn't be said of Debbie. Although slim, the act of holding her own weight may be too much for her thin arms.

"Did we pick up that nylon paracord?" asked Mike, thinking back to the camping shop.

"I don't know, hold onto me," replied Debbie and he held her tight while she removed her backpack. Delving deeply, she pulled out a spool of tightly bound cord and handed it over.

"We will use this. Once I am over I will tie it off. For now, we can tie it around that and I will tie it around my waist," Mike indicated a bent steel strut that would be a perfect anchor point. He knelt down and wrapped it around, tying it in a knot before pulling as hard as he could. It didn't snap so he spooled a ten-foot length at his feet and tied it around himself.

"You want me to be a tightrope walker?" she asked, disbelievingly.

"No. I tie it over there and then use it to support your weight. You will still need to hang from the cross beams, but it will take a lot of the strain from your arms," Mike explained.

"I think I understand," she said. Her vision kept lowering to the reaching carnivores and the grim death that would arise if she fell.

"Wait here," Mike said and winked.

Taking hold of the steel beam, he lifted his legs to put the full weight on his arms. Satisfied that it was manageable, he swung out over the gulf and grabbed the second rung.

"Please be careful," Debbie begged.

Mike was too intent on the job to remind her that he was unlikely to do anything but be careful in the circumstances. Reaching the halfway point, he clutched at the next beam and an unseen edge cut into his palm, causing him to lose his grip. Debbie shrieked as Mike swung precariously from one arm, twisting around until his shoulder threatened to pull from his socket. Ignoring the pain, Mike reached up and took hold of the center support, easing the burden on his protesting joint. The blood ran slowly down from his hand and tickled his underarm as it moved lower. The undead were frenzied at the meal hanging above their heads and groaned even louder.

"Mike, are you ok?" Debbie wailed.

"Do I look ok, you fucking idiot?" Mike growled, "There is something sharp up there."

Instead of trying the same place again, he shuffled down a short distance and swung again. The bloodied hand was weakening and slippery, but whatever sharp edge had cut him was further down the roof beam and didn't reach this far. With three more swings he was relieved to touch down on the other side of the gulf. The fear had been a constant drain on his strength and he was certain that Debbie would have stood no chance if they hadn't been fortunate enough to pack the cord. Opening the injured hand, the cut was deep but hadn't damaged any nerves or tendons. Clenching it into a fist, the pain was receding now that he wasn't hanging by it.

"Hurry up, I want to get out of here," complained Debbie, her concern for Mike replaced with fear of the short walk she would need to take, held aloft by little more than string. Mike's eyes narrowed slightly and she was blissfully unaware that he was weighing the choice of whether to leave her behind, much the same as the other group had decided to do. Sex with her was good; there was nothing she would refuse him, no matter how debauched or painful. The question boiled down to whether he would be more likely to survive by keeping her alive. In case of the worst happening, she would serve as a useful distraction for the dead to feast upon if they got into a bind. All of this scheming went through his mind in the blink of an eye and, decision made, he carefully tied the other end of the cord to a section of steel in the ravaged floor.

"Thanks," Debbie tried to smile through the terror. It appeared as a grimace and contorted her features into an ugly rictus.

"Just be careful of that middle strut, see where my blood is?" he pointed at the sharp edge that he could now see from the other side. Water had been leaking through the roof and the steel had started to corrode, leaving the edge rusty. When had he last had a tetanus booster? Just his fucking luck that he would get another infection so close after his last brush with death. She reached upwards and held tight to the beam, leaning out with her foot and testing the thin rope.

"It will take your weight, trust me. That's it, slowly," Mike coaxed Debbie and she moved out onto the rope fully, only putting as much weight on it as she couldn't hold with her arms.

"Oh God. I don't think I can do it," she cried out, after looking down. She took a pace backwards, trying to reach the solid, yet broken surface of the tilted floor.

"Stop! I believe in you, just look at me, keep your eyes on mine," Mike urged, locking his eyes onto hers, "Now, step by step, move."

She ignored the moans and the horribly springy feel of the cord underfoot. Mike's confidence filled her with a self-belief that had been in danger of disappearing. Her feet seemed to work on their own under the powerfully hypnotic gaze and it came as a shock when she finally felt something solid under her feet.

"There you go; I knew you could do it!" Mike was beaming and the joy was infectious; the hardest part of the tunnel was behind them.

"Thanks for believing in me," Debbie gasped and held him tight.

"No problem," replied Mike, looking over her shoulder. The good news was that if they slipped, they would no longer plough into a mass of broken glass. They would simply fall through the hole in the floor and into the eager arms of the zombies below.

Mike decided to tie them off at each window after finding the cord, just in case. Each window had an upright strut set at eight feet spacing's. If they fell and started the slide to hell, the binding would pull taut and, hopefully, prevent their deaths. No different to climbers who secured safety anchors, they climbed the remaining forty feet without incident and cut the remaining cord to take with them. Mike gave the finger to the small group of zombies at the bottom of the tunnel and looked around at the roof of the south side of the train station. The gently pitched roof was also covered with large sheets of corrugated asbestos, a cheap but reliable material until people started dying from its use.

"You see the heads of the screws?" Mike pointed at the drab, grey covering.

"Yeah, the rusty bits?" she replied.

"You have to make sure you only step on those or you could fall through, they show where the wooden joists are located," he cautioned and lowered himself carefully onto the roof from the torn opening of the fallen tunnel.

Turning, he helped Debbie to get her footing on the delicate surface and was about to direct their route to the access hatch that led down into the main station building below. The sounds of groaning were a constant companion and they didn't notice the increase in the volume until the first crash vibrated through the roof into their legs. Looking up, they could see the open mouth of the southern staircase that once led to the skywalk opening they had just climbed down from. Now, contrasted by the darkness as they came walking into the light, were dozens of cadavers that had climbed to the top of the steps in search of the sustenance they had seen. The dam of rotting flesh burst and flowed over the rim, falling in a heap onto the roof close to Mike and Debbie. The first few had landed on the wooden supports and cracked the asbestos. The others weren't as fortunate and hit the already weakened roofing sheets, crashing through and falling to their doom on the hard floor below.

"Move!" Mike screamed and walked along the screw line, sticking to the strongest part of the roof. Debbie followed and then the dead, who had started to give chase with no fear of the potential dangers. Mike wanted to break into a run, but it would be too risky. The zombies were gaining and they had no chance of making it to the door in time, let alone break through and escape. Mike ushered Debbie past and took out his hatchet. Swinging wildly, he hammered onto the roof, breaking sections away that went spiraling down to join the fallen dead.

"Get to the door, we fight them there!" Mike bellowed and quickly scurried the last twenty feet to the flat, solid platform of the roof access doorway.

89

The trap worked as he had hoped and the first to reach the hacked roof fell through. Similar to films he had seen where people were fool enough to walk out onto frozen lakes, one misplaced step and they were swallowed whole. The zombies that hit the floor below sent up a sickening crunch of sound as they split apart, splashing their rotten green blood everywhere. Out of the eight that had avoided the first pitfall under the staircase, only three survived for the coming battle.

"Get ready!" Mike ordered and Debbie was frantically trying to shuck her backpack off to give her more freedom of movement. The straps had caught on her life preserver and she was caught off balance as the first zombie reached them. Mike swung the hatchet and only managed to cleave a chunk of face away before it fell on Debbie. The other two were intent on Mike, and by trying to hit the one who threatened Debbie, he left himself open. They hit him fully and drove him back against the door with a crash.

"Help me!" screamed Debbie as she looked into the incomplete face of the rotting female. The blackened teeth snapped shut, trying to bite her fighting hands. Green tinged drool dribbled from the open mouth and the breath stunk of rancid flesh and blood.

Mike ignored the plea, only concerned with preserving his own life. Drawing his head back until it hit the door, he threw a vicious headbutt at the male monster, laying open the skin of its forehead and causing it to stumble backwards. The third zombie held on tight and was only inches from taking a bite from Mike's exposed neck. With a roar of revulsion, he grabbed it by the throat and crotch and hefted it overhead, before tossing it over the wall and the waiting carpark below. Like lightning, he embedded the small axe into the back of the head of Debbie's attacker and left it buried as he pushed the other cadaver away again. It fell backwards and landed on the roof hard, cracks radiating outwards and growing until the asbestos crumbled under the weight. The body fell, arms still reaching for Mike as he watched. It impacted the foyer floor and the festering arms and legs exploded from the trunk, spraying viscera and blood everywhere.

"Get it off!" shrieked Debbie under the weight of the dead creature. The twisted backpack and the weight of the figure gave her no room to unburden herself. Mike held up a finger, asking her for a moment while he tried to stop the shaking from the adrenaline surge.

"Are you fucking kidding me? Get this bitch off!" she screamed at the top of her lungs.

Staring down at Debbie as she glared and spat her demands, Mike turned around and sat on the back of the dead zombie. The added weight compressed her chest and the screams were cut off instantly. She desperately tried to draw breath, but it was impossible.

"I can see why the others were going to leave you behind. I've told you to keep your mouth shut, you cunt. Those shouts will bring everything in the area down on us and I still need to try and get away," he told her.

Looking down, Debbie's eyes were rolling and her face had gone a dark shade of purple from the suffocating weight. Her arms and legs were twitching in spasm as she died. All he needed to do was stay put for a few more minutes and he would have peace and quiet. Closing his eyes, he listened to the silence but it was short lived. The groans of the dead approaching the station reaffirmed her value as a convenient source of meat should he need it and, reluctantly, he stood up and pulled the putrescent body off. Debbie was still and her chest no longer rose and fell with the rhythm of her inhalations.

"Now don't be so melodramatic, I was only sat on you for a little while," Mike chastised Debbie's body, "Fucking typical, always after attention."

Mike knelt down and slapped her cheeks, trying to rouse her unsuccessfully. Feeling her neck, the faint pulse was detectable, fluttering weakly. Aggressively, he tilted her head back and pinched her nostrils, blowing two breaths deeply into her starved lungs. The chest rose and fell as her body expelled the air with no visible improvement.

"Don't take the piss," Mike said and repeated the process.

Debbie coughed and drew in a heaving gasp. She started to choke and was in danger of convulsing so Mike turned her onto her side and rubbed her back through the worst of the fit.

"That's it, you're fine," Mike stroked her forehead, ignoring the looks of fear and anger that she regarded him with.

More zombies tried to navigate the shattered roof, but none made it past the existing pitfalls. Just to be certain, Mike destroyed a wide section surrounding their position. A human, with full use of their faculties could potentially balance and make it across the wooden roof trusses. Mobile corpses, who by some means had been given basic motor function to allow them to hunt the living, weren't so lucky.

"Sit up, rest against the wall," Mike said and helped her upright. The worst of the pain in her lungs had disappeared and she started to cry, her fear of Mike matching her infatuation.

"You tried to kill me," she whispered, worried he would attack her again but compelled to get the words out.

"Don't be silly, I just needed you to be quiet," he smiled at her like a father who was trying to explain to a toddler the error of their ways.

"You could have just asked me," she complained, lowering her gaze.

"When do you ever listen when you are having a bitch fit?" he asked, kneeling beside her and stroking her hair that was matted with zombie dribble.

"I…" she started, then fell silent when she accepted he was right. Her tantrums were always an issue and couldn't be controlled.

"Hey. Don't be mad, your craziness is what attracted me to you in the first place. I loved the fact you didn't give a shit what others felt," Mike was in full charm mode, trying to get her back on side so she would continue their journey.

"Really? Most people hate my bitchiness," her inherent need for acceptance was soaking up the praise like desiccated earth.

"Of course. You have a strong personality, like me. We are meant to rule this new world, not those fucking cowards we left behind." Mike was caught up in the fantasy of the power he would wield, those he would control and the world that would become his dominion.

"We will rule it together!" she declared with conviction, believing the implausible scenario. Only six billion shambling monsters stood in the way of their grand plan to become the dark emperor and empress of planet Earth.

"Of course," Mike helped her to her feet, "But first we need to get inside, can you feel how cold it is getting?"

"I hadn't noticed with all the shit we have been through," she admitted. The clouds had gathered and icy winds swirled around them, stirring their clothes. The first flakes of snow accompanied the gust and they looked at each other, then the single door. The coming storm could be fatal if they were on the roof for the settling snow and plunging temperatures. Mike put his ear to the door, trying to judge if any threat lurked beyond.

"I can't hear anything," he said to Debbie, "Get ready, just in case."

She raised her hatchet and Mike raised a boot, kicking out at the door. The lock cracked under the pressure and a second kick drove the door back into the stairwell, carrying a sliver of door frame with it. The access platform was empty and the shadowed void beckoned them with its promise of shelter. The stinging ice particles lashed their skin and the growing banshee howl of the wind pushed them into the opening. Mike looked down the spiral steel staircase and the dull light only served to illuminate the first corner. The light cut through and he traced it down the plastic clad bannister rail. Slimy green handprints were visible along the whole length.

"They have been in here, stay quiet," Mike cautioned.

"Can you see any of them?" Debbie asked and shuddered as a faint moan rose towards them.

Mike put a finger to his lips and shook his head. The beam created spotlights of illumination, but no zombies appeared to be with them. The noise had probably echoed up from the open doorway at the bottom, which cast a murky pool of light on the floor below.

"Shit, why did I have to kick the door open?" Mike asked himself. Anything close enough could have heard the reverberation and would be coming to investigate. Praying their luck would hold, he watched the light intently for any falling shadow that would mean company. Minutes passed and the noise of the shrieking wind may have masked the crash of the upper door.

"I think we are ok," Debbie said, hopefully.

"Come on," Mike whispered and descended, rounding the first bend of the staircase and nearly falling over the corpse at their feet.

The bloodied skeleton was pressed into a corner where the victim had tried to take cover. Shreds of clothing lay in strips around the body as the teeth had delved to the fleshier parts beneath. Only a sturdy utility belt remained around the pelvic bone, filled with tools. The man or woman had obviously been a maintenance worker who had tried to flee the zombies. Driven mad by the agony of being eaten alive, one skeletal hand clutched the end of a screwdriver which had then been stabbed through its left eye. In spite of their growing desensitization to the suffering of others, the horrific suicide would haunt their dreams. Imagining themselves cowering as the teeth tore chunks of flesh away, watching as the hungry zombies swallowed and dived in for more. The glinting point of the screwdriver and the salvation it offered as it moved in towards the soft eyeball.

At ground level the open door had a set of keys hanging from the lock with dried blood encrusting the metal. It must have belonged to the rail worker who had tried to escape the ravenous horde. Snow was falling through the holes in the broken roof and zombies staggered within the station building, stepping around their pulped brethren. Behind them stood another door, smeared with handprints from the frenzied worker as they tried to seek refuge. The door was firmly locked as Mike pressed the handle and tried pushing.

"Maybe the keys open that door?" Debbie whispered.

"It's worth a try," he answered and reluctantly moved out from the concealing shadows.

He withdrew the keychain carefully, closing his hand around the loose bunch to still the jangling noise. Leaning back into the darkness, he slowly pulled the door closed and latched it, before inserting the key and locking it. Debbie switched the torch on and used it to help Mike find the right key from the fob. After four tries the lock disengaged and they pushed through, revealing an office which also doubled as a store for the smaller materials for station repairs; lightbulbs, paint, and various latches for the hundreds of doors and windows throughout the building. One other door sat at the back of the room and Mike knelt down, looking through the keyhole. A freezing breeze blew through the thin slit and made his eye water, but he had seen the carpark that lay beyond.

"We have our way out when the storm dies down," he explained. He opted to avoid detailing the dozens of walking corpses, they would be a problem for another day.

"Thank God. I didn't fancy the idea of leaving through the main station, there were so many," Debbie said over her shoulder as she locked the office door, further securing their safety.

A fresh gust buffeted the rear door, shaking it in the frame. The night was going to be below freezing and they had been fortuitous in raiding the camping shop for supplies. The sleeping bags they had selected were designed for harsher environments than the station office and came complete with hood to protect the head. Pushing chairs and desks out of the way, they laid out the sponge roll mats and then placed the down lined bags on top.

"Do you think we should share body heat? It's going to be a long night," whispered Debbie, biting her lower lip. The attempted murder was forgotten for now, overridden by her carnal desires.

"I think the survival of humanity depends on it," Mike agreed with a leer.

The storm intensified, battering the building with white flurries. Inside, the damaged lovers reached levels of depraved lust, the cold all but forgotten.

CHAPTER EIGHT

Private Morrow sat in the darkened booth, expanding his search grid eastward to track DB and Jonesy. He felt lost and afraid, desperate to find a trace of the men to report to his superior, but equally hopeful he would find nothing. He was certain that if he found them his fear would ensure compliance, the tight knots in the pit of his stomach left little doubt. The possibility of corporal punishment should he fail was an option he craved, despite the pain. At least it meant he would be spared the hatred of his fellow soldiers.

"Please stay hidden, please stay hidden," he whispered repeatedly to the darkness.

The endless farmsteads provided a hundred places to hide and the thermal imaging showed that four of the homes were still occupied. Surrounded on all sides by the dead, still they remained alive which meant they were well defended. The sheer numbers left little doubt that the mini sieges had been going on longer than his friends had been on foot. Each location was marked and referenced for perusal by Baxter on his rounds.

"Keep on hanging in there," Morrow said to the plucky survivors on the screen.

The landscape passed below, more fields and another village. Switching to thermal again he was left disappointed. His searches had so far been fruitless when scanning the more densely populated areas, and with each fly past he felt a small part of himself die. Never married himself, at least he didn't have to deal with the horror of losing children to the plague. His parents lived in London, one of the first cities to fall and he was under no illusion they wouldn't be among the millions of dead shambling in the capital's streets. His attention was lost in the memories of his parents and he almost missed the abnormality on the main screen. The Watchkeeper drone turned around and crossed the railway tracks again and Morrow didn't know if it was important or not. The three carriage train was still, with no heat signatures anywhere near it.

"What are you looking at?" Morrow asked himself. It had been years since he had used British Rail, but he was sure they were normally in four car sections. He had seen the destruction at Chichester station and ran the mental picture through his mind of the numbers, both on the track, and those that had crashed through the building itself.

"Think... think," he muttered, "One, two, three, four. And four off the tracks on the other side."

He assumed a circling flight pattern which allowed the autopilot to be switched on, giving him full control of the camera. Zooming in, the spray of zombie blood was unmistakable on the light grey stone ballast. It was too far to have come from the other three carriages and the row of tidy stone burial mounds were further proof people had been through here.

"Please let it be someone else," he prayed to himself and resumed control of the craft aiming it towards Ford.

A smoke trail drifted in to the picture and it drew Morrow in, finally revealing the blazing carriage perched atop the main bridge towards Angmering. Corpses streamed toward the lure in tight procession but kept falling into the water before it could be reached. The fire belched from the shattered windows which told Morrow it was a recent occurrence. The black smoke was being driven into a frenzy before disappearing completely in the violent winds. The UAS craft was beginning to feel the turbulence and the visuals from the onboard camera were making it difficult to survey the scene.

Picking up the radio, Morrow pressed to transmit, "HQ this is Hawkeye, over."

"Go ahead, Hawkeye, over," came the tinny response.

"My bird is taking a hammering, what's going on? Over."

"Sorry, Hawkeye, there is a storm about to hit along the south coast of England. Get your bird home. Over."

"Thanks for the warning, over," replied Morrow sarcastically.

"No problem, out," answered the operator, ignoring the tone.

"Fucking hell!" Morrow shouted and kicked out at his control station.

The screens flickered with the impact and he immediately relented, stroking the cold plastic, "Sorry, I'm sorry. I didn't mean to take it out on you."

It was the mission and the constant sense of dread on the base that had frayed his nerves. A good meal and eight hours' sleep would be just the medicine he needed, maybe a couple of beers if the store would release them.

"Holy shit," whispered Morrow as he caught sight of the two Foxhounds. One looked as if it was overturned and he could see a group of people surrounding the vehicle. On the path to the yard it had crashed from, dozens of dead had broken off from the train to investigate the noise.

"Run, you bastards, run," Morrow begged at the screen, willing his thoughts to reach the survivors by telepathic means. No sign presented itself, no movement or glance skyward at the attempted psychic message. The picture jumped again and he turned his craft westward, saluting the jumbled images and praying that they would endure. It wouldn't be acceptable to lose the multi-million pound piece of equipment, even though he hadn't been forewarned of the storm. Excitement at his friends' safety metamorphosed into the dry mouthed anxiety he had feared. The swift flight caused no issues and the Watchkeeper touched down safely on the landing strip.

"HQ, this is Hawkeye, the bird is back in the nest, over."

"We saw her land, Hawkeye; Tomlinson is on his way to retrieve her. Get some chow, over," came the reply.

The thought of food curdled his stomach and his chest ached with the stress. The sound of heavy boots marching down the corridor increased the apprehension tenfold until he thought he may pass out from the rapid fluttering of his heart. The door opened and Baxter marched in unannounced.

"Good afternoon, Private," he said.

"Good afternoon, sir," Morrow croaked weakly.

"Report."

"Sir?" the scrutiny of his superior combined with his panic addled his thoughts.

"Am I speaking gibberish, Private?" Baxter asked with scorn, "I asked for the report."

"Of course. Sorry, sir," Morrow said, trying to calm himself, "I have found four homes with living occupants."

"Really?" mused Baxter, rubbing his chin.

"All four dwellings are surrounded by the dead, sir."

"And what is your point?" Baxter asked.

Morrow knew their policy towards refugees and didn't push the point, "Nothing, sir. I just hope they can hold out through the winter."

"Don't let it concern you, Private. Anything else?"

"No sir, all was clear. I will resume at first light as long as the storm has passed," replied Morrow, astonished by the steady tone of his own voice.

"Good work, soldier. We can't be sure that the deserters are not sheltering in one of those houses though," Baxter speculated.

"I doubt it, sir, the dead are quite well entrenched around the positions," Morrow explained.

"I think it is better to be safe than sorry," Baxter affirmed, taking the piece of paper which he had jotted down the coordinates.

"Sir?" Morrow questioned.

With a final salute, the lieutenant turned about face and marched out, reaching down into his belt for the radio, "Fire team, this is Lieutenant Baxter, over."

"This is fire team, go for Baxter, over," answered the new artillery commander.

"Requesting fire mission at the following coordinates, over," Baxter said. From behind, he didn't even acknowledge the sound of someone collapsing and read out the digits that Morrow had handed over, dooming the four pockets of humanity to a fiery death.

CHAPTER NINE

The battle weary survivors gathered in the small bedroom on the canal boat, watching anxiously as Christina gently tried to check DB's head wound more closely.

"The good news is that I can't feel any mobile skull around the wound," she stated as her expert fingers probed at the edges of the bleeding contusion, "Which means there is unlikely to be a compression fracture."

"So he's going to be ok?" Sam asked, grinning at the good news.

"I can't say until he regains consciousness. There may still be a linear fracture which will heal over time, so at the very least we are grounded for a few days while I keep an eye on him."

Jonesy stepped forward and leaned down, placing a kiss on the filthy hair of the doctor in silent gratitude. Christina was still checking DB's vitals and could only reach back and pat his leg in reply. The doctor had found her place in the group and was astonished at how quickly she had been accepted. Building trust in the new world was a rapid process, with terrifying encounters bonding people in hours and days rather than weeks and months as before.

"Stay here, we will be right back," said Kurt. He and John dropped their belongings and made a quick search of the long vessel, but no threat lurked within. Outside? Well that was another matter as the calamitous wail of gale force winds battered at the small windows, reminding them how lucky they were.

The boat was a beautiful specimen and could only have been a year or two old. The attack had allowed little time for inspection and appreciation of the vessel, it had simply been a place to seek refuge from the coming storm. As they left the bedroom, a small hallway led past a compact shower suite, complete with toilet and hand basin. Exquisitely patterned mosaic tiles adorned the walls and the bathroom cabinets were furnished with high gloss white doors, contrasting modern design with the beauty of ages past.

"If that shower works, God is truly watching down on us," John whispered with anticipation.

"He wasn't watching at the hospital," Kurt rebuked, glancing over his shoulder.

A look of sorrow passed over John's face at the memory, "Sorry, Son. That was a silly thing to say."

"It's ok, Dad. Sometimes I do wonder if we have a guardian angel with all the scrapes we have come through, but after Paige I think it was just fear and luck," Kurt replied with scorn.

Gloria had been following with her shotgun and heard the exchange. Her faith was all but gone following the death of the beautiful and compassionate young woman. Her natural mothering instinct had grown into a powerful love for everyone in the group, and the loss was no less shattering than if Paige had been of her own blood. A tear rolled down her cheek and she reached out to rub John's shoulder in support.

"Kitchen and lounge," Kurt whispered after peering through the crack in the doorway which stood in their way. Honey was unfazed and sniffed around their legs without concern. If any zombie had been on the boat, the confined space would mean the dog couldn't possibly miss the scent.

Kurt pushed the door fully open with the hammer head and stepped over the threshold. To his left was a compact kitchen area, with the granite worktops and range cooker overlooking the spacious lounge. Grey sofas were mounted along the sides of the living area with a large screen plasma television mounted on the far wall. John stepped into the kitchen alcove and turned the burner on the hob, which hissed and then ignited with the sparking piezo.

"The gas bottle is still full," John informed them as he opened a cupboard door and tilted the propane tank which fed the appliance.

"I wonder..." Kurt said cryptically, before reaching out and flicking a light switch. The bulb stayed dark and they all sighed with disappointment. The snow had all but obscured the windows and the light inside the boat was dull and grey, with shadows gaining ascendency as the snow deepened on the glass.

The lounge carpet was soft and Kurt felt guilty at the wet, muddy footprints they were leaving in their wake. Sitting on the edge of a leather sofa, he started to take his shoes off until he noticed the amused looks of his father and Gloria.

"Sorry, I just didn't want to make a mess," he grinned and shrugged.

"You are a true gentleman and an excellent house guest," Gloria informed him with a wry smile.

"But your feet stink!" John added and they all laughed.

"I'll keep them on," Kurt said and shook his head at the absurdity of worrying about making a mess in someone's property who was likely to be part of the undead hordes.

"Our noses are most grateful," said Gloria and even Honey had quickly retreated upon getting a closer sniff at the fragrant extremities.

"I really hope that shower works," Kurt said, echoing the sentiments of John and bringing more chuckles.

Two locked doors remained, one leading up a small flight of steps which opened out onto a small veranda for entertaining. The reclining chairs were stacked in one corner and a barbecue was covered for the wet seasons. A canvas canopy had been tied to the fixing points and the snow swirled around and under, creating a maelstrom of white. Seeing there was nothing of value, Kurt pointed to the final door and Gloria raised the shotgun in readiness. Pulling the handle, the door swung wide and Gloria visibly relaxed, lowering the gun. The door only led to a small cupboard with a bank of electricity meters and fuses that were totally different from a standard domestic setup.

"All clear," called John to the rest of the survivors and turned his attention back to the myriad circuits and wires.

"Any idea?" Kurt inquired as John scratched his head in confusion.

"You boys are on your own with this one I'm afraid," Gloria said and took her leave.

"Fucked if I know," admitted John when the teacher was out of earshot.

The others filtered into the room and sat down on the soft chairs, groaning with contentment. Christina followed and only Jonesy was left in the bedroom, keeping a watchful eye on his brother in arms.

"May I have a look?" Christina asked the two baffled men and they gladly stepped aside for the doctor.

"Any idea, Doc?" Kurt asked with fingers crossed.

"We are in luck. The boat has a separate engine and generator, see?" Christina pointed to two separate panels and the information displayed. Refusing to seem less manly, they both nodded without having a clue. "It means we can produce electricity when we are moored as long as we have fuel. Normally the boat would be hooked up to a power point on the dock, but without a supply it's dead."

"I thought as much," John lied.

She made one final check of a small manual that was in the cupboard and nodded to herself, "Good, it's similar to one I have used before. Wait here."

Christina wrapped the scarf around her face tightly and opened the door that led up to the observation deck. The door was ripped from her hands and flung back against the wall with a crack, but thankfully the glass held.

"What are you doing?" yelled Kurt over the din.

"Be right back," called Christina, shielding her face from the biting wind and snow.

She hurried up the steps and Kurt pushed the door closed, stilling the air within the cabin. Kneeling at a seemingly normal section of deck, she pulled on a hidden handle and the floor lifted like a trapdoor. Kurt watched her reach inside and there was purpose to her movements which he couldn't fathom, but he assumed it was the generator housing. The wind increased in ferocity, throwing her to the side and snatching at her clothes and hair like a malicious entity. Kurt was transfixed by the currents of snow and found himself expecting hands to form from the icy tempest to carry her away. The foreboding caused him to shiver involuntarily and he threw open the door to shake the feeling, intending to help.

"No, I'm ok. Go back inside!" Christina shouted after getting back up and with one more hidden action, the trapdoor was slammed shut.

"Take my hand," Kurt said and reached an arm out to help her navigate the snow covered steps.

"Appreciate it," gasped Christina as the door was closed and she took a moment to compose herself, "Bloody hell that was cold."

"Here, take this," Braiden came over and threw a thick blanket around her shoulders.

"Thank you, sweetheart," she said through chattering teeth.

Braiden stood for a few moments, staring at the doctor which caused her to frown in confusion. He suddenly stepped forward and embraced her tightly, "For body heat," he explained awkwardly, "And for saving DB," he admitted.

"Don't get ahead of yourself, he could still be in danger," replied Christina, wanting to keep a modicum of caution in case the worst should happen.

"He will be fine, I know it," declared Braiden, unheeding of the statement.

"Thank you for the heat," Christina smiled and broke contact, before returning to the fuse board, "Here goes nothing."

One by one she flicked the switches, until finally the lounge burst into brilliant light from the wall mounted bulbs. A cheer went up from the group and Christina blushed at the adulation. Kurt smiled at Sarah and it triggered a bout of mutual hugging and appreciation. The renewed electricity filled them with a sense of accomplishment in the face of the adversity they had endured. Maybe, just maybe, their old life could be rekindled. A life of science and technology, modern comforts and, best of all, hope.

"What the hell?" Jonesy exclaimed as he entered the lounge, "the alarm clock just started blinking at me!" Fascinated by the power, he stood by the wall and flicked the lights on and off a few times, much to the amusement of the survivors.

"It's like being in a disco," said Jodi with a smile.

Braiden and Sam spontaneously broke into a dance routine and flailed around the room, energized by the happiness. John grabbed Gloria and started to pirouette around, staring deep into each other's eyes as they waltzed. Not to be outdone, Jonesy started flapping his arms, doing the funky chicken. Sam collapsed in fits of giggles onto the sofa at the spectacle and even Peter was smiling broadly.

"What's that racket?" flowed down the corridor from the bedroom and all activity stopped as if a pause button had been pressed. Wide eyes and a crazed dash ensued as the group ran to see the source of the deep, complaining voice.

DB was still laid on the stretcher with his head supported. His eyes strained to look at the doorway and a pained smile formed on his lips when he saw his friends enter the room. Christina pushed through the well-wishers and was all business.

"Don't move!" she ordered and shone a small flashlight into each eye. The pupils were sluggish and unresponsive to the stimulus, "Well that's good and not so good, you have a severe concussion."

"I always said you had a thick head, now I'm sure," joked Jonesy who took up his friend's hand, holding it tight with love and relief.

"You didn't think you could get rid of me that easily did you?" DB chuckled and winced at the sharp pain that gnawed away inside his head.

"He needs rest! You will have to come back in a while," Christina ordered and turned her attention back to the patient, "I will do some more checks and then you need to sleep."

The survivors could see the agony etched on his face and quietly left for the lounge, wishing they could help, but knowing nature would take its course. All they could do was pray. Not that it would carry much weight if the past few days were anything to go by.

"Can I have some drugs? My head is killing me." DB asked, closing his eyes. The act of talking sent vibrations through his head that felt like razor blades inside his skull.

"Not right now. I need to monitor you for a while to see if anything more serious is going on," commiserated Christina.

"I understand," DB whispered and closed his eyes. The pain was being replaced by a growing weariness and in moments he had drifted off. Christina watched and the steady rhythm of his breathing signaled a sleep state instead of unconsciousness, which was a great relief.

"Sleep now, gentle giant," whispered Christina after finishing her tests, placing a kiss on his fevered brow.

The lounge was full of excitement at the partial recovery of their friend. Although not out of the woods, Christina agreed that his prognosis was infinitely better than she had believed at the foot of the river bank. Recuperation was now required and she explained to the group what that meant.

"He will need several days of bedrest as a minimum. We won't be able to push on for the castle until he is on his feet and the concussion is gone. Any kind of stress or strenuous activity and it could hamper his recovery," she explained.

"We need him one hundred percent," agreed John. He was a fearsome warrior and their chances relied upon as many strong men and women for the coming onslaught.

"We are stranded here for now? Oh my, how will we ever cope?" Gloria joked sarcastically.

"I agree, we are slumming it a bit, what with electricity and cooking facilities. I think we will just have to try and make it work," John shook his head in faux melancholy.

"I have even more bad news," Jodi said, walking back into the room, "The shower is working… and hot."

More applause threatened to echo the length of the barge until they remembered the sleeping soldier. Celebration was limited to a couple of silent fist pumps and quiet back patting. Honey was caught up in the jubilation and wagged her tail furiously, licking everyone who offered their hand.

109

"It seems the boat was fully stocked and ready to go, which means people probably lived on here instead of using it for holiday cruising," Christina explained.

Sam looked at her with a frown, "Why wouldn't they just live in a house?"

"Because this costs about fifty thousand pounds, and the average house is two hundred and fifty thousand pounds," she replied.

"Ah, that makes sense," Sam admitted, nodding slowly. Money and finance hadn't been a concern while he was growing up, and now it probably never would be. Any society that grew from the corpse of the old world would more than likely be based on barter and trade.

"Everyone get comfortable, I will get the dinner on," Kurt offered and Peter started to take requests. The vote was unanimous for macaroni and cheese, so Kurt opened the large tin and poured it into a saucepan that he found tucked in a small cupboard.

"Yes!" Braiden exclaimed when the television blazed into life.

"What? You get to look at a blank screen?" John was perplexed by the wide grin on the youngster's face.

"Nope. We get to watch these," Braiden said, pulling a stack of DVD's from a cabinet below the screen, "But I don't think we can spare the electricity," he finished and put the films away, closing the drawer carefully.

Sarah looked at Gloria and they both smiled at the maturity he was showing. Months ago he had been a hellion and the bane of many student's lives. Now here he was, caught between the urge to capture some small semblance of their old life, and the knowledge that the fuel would serve a better purpose elsewhere.

"I'm sure one film wouldn't hurt. We may never get the chance again," replied John and this was just as surprising as Braiden's personal development.

"Dad, are you feeling ok?" Kurt asked, stirring the food and laughing.

John's cheeks darkened and he shrugged, "Well, the boys have had it hard," he blustered, trying to justify the sudden change in his no nonsense character, "We could all do with a good laugh. Braiden, find a good comedy, lad."

"Ok, Grandad," he replied and dug back into the collection.

"You're a good man, John Taylor," Gloria whispered as her arms encircled his waist.

"Just don't tell anyone," he whispered back and held her close.

The storm raged, pummeling the long vessel with gusts of driven snow. Winds searched for ingress along the seams and sills, shrieking with inhuman need when denied access. With temperatures dropping and the onset of night, the survivors huddled in relative comfort as four friends suffered a calamitous bachelor party in Las Vegas on the big screen. Raucous laughter rung out, cleansing the area with renewed hope. As the movie rolled and the adversity brought the mismatched friends closer, the survivors felt a certain kinship with the fictional characters. The hilarity gradually faded as these feelings triggered memories of the horror and death they had witnessed. Feelings of contentment grew into guilt at their inactivity and before the movie ended they were all fidgeting and restless. Braiden stood and walked over to the television, pausing by the power switch to look at the group.

"Turn it off if you want," Kurt offered and no one objected.

Pressing the button, the picture blinked out, "It didn't feel right. I mean, people are dying and... I thought it would be good... but, with all that's going on..." Braiden tried to articulate the conflicting emotions, finally gave up and looked at the floor in silence. Growing up in an environment that involved differing levels of screaming to

111

communicate was not something he could get over in a few weeks, but he was trying.

"I know exactly what you mean." John came to the rescue, hugging the boy close, "We have been to hell and back and I don't think it's possible to go back to the way things were that easily. Maybe when we are safe and humanity has come back from the brink it won't feel so… disrespectful?"

Everyone nodded in agreement at John's accurate analysis of the situation. Thankfully, before they could dwell too much on the pain, DB's voice rang out from the bedroom interrupting the morbid thoughts.

"Who's a man got to kill to get a meal around here?"

"I'll take it," offered Jonesy. Picking up the plate of warm pasta, he made his way down the hallway with Christina in tow.

"That smells good," grinned the injured soldier from the bed.

"Trust your stomach to wake your fat ass up, you're meant to be resting!" Jonesy scolded him and laughed.

DB was still strapped down on the stretcher, but the doctor decided to try and move him onto the bed for comfort. If they had tried to feed him laying down, he was in danger of choking to death on the cheesy treat.

"Lie still," said Christina as she felt around his head and neck, before moving down his muscular body. She still didn't understand the banter about him being a 'fat ass' but didn't raise the issue.

Blood had ceased trickling from his ears and the swelling had diminished from the egg shaped lump he had worn earlier. By carefully flexing his fingers and toes, a full range of movement and sensation was noted before Christina was ready to try and shift his position. Any hidden damage would have been impossible to pick up without the use of an x-ray anyway, so they unstrapped him and hoped for the best.

"If you have any tingling or loss of feeling, let me know immediately," Christina said sternly.

"You can count on it, Doc," replied DB, nervously. The last thing he wanted was to be paralyzed in the zombie apocalypse, the only cure would be a bullet to the brain. He could just picture himself sitting in the wheelchair, being pushed desperately by one of the group until the inevitable tumble. Laying in the street, unable to move as the zombies surrounded him and started the feast.

"At least it wouldn't hurt from the neck down," he commented.

"What, are you losing feeling?" Christina asked in a panic.

"No, sorry, Doc. I was just thinking if I ended up crippled, it wouldn't hurt much getting eaten," DB explained and Christina wrinkled her nose.

"It would hurt the zombies more, trying to eat your bloated carcass," Jonesy mocked and DB laughed. It caused a great deal less shooting pain in his head than before his afternoon nap, so he said a small prayer to God, the baby Jesus, and whatever else was out there. They continued the maneuver and pulled the stretcher from beneath his bulk. Laying back into the goose down pillows, DB felt he had died and gone to Heaven.

"I can't take this anymore. Why do you keep calling him fat when he is anything of the sort?" Christina demanded, putting her hands on her hips.

"It's nice of you to say that, but look at him," Jonesy pointed at DB who pulled a hangdog expression, "He's a lard arse."

Christina was unimpressed and the fierce scowl she regarded them with caused more laughter. DB started to explain, "When I was younger I was... a bit plump. You could say I was a right little bloater. The kids on the estate used to call me beached whale and threaten to throw me back in the sea. When I hit sixteen I was nearly as tall as I am now, and strangely enough the bullying stopped. Most of the time they would even cross the street in fear."

Christina was still not convinced, "So you were bullied all through your formative years, and now use a nickname that reminds you of your awful childhood?"

"I use it to drive me," he said earnestly, "All the hate and bitterness is my fuel, it's what allows me to push through the pain and be a real warrior."

"That, and you really do love to eat," Jonesy said and patted DB's flat stomach.

"You are both incorrigible!" she complained before walking off, shaking her head and smiling, "I will be back to check on you shortly. Call me immediately if you have any numbness."

"You're the best, Doc," called out DB.

"I know," she replied and was gone from the room.

"You had me scared there, you fucker," Jonesy admitted now the ribbing had come to an end.

"It will take more than a caved in skull to finish me off," DB answered with a tired smile. Despite his high spirits the injury was beginning to take its toll again so Jonesy quickly picked up the plate.

"Get this down you before you pass out on me," Jonesy said and spooned mouthfuls of creamy pasta into the eager cavern of DB's mouth, "And if you ever tell anyone I fed you like a baby, I will kill you myself!"

"Love you, brother," DB whispered after finishing the meal, his eyelids closing with exhaustion.

"Love you, big man, sleep well," Jonesy finished and kissed his friend on the head.

In the lounge, the sleeping arrangements were finalized and instead of bedding down on the couches, the cushions were made into a half decent mattress on the floor. With the generator turned off for the night, the temperature was dropping fast and the decision was made to sleep alongside one another. Christina positioned herself at the furthest end so that she could make routine checks on DB throughout the night. Honey had claimed the foot of the makeshift hospital bed and lay watching the patient as he snored, before drifting off into canine dreams.

"Is everyone comfortable?" asked Jonesy from the opposite end to Christina. As the only one trained with the guns, it was decided he should be free to leap out of bed at a second's notice without falling over the others in the event of an emergency.

"As much as we can be," John replied honestly. The sharing of heat through the long night would be a welcome trade against the opportunity to stretch out on the sofas.

After much fidgeting and accommodation of peoples varying positions, everyone wished each other goodnight. Laid between Gloria and Braiden, Peter thought they must have looked like a packet of vacuum packed frankfurter sausages that he used to buy from Walmart. Debbie had always hated them, but sneaking them into the shopping trolley was one of the only ways he could score a victory, irrespective of how hollow it was. The wind howled outside, reminding him of her tantrums and shrieking fits. Wherever the evil bitch was, he prayed she was suffering.

***

Exhaustion proved to be the perfect sleep aid to endure the chaotic night of wind and ice. Jodi had been woken by the silence, a change in the environment so profound that confusion had mercifully pulled her from the nightmare of Mike and Debbie torturing Paige to death. She looked at the hands of her watch which were coated in a small amount of phosphorescent paint. Five twenty-eight glowed from the timepiece and the others were still fast asleep; some snoring, others struggling with their coverings as they battled whatever inner demon had decided to invade their dreams. The risen moon fought a losing battle with the snow sealed windows and only the feeblest light penetrated into the room.

"Jesus Christ," she whispered with a shudder, remembering.

The horrific visions had been so vivid that Jodi was bathed in a sticky layer of sweat in spite of the chill of the room. Similar to many nightmares, she had been powerless to intervene, merely the unwilling audience for the brutal punishment of the innocent girl. Rooted to the spot, she had listened as Mike had taken perverse pleasure in detailing each violation they would perpetrate. It had been so violent that Jodi had screamed and pleaded, a show of perceived weakness that had only emboldened the depraved pair in their torment. The smell of burnt hair and flesh was still in her nostrils from the torture, the sounds of Paige's bones fracturing as her thin frame was twisted and wrenched still rung in her ears. After the slow and methodical infliction of pain, the killing blow came as a surprise. Wielding one of their machetes, Debbie had locked eyes with Jodi and ran the blade across the bruised and fire blackened throat of Paige, triggering a torrent of blood which could only exist in dreams. The liquid had bathed her and, still caught in the limbo between full consciousness and the fantasy, she quickly checked the moisture saturating her clammy skin. A damp, but clear, hand came away and the final remnants of the delusion were dispelled.

"Fuck you, Mike Arater. Pray we never meet again, because I will fucking kill you," she whispered so vehemently that specks of spittle flew from her mouth.

"Are you ok, sweetheart?" whispered Gloria in the gloom.

"Sorry, I didn't mean to wake you,"

"That's ok, I'm a light sleeper. Bad dream?" Gloria asked.

"The worst," Jodi replied, "You are religious, right? I mean, I've heard the others mention you used to visit church regularly."

Gloria hesitated for a few seconds before answering and Jodi assumed that she had drifted back to sleep, "I used to go to church several times a week, that is true."

"How do you think God figures into all of this? Why would He allow us to suffer like this?"

"Darling, if God exists, and at the present time I have my doubts, I think we can all agree He has monumentally fucked up," Gloria said bluntly and Jodi had to stifle a giggle at the mental image conjured by her profanity; God running around in a panic, hands on his head asking Mrs. God what to do.

Gloria continued, "Whatever happened on that day, we may never know. All that we can take from this whole awful mess is that we are back to a dog eat dog world, survival of the fittest. I just hope that groups like ours can prove to be the dominant force in the world to come."

"I want to kill them both," admitted Jodi reluctantly, hoping everyone else was still asleep, "What would God have to say about that?"

"If God would inflict this horror upon the human race, and then punish us in the afterlife for seeking retribution against evil, then He is not worthy of our faith," Gloria said with a heavy heart. If ever she reached the pearly gates and Saint Peter sat in judgement, her conscience would be clear. Eternal damnation couldn't be much worse than the hell they were living in each and every day.

"You think He would understand?" Jodi asked hopefully. Although never much interested in religion before the apocalypse, the intimate experience of death had awoken a need for answers that couldn't be known. Only when they shuffled off this mortal coil would the searching end, one way or another.

"Worry about it when we get up there. If God tries giving us a hard time we will kick His omnipotent behind!" Gloria declared a little too loudly.

"Testify, sister!" Jonesy whispered and they could tell by the tone he was grinning.

"I'm so sorry," Gloria apologized, lowering her volume considerably to ensure the others weren't disturbed.

"Don't sweat it. I caught the end of the conversation, and if anyone should be worried, it's DB and I. We have done some bad shit serving Queen and Country," Jonesy replied and a darker, remorseful tone had replaced the unseen smile.

"You are a professional soldier, dear. I'm sure you were only following orders," Gloria said, trying to assuage some of his inner guilt.

"I don't know how well that defense will stack up when I stand to be judged," he replied with a bleakness in his soul, "Anyway, let's try and get another hour of sleep."

Gloria knew of the abhorrence of war. Her father had returned from fighting the Nazi's and had never been the same again. The inhuman cruelties witnessed had ripped him screaming from sleep most nights, and only her mother's soothing voice had calmed the tremors. Gloria had watched surreptitiously on more than one occasion, scared and bewildered at his gasping sobs. After sneaking back to bed, the morning had broken and her father had seemed unshakeable once more. It had taken an older cousin to explain that during the liberation, the Germans had taken to spiteful retribution for the impending defeat. Men, women, and worst of all, children had been butchered in their thousands. Passing each tiny corpse had gradually eroded any sense of mercy he felt towards the enemy, and for the rest of the war he killed them out of hand, even the ones who attempted to surrender. Lauded as a fearless warrior, he had despised the adulation that came from murder. Upon return, he had never spoken of the war again and information was only forthcoming from his friends after a few too many whiskeys. Gloria reminisced, picturing herself as a small girl sitting on his lap, her father stroking her hair with his scarred, calloused hand. The fond memory filled her with a warm longing and slumber beckoned, promising a joyous reunion.

CHAPTER TEN

Morrow slumped down at the table in the canteen. His plate hit the surface and clattered, spilling some of the warm sauce over the melamine.

"What the fuck is up with you? You have a face like a smacked arse," said Private Harkiss, moving down the table to avoid the gravy which was slowly flowing towards him.

"Have you been crying?" laughed another soldier.

"Shut your fucking mouth before I kick the shit out of you!" hissed Private Eldridge.

"Yeah, Ok. I was only messing around," sulked the chastened man. He knew she would follow through on the threat after seeing her take apart several of his friends in the boxing ring.

"What's up, Paul?" She reached out and held his hand.

"Did you hear the artillery firing earlier?" He looked up and her face was full of genuine concern.

"We all did. It's about time Baxter started to fight back against the dead fucks, I'm sick of sitting here with my thumb up my ass while they eat the whole world," she said.

"It's not like that…" he managed before the tears flowed. Several of the troops snickered but none dared to insult him again.

"What happened?" Eldridge coaxed.

"I found four pockets of survivors," he said, looking into her eyes which went wide with excitement.

"That's great, why are you so upset…" the sentence wasn't finished as she recalled the four heavy sonic pulses that came with the artillery fire. "He wouldn't fucking dare!" she growled, but Morrow's face spoke the truth.

"Dirty mother fucker!" Harkiss groaned, "There are hardly any survivors as it is…"

"You couldn't have known what he would do, you were only following orders," Eldridge said, pushing the bitter hatred deep down, amassing it for the right moment.

Morrow laughed sickly, "That's what the German SS troops said before they were executed."

"I would have told him to go fuck himself," boasted Harkiss.

"Don't give me that shit. You would have rolled over and showed your belly the same as most people," Eldridge countered.

"Shut it, bitch. You don't know what I am capable of," growled Harkiss, standing up menacingly.

"Well look at Billy-Big-Bollocks here. You are a scary looking bastard, no wonder the women run away," Eldridge laughed.

"Want me to show you how dangerous I can be, you whore?" he started to swagger around the table, fists clenched.

"Please do," Eldridge smiled before turning in her seat, "Sergeant Filton, Harkiss has something he wants to say to the lieutenant."

"What the fuck are you doing?" snarled Harkiss as their superior marched over.

"Now you get to prove yourself, tough guy," grinned the female Private wickedly.

Harkiss sat down, face blanching with fear as he tried to avoid the eyes of Filton.

"Well, what is it, Harkiss?" he demanded, "Stand up when I am talking to you!"

"It was nothing, sir, I was just wanting to thank him for keeping us safe," blabbered Harkiss.

"Are you taking the piss?" shouted Filton as he stood nose to nose with the subordinate.

"He wasn't, sir, we all feel grateful to the lieutenant for his leadership qualities," Eldridge interceded, taking some of the heat from Harkiss. She was a good judge of character and the change that Filton had shown over the past weeks was entirely down to fear at what would happen if the soldiers rose up.

"Well, if that's the case, I will pass it along," Filton saluted and went back to his table.

"You cunt, why did you do that? I could have been killed!" growled Harkiss over the table.

"Calm down," Eldridge whispered, "He is terrified of us. Even if you did tell him to tell Baxter to go fuck himself I doubt he would."

"It was still a dick move," he complained and resumed eating.

"Now listen, all of you. The tide is turning; Baxter is bat-shit crazy and more and more people have had enough. We just need to pick the right moment and the base is ours," she said quietly, looking at each in turn.

"Why would people give a shit. If we just keep our heads down we can ride this out," whispered a Private from the next table.

"Don't you want to know what's happening out there? If your friends and family are safe?" she asked and he nodded sadly.

"Nothing's happening, everyone's fucking dead," muttered Harkiss.

"Those four poor families were surviving, and that is just in this area. There could be thousands of people out there. Not to mention the rest of the Armed Forces, where the fuck are they?" she continued.

"Dead," Harkiss spat.

"Impossible!" replied Eldridge, "Don't you wonder what happened to Graff and Poncho? They are still in communication with people, that is why we haven't seen them for weeks. Baxter doesn't want them spilling the beans."

The group sat in silence, eating their dinner while they contemplated the next move. If others were out there, why hadn't anyone come to take over from Baxter, someone more senior? There were so many unanswered questions on people's lips; the secrecy after the outbreak had been understood, but the world was gone now. What could Baxter possibly hope to gain by brutalizing a small and dwindling regiment? They weren't allowed to fight back against the hordes that waited at the gate. Survivors were turned away under penalty of death, and now they were being blown up. Insanity.

"I think I saw DB and Jonesy," Morrow whispered so quietly that Eldridge had to ask him to repeat it, "Don't tell anyone yet."

"That's fantastic!" she whispered back, barely able to conceal her excitement, "I understand. My lips are sealed."

"If I had told Baxter, those families would still be alive," said Morrow, putting his face in his hands.

"You couldn't know what he would commit cold blooded murder," Eldridge emphasized.

"I should have just kept on flying past without noting their position, their blood is on my hands."

"Knock that shit off. You have one mission now, track them and find where they are going. Feed Baxter as much shit as you need to keep him from finding out," Eldridge said gravely.

"I don't think I have it in me to keep quiet. He scares the hell out of me, it's like he knows things!" Morrow despaired.

"He's not omnipotent, just hold your nerve!" she replied sternly.

"I'll try," offered Morrow.

"I know you will," she finished, but wasn't convinced.

Filton watched her from his table, trying to be casual. She knew there was a target on herself from the show of defiance at the gate. Let them watch, she thought, it may take the pressure from the UAS pilot who was close to breaking point.

CHAPTER ELEVEN

"**S**hould he still be asleep?" Jonesy asked the doctor.

"After the knock he took, I'm amazed he survived," she replied honestly, "I can only put it down to a thick skull."

Jonesy laughed into his hand to muffle the noise, "I can't wait to tell him that."

"I didn't mean it like that," Christina said, frowning and smiling at the same time, "I merely pointed out he has good genetics."

"Oh really?" Jonesy raised a knowing eyebrow.

"Behave yourself," warned Christina, but he caught the blossoming cheeks before she turned away.

"Sorry, Doc, I'll leave you to finish up with him," he said the final words with a lewd inflection and barely made it out of the door in time to avoid the thrown pillow.

Peter was preparing breakfast; the final slices of bread held over the cooker burners in an attempt to toast it. It worked to a fashion, with some corners singed and others left barely touched by the flame. He shrugged at Jonesy who looked at the plate of char patched bread with a look of amusement.

"It was worth a try," Peter offered by way of explanation.

"Absolutely. The smell hit me in the bedroom," Jonesy said and took the plate.

Peter looked crestfallen and could only mutter a quiet, "Sorry, I tried not to burn it."

"I didn't mean it like that, mate," Jonesy clapped him on the shoulder, "I meant it smelled delicious. Although, I am surprised the fire alarms haven't started blaring."

Peter laughed and looked around the cabin at the swirling tendrils of smoke from his haphazard browning. Jonesy bit into the crisp delicacy and the melted butter ran over his tongue. The salted spread was enough to make him close his eyes in appreciation, and he sighed with contentment.

"I heard conversation about going out. Why are we risking our lives when we barely survived yesterday?" Jonesy asked between mouthfuls.

"There's a farmers store in the town," explained Gloria, "We need to search it for supplies before we try and reach the castle."

"Why would we need rotten fruit and vegetables?" he asked, "Surely a supermarket would be a better choice for a raid?"

"It isn't the existing produce we are after. There are a few acres of untouched soil within the castle walls," Gloria explained.

Jonesy shook his head at his foolishness, "We are going for the seeds."

"Exactly!" exclaimed John. "We will need to forage for existing supplies to get through the winter, but as soon as spring breaks we plant crops. A mix of vegetables and fruit will be needed or we run the risk of nutritional deficiencies which will leave us too weak to fight."

"I'm in," Jonesy declared and went to the pile of weapons and ammunition, "Who else is going?"

"Me," Braiden said and held up a piece of paper, "I have the list."

"Me too," replied Sam.

"And me," said Peter.

By the end, it seemed everybody would be going and Jonesy had to gently reject their enthusiastic offers.

"No, I want it low key. Braiden, Jodi, and I will go," he told the group.

"I don't like the idea of you being out there in such small numbers," Sarah said and hugged Braiden, worry etched on her features.

"Trust me, we can move from cover to cover a lot easier if there are just three of us," Jonesy explained. He understood her concern, but stealth would be paramount in avoiding any lingering dead.

"I'm coming too," proclaimed Kurt, "Unless we plan to dig the soil by hand we will need some tools. You can cover me while I bring back as many as I can carry."

Jonesy nodded in agreement. The castle would possibly have a gardening division to maintain the beautiful grounds, but a set of shears and a shovel wouldn't last long when they had to plant hundreds of seeds.

"Let's take a look. We still have the issue of getting to shore safely after destroying the ramp," said John opening the door leading to the covered entertaining deck.

The snow had settled into the corners from the driving wind, but the main deck was mostly clear of the powdery ice. Christina followed and fired the generator to provide some electricity for the small heaters in the narrowboat.

"We are good for a few days at least," she told John, pointing at a fuel gauge that registered at over ninety percent full. With a nod, she closed the hatch and left them to take in the view.

The panorama was breathtaking. Like a scene from a Christmas card, the fields and trees were a crisp, almost luminous white. All that was missing was the glow of welcoming lights from the windows of the homes and lazy, drifting smoke from the chimney stacks, promising a cozy hearth. Further upriver, the bridge and burned out train were the only objects to be lacking a white blanket. The stark contrast between the beauty of the vista and the awful, twisted, burned shell of the carriage ended any sense of wonder.

"Shit. I hoped they would have wandered off in the night towards the train," whispered Jonesy, crouching and looking over the edge of the deck.

The quintessential children frolicking in the snow, making snowmen and playfully throwing snowballs had been replaced by the gathered corpses of the previous day's pursuit.

"I doubt they could even see the fire with the storm raging all around," deduced Kurt.

"How many do you think there are? Fifty, sixty?" asked Jodi.

"At least," John agreed.

"How do we get past them?" she questioned.

"I could pick them off one at a time, no problem," explained Jonesy, "It would only take me ten minutes."

"I don't think we will have much choice," said Kurt with frustration. They had thousands of rounds of ammunition left, but each shell was valuable and to use them on enemies that couldn't reach them seemed a waste.

"Wait a minute," whispered Jodi, trying to see if her eyes were deceiving her.

"What is it?" asked John after a few seconds, unable to understand what she was staring at with such intensity.

"They aren't moving like before…" she said, more to herself than the others, "They can see us, but they are sluggish."

"I'm obviously not seeing what you are seeing." Jonesy pointed to movement within the crowd.

"No, look closely," Jodi continued, "It's the older ones that can move."

They studied the group for a while and she was right. The 'wetter' dead; the ones who had been killed and partly eaten after the outbreak showed little movement, despite the proximity of food. The older, drier ones; those who had decomposed and dug themselves from the grave were the only ones with full mobility. They moved within the larger mass unhindered, trying to get to the survivors but unwilling to wade through the river.

"They must be frozen, that's why they can't move," Braiden understood.

"Exactly," beamed Jodi.

"We can avoid most of them completely. And there I was last night, complaining about the cold," Kurt joked. The recovery would be a great deal safer than they could have hoped for, but they were constrained by time. The sky was clear and the sun was blinding against the white backdrop. The snow was giving off a mist as the rays gradually brought the temperature up.

Seeing this, Jonesy stood up, "We need to hustle. We won't get a better opportunity."

"Why don't we take advantage and just kill every last one of the bastards," Braiden growled, "They are sitting ducks."

"It would give us a much safer route back to the boat," mused Jonesy, "Let's do it. Kurt, get out on the dock and pull one of those boats down here." He pointed to a rowing boat tied further down.

"What are you going to do?" Kurt replied.

"I'm getting my rifle; I will take out the dry fuckers."

Kurt shook his head at the absurdity of the label; they were now differentiating the zombies by how moist they were. "Ok, be right back."

129

CHAPTER TWELVE

The wooden floor was icy, but a layer of anti-slip material had been fitted in the past. It was in a poor state of repair, much like the rest of the dock. Stepping carefully, Kurt pushed the snow clear with his foot and made it to a sturdy looking dinghy.

"Follow in my tracks," Kurt said to Braiden.

The faint coughs of the suppressed rifle spat, breaking the morning silence and the mummified cadavers were destroyed, falling around their immobile companions. They untied the craft and guided it around the empty moorings, before securing it to the side of their floating abode. Heading back inside, they found Jonesy suiting up into his tactical vest and loading up fresh magazines. Jodi, Kurt, and Braiden gathered their weapons and the expedition was ready.

"Do we have any scarves?" asked Braiden, rubbing at his aching ears.

"That's a good idea. The cold will affect us as much as it affects them," Kurt agreed, blowing warm breath into his cupped hands, trying to ease the numbness in his fingers from reclaiming the boat.

"Gloves would help too, but I don't want the bat flying out of my hands," Jodi explained.

Gloria dug through their belongings and found three woolen scarves. Jonesy waved her away, he would make do without one. He had never liked the feeling of the wrapping, especially around his face. When carrying out special operations, they were forced to wear dark fabric face coverings under the helmet to mask their identities. It felt like being slowly suffocated.

"Please be safe," Sarah said, hugging them all close and giving Kurt and Braiden a kiss.

"It'll be a walk in the park," replied Jonesy with an almost imperceptible nod to her. He would keep them safe, no matter what.

They stepped carefully into the bobbing boat, and were waved off by those remaining. Sarah mouthed 'I love you' and Kurt blew a kiss to her. Braiden rowed slowly, watching the horde for any sign they had regained enough flexibility to pose a direct threat. Some heads turned in slow motion with a great effort, splitting frozen flesh in their desire to see the warm meat.

"I think we are good. Another hour or two and we would be in trouble," Jonesy judged and they all climbed out onto the frozen riverbank. The snow was ten inches deep, crunching with each stride as it compacted under their weight.

"We take it slow, choppers only. Strike quickly and then back away, I will watch for any activity from behind," Jonesy said and shouldered his rifle.

The crowd were like statues in a horror film. Milky eyes turned, watching the survivors as they moved behind the frozen zombies. Limbs cracked as the monsters started to strain in their frozen state, desperate to feed. It was soon apparent the two-hour window was too generous and didn't account for the tenacity of their foe.

"Jonesy, we don't have that much time. Keep an eye on us as well, the natives are getting restless," Kurt told the soldier.

"I've got your back," Jonesy confirmed, "Go to work."

One by one, the zombie's skulls were split open, spilling an icy, green slush. Darting in and slashing down, the three then leapt back to ensure they wouldn't be surprised by a freshly moving arm. The massacre lasted only minutes and the release of fearful, pent up breaths could be heard from the watchers on the narrow boat. With a final wave, the four-person team moved off into the frigid day, leaving a pile of frozen undead corpses at the riverside.

"Stay to the fence line and if I drop to the ground, you do the same," Jonesy ordered and moved off up the track that led to the decrepit boat enthusiast building.

Time had not been kind to the ailing business and a new coat of paint was long overdue on the flaking structure. A few zombies stood in the abandoned car park, but were rooted to the spot and facing away from the survivors. The track joined the main Ford road that led south to Bognor Regis and north, over the railway to Arundel. Before the dead took over the world, salt spreaders would have covered the roads to keep traffic flowing. Now, the snow topped cars were still, the black tarmac layered with white.

"The farm store should be to our left if Christina remembers correctly, set back between those businesses," Kurt whispered, pointing to a small promenade of shops.

A café, hair salon, and an iron mongers had been broken into, the glass shattered inwards. He could imagine the terror as the zombies hammered on the display window, the first cracks appearing as it weakened. The screams as the dead breached the shops, feeding on those within.

"I don't get it," said Braiden.

The others looked at him quizzically and Jodi spoke up, "What do you mean?"

"Ford isn't a big place, but we haven't seen anywhere near enough zombies," he explained his concerns.

"Don't forget the train station," Kurt said. But thinking back, there were only hundreds, not the thousands there could have been and his brow furrowed in confusion.

"I say we just thank our lucky stars they have walked off somewhere. Let's go," Jonesy finished the conversation and ran low between the cars, kicking up drifts of snow.

A sign mounted on the brick wall above an untouched antique shop proclaimed 'Weston's Farm Store, fresh produce daily' with an arrow guiding the public between the buildings. Ducking outside the shop while Jonesy surveyed the short alley, they all jumped when a metallic gonging commenced. An ornately carved Grandfather Clock was chiming for the turn of the hour, standing proudly behind the shop's window, pendulum swinging within the glass fronted housing.

"Fuck!" growled Jonesy. "Let's move, I don't want to be here if anything comes to check the time."

Following his lead, the others jogged behind. A delivery truck was parked with the rear doors open, partly unloaded while other containers had been spilled when the first dead had attacked. The smell of rotten fruit was sweet and acrid, but the low temperature kept the decomposition under control.

"I think the coast is clear. Jodi, would you mind keeping an eye out?" Jonesy asked, looking through the open doors.

"I'll whistle if I see anything," she replied, finding a good spot to keep watch.

The building comprised two sections, the original brick structure containing all the fruit and vegetables. Adjoining this was a corrugated metal building; a cheaper way to extend the property for the equipment and farming materials. Kurt stepped inside and gently struck a metal rack with his hammer, making enough noise to alert anything inside. The silence wasn't broken by shuffling or moaning and they entered, searching for the supplies.

133

Jodi clenched her bat tightly, ready for any sign of the dead. Deciding to be proactive, she moved to the side of the building and checked down the side. It led to a small wooden fence and then nothing but open fields for miles around, the source of much of the goods that used to be sold. Backtracking, the other side was also clear, which left only the alleyway and either end of the promenade of shops to observe. Quiet conversation flowed from the open doors and she caught snippets as a discussion took place over what to prioritize. The cold was beginning to seep through her layers of clothing, so she decided to walk back and forth, patrolling the front of the building to get the blood flowing. On the third sweep, more conversation caught her attention but it wasn't coming from the store. It was hushed and angry, coming from the ground ten feet from where she stood.

"What the hell?" she whispered to herself.

The snow started to shift and she quickly ducked behind a car, puzzled at what was occurring. Ignoring the chill, she lay down to look beneath the vehicle, trying to get a better view. A sheet of wood lifted and the light revealed the top of a head, looking warily around. The snow cascaded down, falling into whatever hole he was stood in.

"I don't see any, let's get this done and get the fuck back," rasped an unfriendly voice and the sheet lifted completely, dropping to the rear. The man climbed out of the hole scowling, and the visible tattoos were unmistakable. Poorly inked prison markings stretched around his neck and covered his hands, even the fingers.

"Help me up," came another voice, and Tattoo hand reached down, pulling another man out of the hole. Though sporting fewer markings, his eyes were shifty and calculating, making him seem just as dangerous.

"Hurry up, you fucking pussy," Shifty Eyes growled down the hole.

A third man rose into view, but had a look dissimilar the first two. His face was heavily bruised and fresh blood was running from the nose. Dabbing at the injury, he shied away from the attention of the two violent looking thugs.

"Stay here and keep watch," said Tattoo, staring menacingly at the cowed figure.

"You move an inch and I may just take my turn on your wife tonight," said Shifty, banging him in the chest. It was a challenge, but the terrified man stared at the ground, refusing to rise to the bait, "Nothing to say?"

"He's a faggot. I'd cut the heart out of any man who looked twice at my bitch," declared Tattoo.

"You are lucky she was such an ugly cunt then aren't you?" joked shifty and Tattoo laughed.

The beaten man coughed and Tattoo grabbed him by the throat, "You think that was funny?" he snarled.

"I'm sorry, I was just coughing," he struggled to choke the words through his compressed neck.

Pulling him close, Tattoo spat in his face and backhanded him, sending him sprawling into the snow. Jodi had to fight every instinct to jump up and smash their heads with her bat. As it was, she might have to do it anyway if they were here for the farm store. Watching closely, they sauntered off down the alleyway and she waited until they were gone from view before standing. The man gaped at her, astonished by the woman standing only ten feet away.

Hurrying around the car, she said urgently, "Quickly, come with me, you will be safe."

He backed away and nearly stood in the yawning hole in the ground, "No, just get out of here. They will hurt you if they catch you, please just go."

"Don't worry about them, we have guns," she tried to convince him.

"You don't understand, they have my family," he said, anguish contorting his face.

135

"We can help, just come with me. I will get my friends and we can take out those two bastards," Jodi attempted to take his hand but he slapped it away.

"That will be even worse, if we aren't back in time the others will know something is up and they will torture my wife again, maybe kill her," he sobbed, dropping to his knees.

"But we have guns, we can come back with you and rescue them," Jodi was acutely aware of the ticking seconds and the fact she had no idea how long the thug's errand would take.

"They have guns too, and they watch the tunnels. If I brought you and your friends back, they would just collapse it on top of us without a shot being fired. One of the things I was made to design was a failsafe in case the zombies ever managed to breach the tunnel. There is a rope system attached to the side braces which they can trigger in seconds, dropping tons of earth on top of them," he explained.

The predicament of the poor man was insurmountable at the moment, but his evident weakness threw up another question, "Why did they bring you out here instead of one of their own?"

"You mean a thug, or murderer, rather than a coward?" he said, finally standing.

"I wouldn't say you are a coward; you've made it this far. But yeah, why not another prisoner?" she confirmed.

"My name is Jason Rechtman, I lived in Ford when the dead came for us. I was a structural engineer and worked from home a lot, so we fled for the prison hoping the guards would take us in. They did, but after a few days, the prisoners broke out and took over the place. Now they use us as their playthings, the sadistic bastards." His face twisted into a mask of pure hatred, "They made me help build tunnels so that we could get past the thousands of walkers. I come with each raid to check the supports and general stability of the excavations. They threatened my wife and daughter if I didn't comply... not that it helped." A glazed look came over his eyes at the unspeakable acts he had seen carried out against his kin.

"How many of you are there? Families I mean," Jodi pressed, hoping to glean as much information as possible from the exchange.

"I led almost thirty people here, and then a dozen or more arrived. After that, nobody living," he said, shaking his head in guilt, "I wish I'd never bothered."

"That was so heroic. Listen, don't lose hope," Jodi took his reluctant hand and met his bleak gaze, "We will come for you, I promise."

"You will die."

"After what we have fought through, a bunch of killers would be nothing," she disagreed.

"Ok," he whispered. Was that a faint glimmer of hope she detected?

"You said tunnels, plural. How many have you dug?" she asked, knowing their time was probably coming to a close.

"Two. One here to raid the shops, and one more into a section of field so that there is an escape route. There are more planned when we can get supplies from the railway storage yard," he explained. There would be enough lumber to build a dozen or more if they could reach it.

"How is it even possible?"

"When you have a labor pool of two hundred strong men, anything can be done. The tunnel itself is only six-foot-high and three-foot-wide which saved us time. It's only purpose was to bring food and small goods back, but I'm sure future excavations will be larger. They have us working around the clock and we average about twenty-five meters a day depending on what we find in the ground."

"That's amazing. You and your knowledge are going to be invaluable when it comes to fighting the undead."

"Thanks," Jason said, blushing. It was the first kind words he had heard in many weeks.

"Jason, what I want you to do is draw a map of the area if you have the chance. Mark any new tunnel locations and leave it in this car the next time you come back. Update it every time you are here," instructed Jodi. The chances of a rescue would be hampered by the winter, so it would be months before any attempt could be made.

"I can do that," he confirmed with a weak smile.

"Stay strong," she finished and squeezed his hand.

Reluctantly walking away, she looked back and saw Jason was filling in her footprints with loose snow, concealing her passage. If the brutes had seen the footprints with no sign of a zombie the questioning would be harsh. Those marking the alleyway could be explained by earlier undead movement. With a last wave, she stepped into the farm store and nearly bumped into the men leaving. Kurt was heavily laden with tools strapped to his back; hoes, shovels, and picks clanked in the gloom. Holding a finger to her lips, she signaled for them to be silent. Outside, the faint voices could be heard and it was only the look on her face and the way she slowly shook her head that stilled them. With a thud, the sheet of wood had been dropped back into place, covering the tunnel from any wandering horror that may fall down it.

"What was that all about, who were they?" demanded Kurt.

"We have a lot to talk about," she replied.

CHAPTER THIRTEEN

axter paced the quiet corridors, looking in on the slumbering troops in their bunks. He envied their respite from the savagery of modern life, rarely sleeping more than an hour at a time himself these days. His jumbled thoughts and decisions kept his mind turning over in an endless loop of conspiracy and scheming. Was he really losing his mind, were the soldiers right after all? Impossible! Only the truly insane are certain of their own sanity, seeing bedlam in the eyes of others.

"I was chosen," he said to himself, looking out in the morning light on the snow covered scene.

Sergeant Rabson came sprinting around the corner, interrupted his thoughts, "Sir, we have a problem," gasped the huge communications room guard, saluting.

"Oh?" Baxter raised an eyebrow.

"You need to hear this, we are being hailed by HMS Dauntless again," Rabson explained.

"Lead the way, Sergeant," Baxter ordered and marched towards the radio room.

Corporal Graff was holding his head in his hands, scared witless. The sight of Baxter in the doorway was enough to make him drop to his knees and start wailing.

"Sir, I promise I didn't have anything to do with it," he cried, clutching at the legs of his superior.

"What on earth are you sniveling about, Corporal?" Baxter said with disgust and kicked him away.

139

"Dauntless have ordered a chopper to investigate our continued silence. They will be here in less than fifteen minutes. Sir, I swear I told Sergeant Rabson as soon as I heard," Graff sobbed. He hadn't forgotten the death threat from before should anyone feel the compulsion to investigate the barracks.

"Which direction are they approaching from?" demanded Baxter.

"Unknown, sir, they didn't say."

Baxter reached for his radio, "Fire team, is your radar surveillance operative awake? If not, get his ass out of bed, over."

"Sir, I'm sorry but she went AWOL weeks ago to reach her family. I thought you had been informed, over," came the apologetic reply.

"Fuck!" shouted Baxter. It was true, he had been told each and every person who had gone missing, as well as the gap it left in their battle readiness.

"Orders, sir?"

Baxter calculated the likely outcome of letting them land and trying to brazen the investigation. It would put his plans back, if not destroy them completely. The mistreated soldiers would not miss the opportunity to inform the hierarchy of what had occurred under his stewardship. That mustn't be allowed! How many helicopters would be still in commission, along with trained pilots to fly them? The remaining Chinooks on Thorney barracks were fueled and ready to go at a moment's notice, with at least one crew being loyal to the new commander. Could the top brass keep sending them should an unfortunate "accident" befall the coming team?

"Sergeant, go to the armory and bring me an L115A3 sniper rifle. I will meet you at the gate, go!"

"Yes, sir!" Rabson yelled and sprinted off.

"Logistics, this is Baxter, over."

"This is logistics, go for Baxter, over," replied the ammunition technician.

"I want a Starstreak missile and shoulder launcher at the Vikings in three minutes, over," Baxter shouted into the radio as he ran for the main parade ground.

"Affirmative, be there in three, sir. Over."

The gate guards regarded Baxter with confusion as he raced across the snow covered ground, twisting around to look in all directions. The dawn was preternaturally silent, even the groans of the dead had ceased. The only noise was Baxter's inhalations and the sound of the compacting snow underfoot as he turned.

"Sir, is everything alright?" called out one of the soldiers.

"Everything's fine. Get back you your position," Baxter shouted back and ignored the salute.

The first faint throbs pierced the still air, but it was impossible to ascertain a direction. Rabson came trotting, the long barreled rifle slung on his shoulder.

"Orders, sir?"

"Get in that tower," Baxter pointed to an abandoned guard post, "Give the approach vector of the helo."

Rabson reached the steps and climbed in double quick time. Pulling the dust caps from the scope lenses, he shouldered the weapon and started a scan in all directions. A Land Rover rolled slowly into view, opting for caution on the icy road with its explosive cargo. Pulling alongside Baxter, the young soldier climbed out and opened the rear doors of the vehicle. A thick metallic tube was secured firmly and a heavy box sat on the floor. Pulling the case out and laying it at their feet, Baxter unclipped the latches and laid the lid on the snowy ground.

"Get the missile ready," said Baxter as he turned on the aiming unit of the shoulder launcher.

"Aye, sir," replied the technician, lifting the sealed explosive and carefully sliding it into the firing tube.

"Sergeant, what do you see? Are they approaching by sea?" Baxter called out to his scout in the tower.

"Negative, sir. No sign of target over the water," he shouted back, resuming his exploration of the low lying hills of the surrounding landmass.

The pitch of the rotor blades was increasing and the air hummed with the approaching craft. The guards were looking around for the source of the disturbance too, though for entirely different reasons.

"North- North East, sir. Coming in low," yelled Rabson, gesticulating at the dark speck in the distance.

"Range?"

"About one mile," replied the Sergeant.

Baxter knelt in the inches of snow, bringing the heavy launcher up to his shoulder and placing one eye over the targeting lens. The barrack's windsock was unmoving, laying gently against the pole so no air movement needed to be taken into account. The aiming unit enhanced the image and he could make out the shadows of the two pilots in the helicopter.

"What the fuck is he doing?" shouted one of the guards in horror.

"Stand down, soldier," ordered Rabson to the defiant man who was scrambling down the flight of steps to stop his superior, all too late.

The trajectory had been calculated by the onboard computer and the tube belched out the missile with a puff of quickly extinguished fire, a feature designed to protect the gunner. Hanging in midair for a fraction of a second, the rocket ignited it's second propulsion system and blazed towards the approaching airship. Being totally unprepared for a hostile reception, the helicopter pilot barely tried to avoid the impact, only veering right at the last second. It was too late for the doomed men, and the impact delayed fuse ignited the explosives, destroying them in a white hot fireball. It dropped from the sky like a falling sun, trailing black smoke and debris before landing among some homes with an ear ringing blast and a roiling cloud of fire as the excess fuel erupted.

"You fucking lunatic, that was an Army chopper," snarled the furious guard.

Swinging a punch at Baxter, the commander only needed to twist slightly to the left. The knuckles impacted the side of the aiming box and the skin split open, causing the soldier to cry out and clutch at the wound. Passing the launcher to the technician, Baxter opted for the tried and tested kick to the groin, laying the man flat out on the ground.

"You really shouldn't have done that," said Baxter to the man who was trying to claw at the vomit inducing agony between his legs.

"Sorry, sir. I didn't want to take the shot in case I hit you," apologized Rabson who came rushing over, pistol at the ready.

"Not to worry, Sergeant, take him away and prepare the troops for another execution at midday."

Baxter moved away, ignoring the gawping stares and looks of hatred from the freshly woken soldiers staring out of the barracks windows. The fire raged in the distance, consuming the neighboring properties and threatening to spread out of control with no emergency services to respond. Private Beth Eldridge glared pure poison at the psychopath, one face among the masses.

CHAPTER FOURTEEN

"You bastard, I think you broke me," Debbie whispered, one leg draped over the warm body of Mike.

"I didn't hear you complaining, though you did scream loud enough to wake the dead. I nearly had to smother you again," he joked, placing a hand over her mouth and nose.

"It's not funny, you could have killed me!" she complained and swatted his hand away, turning her back to him like a petulant child.

"And your tantrums could have got us both killed," Mike responded, moving in behind and reaching around to squeeze one of her breasts.

She replied with a sulky harrumph and tried to pry his hand away with little conviction. It was nice to be getting some attention, to have him fawning over her for however short a time it may be. She knew it was purely his need for sexual release, he was a man after all. But it gave her some small measure of power over him, and that was something to be grateful for. Pushing away with more intent, he only squeezed harder until her flesh sang with pain. Another hand roamed between her legs, delving, and she was helpless to resist. The power struggle was lost again, but the intense pleasure made it a price worth paying.

***

"You're a letch," Debbie giggled, forcefully squeezing her legs together to prevent another performance.

"I can't help it if I have needs," Mike said, trying to worm his fingers between the tense flesh.

"Your needs will see us fucking until we either starve or freeze to death. We need to get moving," she said, allowing one last gentle tease.

"Ok, I'm moving," he moaned, shucking off the sleeping bag, "Fuck me, that's cold!"

"No shit, Sherlock," she laughed and passed him a jumper.

Tossing it on, he managed to try and squeeze his head through an arm hole in his haste. In fits of laughter at the spectacle, Debbie helped him to twist the garment and pull it down. Their eyes met and for a moment, they just looked at one another.

"I'm really sorry I hurt you yesterday," he said tenderly, stroking her face. It was one of the rare gestures of compassion and she held his cold hand to her warm skin, before kissing the palm.

"I know I can be a bitch. I will try and keep my mouth shut in the future, ok?" she said earnestly. She knew that her outbursts could be fatal in the new world and would try to control her temper.

"About fucking time," he replied, back to his sarcastic self. In spite of her flaws, she was growing on him and he felt mildly guilty for the attempted murder.

"Asshole!" she smiled and punched his tattooed arm playfully.

After dressing and repacking their gear, they were ready for the next leg of their journey. Mike had looked around the shelves at the supplies and wrapped two hammers, some nails and several boxes into a blanket to dull their noise.

"What do you need that stuff for?" Debbie inquired. She glared fearfully at the hammers, a talisman of their enemy; Kurt Taylor.

"If we find somewhere to hide, I want to be able to secure it to buy us some time. The boxes hold some solid padlocks, hasps, and staples," Mike explained, showing her. The sliding steel pins would hold for a while before breaking, and every second counted if the dead came knocking.

"How far do you think we will make it today?" she asked.

"In the snow, with those things on our asses?" he said, kneeling and looking out through the keyhole. "A few miles at best. Less if the cold gets to us."

"I don't want to be stuck out in this weather, especially in a tent," she whined, heard herself and stopped. Mike caught the self-control and smiled at her.

"Neither of us do, they were only going to be used in the event of an emergency. On top of that, we would have to keep watch all night so we would be exhausted. I don't want a fight if we can help it. Anyway, there are plenty of farms across the fields we will be travelling, one of them should do the job," he stated.

He could see the carpark had a few guests, but they weren't as animated as usual. The snow had covered everything and even some of the zombies wore a crown of white.

"What can you see?" Debbie wondered, noticing how closely he was studying the outside world.

"I think they are frozen," he whispered, "Or at least slowed down by the cold. Let's get moving while we have the chance."

Mike unlocked the door and pushed it open, checking for lurking horrors behind it and cutting a furrow through the settled snow. The light reflected from the whitened ground was dazzling and he quickly donned a pair of

146

expensive Raybans he had stolen from the camping shop. Debbie followed and pushed the door closed gently, locking the door behind them and pocketing the keys.

"Planning on coming back?" Mike asked with amusement from the cover of a parked truck.

"You never know, we might have to run back here if things don't work out," she replied, too nervous to take offense.

"That's actually a fair point, good thinking," he commended her, before returning his focus to the surrounding area.

"I think they really are frozen," she whispered. Two zombies were looking directly at them, but they made no move to attack.

"We need to get a move on though, I think they are starting to defrost," hissed Mike hearing the first faint groans issue from the glacial lungs of the dead.

They broke into a run, keeping to the center of the road between the abandoned cars to avoid any obstacles that could have twisted an ankle. Heads turned to watch them, and Debbie could see signs of movement in the mannequin like figure's limbs which they passed.

"Stop... have to stop," gasped Debbie after only two minutes.

"Are you fucking kidding me?" Mike snarled through gritted teeth, "We have another mile until we reach the open fields!"

Debbie was caught between trying to draw breath and crying at the abuse she was receiving. "I don't... run. Sorry... just leave... me," she sobbed.

Mike was glancing around and the locals were now mobile, albeit still slower than normal which was their only chance.

"Why did you let me fuck you this morning? We could have been long gone!" Mike shook her violently, which only served to increase the gasping and running snot. He

147

was furious at himself as much as her, but this wasn't something he was willing to divulge. It was only this shared guilt that stayed his clenched fist, and instead he pulled her backpack off and threw it away. They would have to take their chances without her sleeping bag and other essentials. If this fucked them both, he would kill her before the zombies got close.

"No… just go…" She tried to push him away.

"Come on, we fast walk while you get your breath back," Mike took her by the arm to help ease the burden and he looked back with remorse at the fading backpack.

"Thank you for not leaving me behind," she said eventually. Embarrassment and fear had kept her quiet for nearly ten minutes which was a record.

"I don't understand how you are in such good shape but so unfit." He looked sideways as they started to jog slowly.

Debbie could only look at the ground, racked with self-disgust.

"Ahh," Mike said, knowingly, "You're a puker."

"Don't say that, it sounds awful."

"Hey, I'm not judging. Whatever you do, it works," he replied, a strange compliment to her eating disorder.

"Thanks… I think," she huffed. His steady breathing was a constant companion to her own labored panting. Her lungs and legs screamed in agony, it was as if someone had poured acid in her veins. She nearly collapsed to the ground with relief when he stopped them behind a wall to scout the next obstacle. To reach the fields, they would either have to cross the motorway and the teeming zombies that swarmed there, or use the pedestrian flyover.

"Catch your breath," Mike ordered unnecessarily. Debbie was hunched over, vomiting the cereal bar she had eaten for breakfast. This time she would have given anything to keep the food inside her.

"Old habits die hard I guess?" Mike laughed with derision.

"Cunt," was all Debbie could muster between drawing breath into her tortured lungs, and trying to stop heaving. Nothing was left in her stomach to expel and the spasms left her weakened.

"Decision time," Mike looked at her, "We either cross the six lanes and hope for the best. Remember the game Frogger?"

She did. It hadn't worked out too well for the poor frog much of the time; either squashed or drowned, which had always struck her as a strange death for an amphibian.

"Or?"

"We take the bridge, but if any follow or block our way we may as well just jump from the top and kill ourselves," he replied candidly.

She mulled the choice, knowing she was the weak link and would doom them both if it went wrong. It didn't occur to her the sly looks he was giving her were the reaffirmation that she would be fed to the walking dead to save himself. She assumed it was his own inner thoughts. The dead were sluggish in the lower temperatures, but their sheer number in between the wrecked cars terrified her. If they got cornered or slipped on the icy ground, it would be their end.

"We risk the bridge," she stated, decision made.

He nodded and they quickly skirted the wall and a vehicle that had ploughed through the brickwork. The bridge was made of painted steel and through the safety bars they could see no zombie was lurking, which was a miracle considering the numbers that waited below.

"Quickly," Mike urged her, as they reached the disabled friendly bridge ramp.

He could remember the uproar that had greeted the plan to replace the old steps with the ridiculously expensive slope. When pressed, the local Council had been unable to

149

provide a shred of evidence that anyone with a disability had even asked for the alteration. Some had called it a vanity project by out of touch bureaucrats, others had argued that anything that encouraged those with impairments to get out was to be championed. After much fanfare and a mayoral unveiling, the lack of use by a single wheelchair user had led to a massive voter backlash that saw the incumbents ousted for the first time in years.

"Mind where you step, the snow has made it slippery," Debbie warned.

"Thanks," Mike replied, holding on to the railing for support just in case. He didn't know what had triggered the flashback. Perhaps it was the knowledge that governments and politicians were now dead and buried, so to speak. The powerful and ruthless would forge the new ways of the future and he was certain that he and his sibling would have a part of the glory.

Below, the dead clawed upwards, beseeching the pair to spare a chunk or two of their flesh. Just enough to take the edge off the inhuman hunger which drove them. The lack of intelligence in the corpses working in their favor and drew many dead away from the exit ramp on the other side. If any sense had remained, they would have just marched up to greet them and devour them screaming.

"Take the backpack, I need my arms free to kill those," Mike pointed at a small handful that remained and she took the pack without complaint.

"Be careful," Debbie cried. The walkway was narrow and if she tried to help, it was likely she would just get in the way at the wrong moment.

Mike was all game as he reached the bottom of the slope, psyching himself and crashing the axe against the metal railing in a frenzy. The narrowness that could have caused issues for the pair, also worked in their favor as the zombies struggled against each other with their need to feed. Mike planted his feet and met each monster as it got in range, slashing wildly and tearing chunks of skull away in a rotten spray. The bodies sprawled and provided a further barrier, so Mike climbed on the corpses, the bones fracturing under his weight. Hacking at the last three zombies, he cut them to ribbons and parts of limbs, heads, and torsos were scattered around his feet. Turning to look at Debbie he looked insane, with adrenaline coursing through his system and a bloodlust that wanted more. Instead of being afraid, she felt aroused at his ferocity, like maidens of yore who had bedded the mightiest gladiators.

"Mike. No!" she ordered when she caught him eyeing the approaching group.

With an almost animal whine of yearning, he lowered his chopper and took a deep, shuddering breath.

"We need to go," she said, gently calming him as she stepped over the fallen.

He couldn't speak, only nod his agreement through the adrenaline dump tremors. With one last look at the gathering horde, they ran across the overgrown shrubbery of the motorway embankment and disappeared through the thick hedgerows, leaving their pursuers to bewail the loss.

"That was close," Debbie said, stating the obvious, "Let's put some distance between us."

"Ok, we need to head east towards Hunston, then north-east will take us to Ford Prison," he replied, wiping the chunks of clotted gore from his face and clothing.

With a cracking and rustling crash, the groans of the dead increased in volume as the swarm crushed through the foliage. The snow was rapidly becoming a slush underfoot and the undead showed little sign of their previous affliction. Whether their missing arms and legs had broken off while frozen, or been eaten before death, neither Mike or Debbie wanted to find out.

"Persistent fuckers, aren't they?" Mike fumed.

"How are we going to get away from them?" Debbie whimpered, "We need rest, they don't."

"Just shut up and walk, mind your footing though. I think this field was ploughed before the winter," Mike warned and Debbie could feel the contours of the earth beneath her feet, the rising piles of shifted earth.

"I want to go back to the train station," she cried. The mixture of aches and pains, combined with their entourage was pushing her to breaking point.

"And how the hell do you plan on accomplishing that?" Mike barked, casting a fearful look over his shoulder. The dead had spread out and now covered half the span of the field.

"I don't know…" she sobbed.

Mike looked at her, the way she staggered with slumped shoulders, like she had already given up. All it would take was a punch or a kick to send her sprawling and the zombies would have their fill of her warm meat. If it had been a smaller following, he would have sacrificed her life there and then, but the walking corpses numbered close to two hundred. It was possible the ones who couldn't reach Debbie would continue their pursuit and he would be alone.

"Come on," he threw one of her arms over his broad shoulders to help her run, "We will change direction to throw them off our scent."

Mikes resolve was infectious and she found reserves of strength that were heretofore unknown. She nodded and lifted his arm, breathing fast but with a steady rhythm in place of the near hyperventilation. The field ended with a barbed wire fence that bordered a smaller road.

"Get through, this will buy us a minute," Mike said, holding the wire apart while she climbed through. She offered to take his pack to allow him through, but he took hold of a post and vaulted it instead.

"The nunnery!" Debbie exclaimed.

"What?"

"Hunston nunnery is close, we could hide there. Follow me," she said excitedly, grabbing his hand.

The road was empty which gave them a clear run. It was unusual to find a zombie free route, maybe it was the proximity of the city drawing them in, they just didn't know. They had made it three hundred feet before the dead ripped themselves to shreds pressing through the spiked barrier. It gave them a chance to catch their breath while they planned.

"What is this place you are talking about, do nuns really live there?"

"So Sam said. I was eavesdropping while they talked in the farmhouse and he mentioned this place. It is set back from this road and has high stone walls surrounding the grounds. There is only one side of the living quarters and chapel exposed with windows set high enough to be unreachable. One door in, that's it," she explained.

"It sounds like a fortress."

"It almost is. It was designed to be a sanctuary during the dark ages for priests and their followers who were fleeing persecution. When the danger had passed, the archbishop assigned it as a convent for ladies who wanted to serve God. What a crock of shit," Debbie laughed. Who wanted to waste their whole life being faithful to a made up sky fairy?

"I don't like it. What if we get trapped inside and they surround us?" Mike pondered, analyzing every conceivable angle. He would be happier on his feet, at least that way they could feint and dodge to avoid the dead.

"It was just an option, I thought it may help," she replied.

"We can take a look, but I think we should stay mobile."

The high laurel hedgerows stretched into the distance, with gated entrances every half mile for agricultural access. A faded wooden sign read 'Hunston Convent, Private' at one opening. Mike looked down the snowy driveway, thinking. The walls were high and made of heavy stone, not unlike the color of the rock from Winspit mine. It would be a fine place to hide if they didn't have the prison to reach. Curiously, dead zombies littered the pathway, piled either side of the road. The snow had encased most of the bodies, but patches of rotten flesh showed through.

"What do you make of that?" Mike pointed to the neat rows of corpses.

"Someone has put them there. Do you think it's to scare people away?" asked Debbie, frowning.

"I don't think so. It's almost as if they wanted to keep the driveway clear," Mike mused.

"We can take a quick look. I'm intrigued now," Debbie offered, shrugging her shoulders.

Mike glanced back at the horror choked road, the shambling, crumbling wall of death that was coming for them. "Ok. If we need to we can just draw them in and circle the wall."

They trampled through the snow, watching the heaped corpses for signs of movement. Mike paused when he caught sight of something through the melting snow. Kneeling down, he brushed away the slush and a small wooden crucifix was bound to the forehead with twine.

"What do you make of that?" Mike asked as he looked at the religious symbol and the gaping wound in the split skull of the deceased.

"I have no…"

"Quickly child, get inside!" cried an unfamiliar voice, causing them both to start.

Mike fell back onto his ass after mistaking the source to be the zombie, but peering out from the heavy door of the convent was a nun dressed in traditional habit. Her face was full of concern for the two unannounced visitors.

"Hurry!" she beckoned them with a wave of the hand.

They looked at each other and a malicious grin spread on Mike's lips, "Follow my lead."

"Are you being followed?" the sister asked. The growing chorus from the approaching hundreds answered the question for her and she became even more frantic.

Sprinting the last fifty yards, they barreled in through the open doorway, narrowly missing the nun. The entrance hall was exactly as Mike had expected it to be; adorned with a variety of crosses and religious artifacts, but little else. Those in service to God rarely had anything of material wealth or luxury. Even the chairs, though antique and beautifully made, were worn and uninviting. The opulence of the higher tiers of the clergy didn't filter down to those who willingly chose abstinence. The smell of age hung in the air, as much from the ancient dwelling as the elderly sisters who came through to see what all the ruckus was about.

"What on earth is going on here? Who are you?" demanded a stern looking nun of advanced years. The way the others gave her space indicated she was the mother superior.

"Sister Mary, they were out in the cold and in danger. I had to let them in," answered the sister who had opened the door.

"How dare you disobey me?" shouted Sister Mary, ignoring the newcomers. "I told you we were to maintain anonymity and pray for salvation!"

"But... God wouldn't have wanted them to be left to die," agonized the younger nun.

"I decide what God wills. Do you understand me? Look at the trouble the others have already caused us with their impact on our scant supplies," she screeched and the younger nun was cowed, her head lowering in submission.

"Yes Mother Superior, I understand."

"Good. Now I am sorry, I truly am, but there is no place for you here. We simply don't have the space or resources. You will have to leave, and know that God goes with you," Sister Mary ordered, full of pomposity and righteousness. With a flapping of the arms, she tried to push the pair out through the open doorway until Mike produced a pistol and slammed it into the side of her face, sending her sprawling to the floor.

"I don't think so, you arrogant cunt," Mike said and the nuns blanched and crossed themselves. All except for their would-be savior, who was transfixed with fear at the sight of the firearm. On the floor, blood gushed from the cheek of the mother superior and her eyes fluttered in unconsciousness. The others had gone to her aid, dabbing at the open wound to try and staunch the blood.

"What's your name?" Mike demanded of the younger nun.

"Sister Belinda, sir," she answered meekly, still looking at the sleekly shining weapon, "I'd better close the door now."

"That won't be necessary, we won't be staying," Mike explained with a smile that chilled Debbie's blood.

"Then why did you strike our sister?" scolded another nun from the side of her injured companion.

"Because I'm not going out that way," he answered as if he was answering an imbecile.

"I don't understand," complained another.

"You will soon enough," Mike said, stepping further into the hallway with Debbie, placing the nuns closest to the door.

"I need to close the door, they are nearly here," begged Sister Belinda.

Mike only shook his head and made a mock sad face, "No, you *want* to close the door. But I want the door left open, I have some friends who are coming to say hello."

"Ignore him, close that door now!"

"Don't you fucking move!" screamed Mike, pointing the gun straight in Sister Belinda's face.

"But we will all die!" wailed another voice and Mike burst out laughing.

"No, silly, you will all die and we will escape while they feed on your carcasses," Mike rubbed a knuckle into his eye as if he was wiping away pretend tears, but his evil grin left no doubt he was loving every second of their fear.

"You are damned for all eternity, your soul will burn in the fires of Hell," cursed the mother superior who had regained consciousness.

"We are already in Hell, you fucking whore!" Mike yelled and Sister Belinda made her move for the door. The gun cracked and Mike was so shocked at the sudden recoil and noise it fell from his hand and bounced on the tiled floor, finally settling by one of the nun's feet.

"Ack…" coughed Belinda and a gout of blood erupted from her mouth. The bullet had ripped through her neck and the torn artery sprayed the white frost with deep claret through the open doorway.

The momentary shock wore off and the nun tried to reach for the gun. Unused to confrontation, her hands shook and the blood from the cheek wound of her friend made the metal slippery. Mike wasn't so disadvantaged and stepped forward, kicking as hard as he could and connecting with the jaw of the elderly woman. The bone cracked from the power of the blow and broken teeth spilled from her bloodied mouth.

"The guests of honor have arrived," Mike announced darkly after retrieving the gun.

The first zombies fell on the dying Sister Belinda, whose blood was barely trickling from the wound. Tearing at her clothes with skeletal fingers and teeth, they ripped the black habit into pieces to reach the tender meat beneath.

"Dear God in Heaven. Save us, your loyal subjects. Hear our plea," the nuns begged, falling to their knees and praying.

"You are both going to die, and it won't be quick. You will scream as the Almighty delivers his retribution, you motherless bastards!" shrieked the mother superior and Mike had to admire her moxie.

"Language, Sister. You will be meeting your Lord soon and don't want any stains on your soul," he chided and lifted the broken jawed woman by the back of her dress, throwing her towards the advancing monsters like a treat tossed to a family pet. The ravenous creatures wasted no time and began the process of devouring chunks of flesh from her body.

Enough were pouring through the door to ensure the rest of the swarm would follow, trapping them within the confines of the convent walls while he and Debbie made good their escape. The dead reached the nuns and attacked without mercy, their prayers going unanswered. Noses, ears, chunks of scalp and protesting fingers were bitten off and the gargled screams rang out through the building. Crucified Jesus watched them with painted tears running and a mournful sadness at the fate of his loyal disciples.

"Time to go," Mike urged, pulling Debbie away from the butchery that was occurring.

"In agony," spat the dying Mother, blood frothing from her mouth as the zombies tore her insides out, entrails spilling on the floor.

"What did she mean? That she was in agony or we will be in agony?" Debbie fretted.

"Who gives a fuck. We can get away free and clear, now come on!" Mike pulled her along and through a door which led to a long dining area.

This room was also austere; a stout wooden table ran the whole length of the shadowy hall, with the stains of centuries ingrained in the wood. Paintings of anointed saints observed them with silent accusation and Debbie was sure their eyes followed her every step. Mike clutched at the handle of a closed door but it was pulled from his grip.

A young man gaped at the new faces who had appeared, but this quickly turned to fear when he saw the splashes of blood and their general disheveled appearance.

"What's going on?" he asked, looking over their shoulder where the sounds of screaming had now stopped.

"Nothing. Just a bit of trouble at the door, but it's all sorted now. You should go and see if the sisters need any help," Mike said and patted him on the shoulder as he ran past. They watched his disappear through the dark doorway to the entrance chamber, and new agonized screams began.

"Why did you do that? What is he even doing here?" Debbie asked with confusion.

"Fuck knows, but he doesn't look like a nun. If he is stupid enough to go rushing towards screams with the dead roaming the earth, he's too dumb to live anyway," Mike laughed and pulled her through to the room beyond.

It led down a short hallway and then through another small door which was a side entrance to the main church. They came out on the eastern side of the transept, which adjoined the nave and aisles. Dozens of terrified faces huddled between the pews watching them; men, women, and children. They couldn't have been more afraid if the actual zombies had burst through into the Holy place of worship.

"So many people, Mike, what are we going to do?" Debbie whispered as the group started to stir, questions about the screams overcoming their initial fear.

"We escape. You can see the light through the main doors over there," Mike pointed and they hurried through the converging masses, ignoring their inquiries. When one man stepped in front of them and placed a hand on his chest to demand answers, Mike head butted the stranger on the bridge of his nose. It was an injury that would incapacitate him, and also prevent any more delay from the others. Bewilderment at the sudden violence escalated to screams of terror as the first undead burst through into the church.

"I guess they don't fear holy ground then," Mike said nonchalantly, pushing through the double doors and out into the chilly day.

"Can't we help them at all?" Debbie asked naively. The curse and the outraged stares of the painted saints had worried her.

"You can stay and help, I'm jumping that wall and running for my life," Mike said and strode off, leaving her to decide her fate.

Her newfound compassion lasted all of three seconds and she left the children begging their parents to save them from the monsters. The onset of their high pitched wails showed how hopeless their request was.

"Use my knee to reach the top of the wall and pull yourself up," Mike said, bending a leg to provide a hop-up. With a lithe grace, she leapt and straddled the wall, reaching down to help Mike who ignored her. Taking a few paces back, he ran full pelt at the wall and jumped, planting his feet on the stone to give extra lift. In one fluid motion he was also sat on top, facing Debbie and with a perfect view of the ensuing carnage.

"Shit!" Mike complained when it was clear all they could see was the outside of the slaughterhouse. The battle was taking place within the main church building, with screams and crashing noises rebounding within the walls.

"I think we should go," Debbie said, preparing to drop down from the wall.

"No wait, look at this," Mike was slapping his thighs with mirth.

In the gardens, an obese teenager had followed them through the doors and was trying to run away from two horrors that wanted to taste his soft doughy meat. The size of the youngster left him unable to run properly, only waddle as his flabby thighs got in the way of each other.

"Run, Forrest, run!" yelled Mike and roared with laughter. Even Debbie giggled into her hand at the sight.

"Life is like a box of chocolates!" the boy called back as he deftly dodged the grasping arms of one of his pursuers.

"Fair play, you fat fucker," Mike said with respect at the comeback.

The second zombie had managed to get hold of the collar of his coat and was trying to take a bite from his neck. Surprisingly, instead of screaming and wailing like they expected, he twisted and snapped the arm, before throwing the zombie to the ground. Using his weight, he leapt and stamped down with both feet onto the fallen corpses head, crushing it flat and spraying gore in all directions.

"Snowball fight!" screamed the boy and he scooped up a compacted ball, throwing it at the advancing ghoul. The hard packed ice hit the zombie full in the face and it staggered backwards, spitting out the slushy mixture.

"Well I'll be damned," Mike said with awe. He had completely misjudged the teenager, thinking him to be a sad, pathetic weakling due to his girth. Jogging over to the pair of onlookers, his flesh wobbled and jiggled like jelly. Debbie made a disgusted sound as he came to a stop below.

"Hey, do you mind if I come with you guys? I don't think this place is safe anymore. I'm Winston by the way," he held out a hand and shook the air, mimicking a handshake in place of the real thing as Mike was out of reach.

"Winston, who the fuck calls their kid Winston? How old are you, seventy?" Mike said, mockingly.

"Nope, seventeen years young. My parents named me after Winston Churchill," he answered, looking behind to see how close the second zombie was.

"I'd get moving if I were you, she looks like she wants to eat blubber tonight," Debbie giggled at the festering woman who still had snow buried in the back of her mouth from the snowball.

"What can I say," he shrugged up at her and smiled, "The ladies can't resist me."

With that, the woman reached him and with a speed that belied his weight he feinted to the side and grabbed the back of her head, propelling her face forward into the wall. With a wet smack it came away and the nose was pulped, spilling green blood onto the snow. He drove the head again and again into the stone until the zombie fell dead at his feet.

"Good work," Mike nodded his admiration.

"So can I come with you? I won't slow you down," Winston begged.

"I'll tell you what, Chunk, if you do the truffle shuffle for me, I may just think about it," Mike offered spitefully.

"A fat joke!" Winston slapped his thigh and laughed, "I've never heard that one before."

"Yeah, right," mocked Debbie.

"And anyway, it's glandular," he explained with a sad face.

"Really?"

"Nah, 'course not. I just eat too much crap," he grinned up at them.

The dead congregation were leaving the church and stepping into the daylight. Fresh blood covered the zombies, with red liquid cascading from their open mouths like the communion wine of Hell.

"Sorry, Winston, but we have to go now," Mike said morosely, "Plus you would probably rip my arm out of its socket if I tried to help you up."

"Another fat joke! Brilliant. With a comedy genius like that, you should be on the stage," Winston nodded, "Sweeping it," he finished.

Mike laughed at the quip, but time was running out, "Good luck with your new friends," Mike saluted and dropped effortlessly to the ground on the other side, tucking his legs and rolling to minimize the impact.

"Hey, don't be like that," Winston called from the other side.

"Ready?" Debbie asked, and dropped into Mike's waiting arms.

The screams of the dying were fading as the zombies finished off the last of the survivors. Winston had also fallen silent and they assumed he was wobbling away to try and escape.

"That's a shame, I kind of liked him," Mike said as they pushed through the hedges and back out onto the road.

"He was a fucking slob, what was there to like?" Debbie asked, unable to see any qualities in the teenager.

"He made me laugh, which is more than can be said for your repartee," Mike replied and she scowled at the insult.

"I bet he doesn't suck dick like I do though," she countered.

"How do you know?" Winston called out as he pushed through the same gap in the branches.

"How the fuck did you get over that wall?" Mike demanded, pointing the gun at him.

"Don't shoot!" Winston threw his hands up in mock surrender and laughed. "There is an apple tree that overhangs the wall. I just climbed it and hopped over," he answered putting his hands back down, certain that Mike was only joking with the gun.

"Tricky little cunt, aren't you?" Mike grunted.

"Not so little," Winston laughed and patted his jiggling tummy.

"Why would we want you tagging along with us?" Debbie sneered.

"Because, my raven haired beauty, I am a lean, mean, zombie killing machine," Winston bowed.

"Don't call me that, you vile blob," Debbie scowled at the compliment.

"You'd rather I call you ugly?" Winston raised a confused eyebrow.

"No, that's not what I meant. I meant…" she blustered and Mike chuckled.

"At the very least I make a convenient distraction if you ever get in trouble," Winston said, doing a less than gymnastic twirl.

"So we get to feed you to the dead fucks if we ever get in trouble, is that the deal?" Mike asked with no humor.

"And what a meal my gorgeous body would make," Winston joked, pelvic thrusting towards Debbie who stepped forward and slapped him.

"Fucking pervert," complained Debbie.

"She's got some fight in her, I like it." Winston patted Mike on the back, a brotherly gesture that wasn't reciprocated, "I'll grow on you, I promise."

"Like a tumor, I expect," Debbie finished and they recommenced their journey eastward.

CHAPTER FIFTEEN

"The prison is full of survivors, but the inmates have taken over," Jodi explained to the rest of the group in the lounge.

"We have to do something to help those people," declared Kurt.

John shook his head; history was in danger of repeating again. "There is nothing we can do."

"There has to be!" Kurt shouted back.

"You didn't let me finish." John tried to remain calm, "I meant there is nothing we can do *yet*."

"But you heard how they are being tortured, how can you sit there and do nothing?" Kurt looked at his father with disbelief.

"Ok." John decided on a different approach, "Explain to us how we are going to get inside."

Kurt looked confused for a moment, "Well, the tunnels."

"You can't, they are being watched around the clock. As soon as they see someone trying to get in they have rigged it to collapse," Jodi reminded him.

"Then we go over the walls," Kurt continued.

"The dead have the place surrounded. By the time you have fought through them, the guards would have seen and would organize a welcome party," Jonesy added.

Kurt paced back and forth, a familiar trait when he was frustrated, "We can't just leave them to suffer!"

"Kurt, you are a brave bastard." Jonesy stood and placed a hand on his shoulder, "But you can't go into this halfcocked."

"Winter is almost on us and we are sat on a boat. We need to get to the castle and take it, then we will have a base to work from," Peter added.

"And in that time, how many of the survivors will be killed or raped?" Kurt asked, trying to be contrary.

"Less than if you get yourself killed and they are trapped inside forever with those brutes," Gloria said logically, trying to make him see sense.

Kurt slumped into the chair in resignation. His mind was filled with visions of brutality and screaming women and children. He knew he was being unfair on himself, he couldn't bear the burden of the whole world on his shoulders. His family must be his primary concern, getting them to shelter and sanctuary within the massive walls of Arundel castle.

"I'm sorry," he said to the group, "I understand that it is hopeless for now."

"Hopeless? Yes," Jonesy agreed, "But we don't need to sit here doing nothing. Tomorrow, we can go and scout the prison, see if there are any weaknesses."

"And if there are?"

"Then we bide our time and come back in the spring. If Jodi is right, they will have constructed more tunnels by then, which will spread them thinner and thinner. In the meantime, we will train you all in the use of these." Jonesy held the rifle out and patted his sidearm.

"I'd feel better going against armed criminals with a gun, rather than this." Kurt raised his trusty hammer.

"We won't have anything too heavy to worry about. Thanks to the government confiscating everyone's weapons, they are only likely to have shotguns and the odd bolt action rifle. We may be outnumbered, but they will be outgunned," Jonesy said.

"Can we save everyone?" Sam asked hopefully.

"In my experience, it depends on how far they are willing to go. If they use the hostages as human shields, I have to be honest and say no. Sorry, Sam," Jonesy responded sadly.

"I understand. We will make them pay though," Sam growled with a fire in his eyes.

"You bet we will," Braiden agreed. They made a fearsome pair, young and brave. In time, they would fill out and become quite the warriors, fighting together for a better tomorrow.

"Did I hear something about payback?" came a familiar voice from the hallway door and DB ducked down to avoid banging his head on the door frame.

"What on earth are you doing out of bed?" gasped Christina, rushing over.

"I heard parts of the conversation. Sounds like a good old search and rescue op," DB said to Jonesy.

"It will be, but not for a few months. Get your ass back to bed before you fall over and crack your head open again," Jonesy replied.

"Go! Now! Come on, back to bed." Christina bustled the huge man out of the room, much to the amusement of the others.

***

The snow had all but melted with the climbing temperature, only the thickest collections holding out against the thaw. The group had planned throughout the evening, working from a laminated map that all soldiers took with them. A course was plotted that would give them a full view of the perimeter of the prison.

"Can I have a word?" Jonesy asked as he joined Kurt on the viewing deck.

"Of course, I was just thinking." Kurt pushed away from the edge and stood up, "What's up, are we ready to go?"

"That's what I wanted to talk to you about."

"I'm ready when you are," Kurt said, mistaking his intent.

"No. I want you to stay here," Jonesy replied, "You are a great man to have at your back if shit goes south, don't get me wrong."

"So why do you want me to stay?" Kurt was confused.

"You are a hot head and it's what has kept you alive. For this mission I want calm and collected, I want to take Sam and Braiden," Jonesy explained.

"I don't want my boys out there alone," Kurt protested.

"They won't be alone; they will be with me. I think they have what it takes to be great soldiers."

"So they can fight, what of it? We can all fight when we need to." Kurt was starting to get angry.

"Being a good soldier isn't always about fighting. I want to teach them to blend in, to move unseen among the ashes of our old world."

"I don't think Sarah will go for it," Kurt protested. He knew the soldier was right and any skills the trained killer could impart would increase the chances of survival for his children.

"She said to ask you."

"Fuck!" Kurt tore at his hair, conflicting emotions running through his mind. "I know you want to help, but they are my boys."

"Kurt, you have my word. If it looks dangerous, we will abort and come straight back. If anything happens, I will die to keep them safe," he proclaimed and Kurt knew he was speaking true.

"Ok," Kurt sighed.

"Yes!" Sam and Braiden cried out excitedly, running up the steps from the main cabin and high fiving each other.

"How long have you been listening?" Kurt asked with a scowl.

"Not long, Dad."

"Only for a minute."

"Boys, this isn't a game," Jonesy scolded the pair.

"We know, sorry," Sam apologized.

"We are just happy to be doing something to help those people, Dad. We may be able to see something that can help us in the spring," Braiden pointed out.

Kurt looked at all three; Jonesy with his look of determination and the two boys who were almost bouncing with nervous energy. "You better come back to me in one piece," Kurt demanded and hugged them both close.

They rejoined the others and Sarah shrugged her shoulders at Kurt apologetically. It was impossible to know what was best for the boys, but hiding from the reality of their new existence would not be it. She had heard from Jodi that the streets were unusually quiet, which was the only reason they were being allowed to go. After dressing in dull greys and whites to blend in, they geared up and moved out onto the dock. Jonesy carried his suppressed rifle, and Sam had his slingshot whose rubber banding had been replaced. The steel bearings sang as Sam destroyed the small group of dead that had gathered at the bank, falling amongst those slain the day before.

"Ok, let's move out," Jonesy said and they rowed to the muddy shore, leaping out and running up the boat ramp.

"Be safe," Sarah whispered, holding Kurt tightly.

"They will be fine," Kurt said, keeping his fingers crossed, out of sight.

***

169

"Ground rules," Jonesy looked at the boys who listened intently, "You are my shadows. You do not move unless I move, you do not speak unless I speak. Understand?"

They both nodded.

"After the shops we are going to move through a small housing estate. It's a bit out of the way, but it will bring us out in sight of the main entrance of the prison," he pointed at the map, drawing a line with his finger on their route, "We can watch for any signs of life and then scout around the walls."

They nodded again.

"Let's move."

Jonesy ran from car to car, closely followed by the youngsters. After the first few maneuvers he was confident enough in their ability that he risked a glance over the top of the vehicle they were crouched by. They looked up at him expectantly, keen to impress. Nothing moved apart from a bedsheet that had been trapped by the overhead power lines. How it had got there he couldn't say, but he watched it flutter gently in the breeze for a few moments. It triggered a memory of the barracks and his old friends. At dawn, the British flag had been raised to the familiar bugle call, a sound he remembered fondly.

"The coast is clear, stay low and stay vigilant," Jonesy said, relaxing a little.

"Where are they all?" asked Sam.

"They must be at the prison, it's all I can think of," Jonesy guessed.

The shops were still dark and silent. No person, living or dead, remained inside as they carefully passed each frontage. An abandoned wedding dress shop gave Jonesy the creeps; the mannequins stared out, smiling coldly in their frozen poses. No one would ever wear the carefully crafted dresses, the work of many hours of loving assembly. Would anyone even honor the institution of marriage in a world abandoned by God? Sam followed the others and caught movement from the corner of his eye, a shadow moving amongst the darkness.

"Look out!" he called as the zombie pushed through the inanimate figures.

With a crack, the corpse slammed through the plate glass window which showered them in shards of glass. Braiden shook his head, scattering the fragments out of his hair. Before the monster could regain her footing, he slashed cleanly through her skull with his hatchet, spilling the brains.

"Hustle," Jonesy whispered and started to run, seeking to put distance between them and the noise.

The road veered to the right and opened out onto the housing complex. They caught their breath while looking around the side of the first house.

"Good eye, Sam, I missed the bitch," Jonesy complimented him.

"I didn't see any more of them," Braiden said, wiping the smeared blood onto the wet grass.

"They have to be at the prison. Where else would that racket not bring a hundred down on our heads?" Sam wondered.

"Nowhere," Jonesy agreed and walked off down the road.

The scene was surreal. Cars sat in driveways. House and garage doors stood wide open, the valuable contents on show for any potential thief. Gardens that had been left untended suffered overgrown grass and dead flowers that should have been removed at the turn of the season. A set of swings rocked in the morning breeze, the seats now empty. Sam could imagine how much joy the simple toy had provided as a parent pushed them higher and higher, his own yelps of pleasure and fearful giggling as the ground rushed away were not forgotten. Jonesy walked up one driveway, checking if he had seen what he hoped. A rack of

171

fishing rods, secure in their canvas holders stood in one corner.

"We will return this way and take these back with us to the boat. I haven't been fishing in ages and it would be a good supplement to our diet."

"I love fish!" Sam declared, salivating at the prospect of the warm white flesh.

"We could do with taking some of these tools with us too," Braiden looked over the rows of neatly arranged equipment.

"And I'm supposed to be the mature one," Jonesy chuckled, "All I was worried about was my stomach."

"They may have tools at the castle," Braiden admitted, "But it won't hurt to be on the safe side."

"Agreed. Wait here and keep your eyes open, I'm going to look for the keys for the four by four," Jonesy directed and raised his rifle.

Standing by the side of the door, he dropped low and swept inside, disappearing from view. Reappearing minutes later with a set of keys he pressed the button, but nothing happened.

"Shit," he muttered and threw them on the lawn, "Wrong keys."

"We can find a vehicle later. There are plenty of homes on the way," Sam said and they continued the journey.

They felt watched as they navigated the streets. The upper windows of the homes looked like eyes, judging them as they passed for their continued existence, while their owners wandered the earth, forever doomed. The rows of identical houses gave them a feeling of déjà-vu as they moved street by street closer to the prison.

"Can you hear that?" Jonesy asked the boys quietly.

"I think we have found them," Sam agreed.

The unmistakable commotion grew with each step, the mournful wails of the missing villagers assailed their ears.

"There must be so many," whispered Sam fearfully.

"Get down, I will take a look," Jonesy ordered and they crouched obediently as he rushed to the corner of the street which, according to the map, led back to the main road through town. He crawled the last few feet, looking carefully around the low fence of the property. After a few seconds, he shuffled backwards and jogged back to the waiting teenagers.

"What did you see?" asked Braiden.

"Let's get inside. That house overlooks the main gate." Jonesy took them to the open front door of the dwelling. "We are too close for anything but axes."

They made ready the sharp weapons and followed in low, imitating the soldier. The hallway smelled damp and musty, a common issue in derelict homes. The carpet was saturated from the snow which had blown inside and small fungi grew in the darker corners. Jonesy held a finger to his lips and pointed at his eyes, before directing them through into the living areas. They had seen enough movies to understand they were to search the lower floor. They moved as one unit, through the lounge and into the wide kitchen and dining area. The plates of maggot riddled food were not an unusual sight, and Sam found himself wondering if this was one of the families that had made it behind the prison walls. A crumpled picture was stuck by magnet to the fridge, depicting a crayon family having a picnic. The smiling green, blue, and pink faces beamed at the three who felt like interlopers under the waxy scrutiny.

"Garage," Jonesy dared to whisper, pointing at a wooden door with a heavy lock designed to keep any burglars out should they make it through the metal rolling barrier.

Braiden and Sam watched the rear as he pulled the handle, exposing the pitch black interior.

"Anyone home?" Jonesy asked the darkness and paused, "All clear."

"Upstairs?" whispered Braiden and Jonesy nodded.

The stairs creaked under the pressure, so Jonesy showed them to spread their legs and only walk on the edges of the wooden treads.

"They are the strongest part, no noise," he said.

The hallway at the top of the steps was deserted and every door stood open.

"Housekeeping," Jonesy called out quietly and, as he had assumed, the place was empty. The constant murmur of the dead would have pulled any residing within to the prison walls.

Jonesy took them into a rear bedroom; well-proportioned with a king sized bed and a plasma television mounted on the wall at the foot. The bed was unmade, sheets ruffled and the pillows still had the sunken impressions of their owner's heads. The curtains were open but the lace underneath camouflaged them from any attention. Looking through the delicate fabric, they could see the fortified entrance to the prison. Built during the reign of Queen Victoria, the entrance comprised two viewing towers sat either side of the main wooden gate. The stern visage of the long dead monarch stared out from the brickwork where the artisans had inlaid two stone portrait carvings. The main gate had been forced open by the sheer weight of the undead, but they had been prevented from gaining entry to the inner prison by the reinforced steel inspection cage. The transports would be sealed within the area while checks were carried out, to ensure the paperwork was in order and no prisoners were trying to stow away and escape.

"They can't make it inside can they?" Sam wondered.

"No, the steel bars are strong and it looks like they have been reinforcing them too," Jonesy added.

The cage struts were joined with what looked like rectangular iron bed bases. The inmates must have unbolted them from the cells and welded them to the cage, strengthening the structure. The towers were adjoined by high brick walls, not unlike those of the castle they were hoping to reach, except for the coiled razor wire that stretched into the distance. Set along the perimeter were smaller watch towers and large mounted halogen spotlights for scanning the site during the long dark nights. The bulbs would likely never again burst into life, unless humanity could fight back and restore electricity. Jonesy lifted the binoculars and there were guards along the whole wall, certainly enough to ensure no raiding party could climb them unexpectedly.

"I think we know where all the locals went," Braiden said, looking out, "And a few more besides."

The walls were besieged by thousands of zombies, all beating uselessly against the stone. The closest had rubbed themselves raw, smears of gore were like a shiny skin on the dull brickwork. No patch of ground was left clear, so the worry of a raiding party would be even further down the prisoners' concerns. It would have been as they had guessed; a battle through the dead, all while being observed by the dangerous looking men. They were unarmed, but Jonesy had no doubt they could muster firearms quicker than the group could fight through and climb the wall.

"I think we have seen enough," Jonesy noted and moved away.

Sam stood a bit longer, watching and listening to the clang of bone on steel from the inspection courtyard. The dead were tightly packed inside, unable to move freely.

"Why don't they just kill them through the bars?" Sam asked, "They would be safe."

"Knowing what we know about the hostages, I think they are a convenient way to ensure they stay inside the walls, regardless of how they are being treated," Jonesy offered but couldn't be certain.

"Plus the secret tunnels mean they can get outside to raid anyway. There's no need to destroy them," finished Braiden.

They left the house and jumped through a neighboring garden to stay out of sight. Slowly but surely, they moved between cover using trees, hedges, and anything else offering concealment. Passing through a field that ran parallel to the prison, they heard a ruckus that wasn't caused by the dead. A line of razor wire had been peeled back and a rickety platform had been constructed, projecting out and over the massed zombies. A group of men were standing on the platform that Braiden thought would collapse at any moment. In the background, lining the wall, stood weeping women and children.

"What the hell are they doing?" wondered Sam, crouching under the shadows of a mighty oak.

"You may want to look away, boys," cautioned Jonesy. He had seen the aftermath of executions in Afghanistan, the inconsolable families of the slain.

"Why?" asked Braiden, until the men pushed one of their number to the fore. "Oh."

He was dressed in the filthy uniform that had he had been wearing when the dead had risen. A prison guard, one of the kind souls who had thrown open the gates to offer the locals a chance at survival. Now he was to be used to make an example to the others, in case they had any ideas. One of the captors was obviously the leader, the way the men parted in deference to his passage.

"Do you think that's him?" Sam asked Braiden.

"I don't know, could be," he replied.

"Could be who?" Jonesy was baffled by their discussion of the stranger.

"Mike's fucking brother," Sam muttered and took the binoculars.

The distance was reduced to nothing and the face that glared out into the day was indeed a sibling to Mike, the one and only Craig Arater. The similarities were many and Sam passed the viewing lenses to Braiden who agreed with the identification.

"It's him. That's who Mike and Debbie were trying to reach. Maybe still are if they survived the city. I hope they did so I can kill them," he snarled with hatred.

"We could shoot him right now, that would teach them a lesson," smiled Sam with malice, "You can hit him from this range, right Jonesy?"

"I could, but I won't," he responded quietly.

"Why the hell not?" Braiden demanded.

"Listen, you have to understand people. In a place like that, with the mad dogs running around without leashes, it takes an amazingly strong personality to keep them all in line. How do we know that by killing him we won't be killing every survivor inside?" Jonesy tried to explain the psychology.

"We don't," admitted Braiden, "But they are murdering people already, what difference will it make?"

"I know it looks like random, cold blooded murder, but it isn't. There is a purpose behind the platform, a sense of order. By sacrificing one person, they can probably ensure submission from everyone within the walls, prisoners and civilians alike. It's a show of power over life and death," he continued. Across the known world, despots used exactly the same tactics to cow their populace. It was a trick as old as time.

"I feel so useless," admitted Sam sullenly.

"You aren't," Jonesy declared, "This is just the way things are now."

"Oh God, look." Braiden pointed.

They had tied a rope around the man's ankles and moved him to the edge. Craig's speech carried across the open field.

"You all know the punishment for breaking my rules. Yates ignored those rules, he tried to help some of you escape. I ask myself why? What is out there but death? In here you are safe. Well, almost safe," he laughed.

"Mercy," called out a female voice.

"Mercy? I don't think so," Craig bellowed and pushed the man in the back.

His cry of fear was cut short as he fell face down towards the zombies, the rope pulling taut and nearly wrenching his hip joints loose.

"I'm sorry, I didn't mean to break the rules!" screamed the man as he swung in the air, inches above the grasping arms of the zombies.

"Yes you did," Craig said sadly, "Now it's feeding time."

"Noooooooooo!"

The others on the platform started to lower the condemned man toward the eager mouths. Thrashing around, he bent at the waist trying to avoid the inevitable, but his injured state made it impossible. The weakened muscles gave up and he stretched out once more, straight into the greedy maws of the dead.

"Tie it off!" shouted Craig and his henchmen obeyed.

Sam wanted to look away, but his brother and the soldier watched the horror with steely eyes. The worst of the feast was masked by the thronging mass of corpses desperate for a taste. Shrieks of agony were cut short and the exposed legs of the poor guard still flexed and kicked. Jonesy couldn't be sure if the man was dead and the movement was caused by the reaching arms.

"Up!" called Craig.

The rope raised what remained of the man. The legs were intact, but his head, arms and trunk were missing. Entrails swung from the ragged flesh of his pelvis and spinal column and these too were plucked out of the air and stuffed into blood soaked mouths.

"I want every one of you to remind yourself what happens to those who ignore the rules," Craig ordered and the captives reluctantly shuffled past the platform, looking at the remains.

The children bawled and hid behind their parents, who in turn tried to ignore the streaming blood from the bisected remains. Prayers were uttered by some, while others threw up over the side of the wall, soaking the uncomplaining zombies beneath. Craig laughed at the discomfort and retching, pulling on the rope and making the legs dance in the air.

"Cut him loose, they won't need another lesson. For a while, anyway," Craig ordered and the men untied the rope, throwing what was left down like scraps to a pack of dogs.

"Fucking bastard," snarled Braiden.

"Dad won't let this go if we tell him," Sam pointed out and he looked at Jonesy who was grinding his teeth, fighting the urge to shoot as many of them dead as possible.

"For everyone's sake, we need to keep what we just saw between us for now," Jonesy appealed to the boys, "When the time comes, we have at least one infiltration point."

"We have company," Sam pointed to a pair of zombies meandering across the field.

"Are those handcuffs?"

Jonesy waited until they came closer and one was definitely fastened to the other, their wrists joined. It looked like a policeman had apprehended a suspect and, ignoring normal protocols, had bound them together. It was clear the criminal had turned after being bitten on the neck, then devoured the police officer whose whole body hung in tatters. Now they walked together, always.

"Sam, take care of it. Then we finish our circuit and head home," Jonesy instructed.

"You got it."

Sam felt more inclined to shoot the arrested zombie as opposed to the police officer, a peculiar response to the equally deadly pair. The bearing found its mark, punching cleanly through the forehead and mashing the brain. The police officer was now forced to drag the corpse of his prisoner, but before Sam could finish the job, a shout rung out.

"What the fuck? Get the boss, quickly," shouted one of the lookouts.

"Shit!" Jonesy muttered, "He must have been watching those two cross the field."

"What's the problem?" shouted another gruff voice.

"I think someone just took out a dead fuck in that field," the man explained.

Jonesy risked a quick look and he was pointing straight at them.

"He's seen us," whispered Sam in a panic.

"No, I don't think so. He can see the body but it's too far to see what happened, plus we are in the shadows," Jonesy surmised.

"Get me the glasses! Where's Craig?"

"They're called binoculars, you fucking moron," laughed another voice.

"Well aren't you the English champion," spat the watcher.

Jonesy knew that as soon as the men could see with the binoculars, their cover would be blown.

"Boys, we need to stay low and quiet. Watch your footing, soft ground only," he directed and they moved from shadow to shadow, trying to reach the curve in the prison wall behind the shrubs and trees before being discovered.

"Over there, boss, look," said the man, directing Craig's eyes.

"So what the fuck am I looking at?" Craig's voice was getting fainter with distance.

"In the field, one of them fell down," spluttered the watcher.

"You called me back because a fucking zombie fell over?" roared Craig, stirring the crowd into a frenzy.

"No, I mean I saw it fall over. I think it was shot."

"By who? Arnold fucking Schwarzenegger? Did you hear a gunshot?" Craig was dragging the man closer to the edge of the platform.

"No. They must have a silencer," he protested with confusion.

"So, you are telling me that we are being watched by invisible people in the middle of the fucking zombie apocalypse, who just happen to be armed with silenced fucking weapons?" Craig had turned the man around and only the balls of his feet and Craig's firm grip prevented him tumbling into the horde below.

"Yes. No. I don't know. I'm confused," he started to cry.

"Have you taken anything today?" Craig asked like a disappointed parent.

"Only some pills from the pharmacy, they keep me mellow."

"You fucking twat, you're hallucinating. Get inside and start scrubbing the shitters, that's your job now," Craig pulled the man back and threw him down onto the deck, "Blake?"

"Yes, boss?" came a new voice.

"Consider yourself promoted, you are now part of the watch," Craig ordered, then pulled his foot back and kicked the previous guard in the ribs.

"I won't let you down."

The three watched as Craig continued beating the man from the platform as he tried to crawl away. Whoever stood out of sight below the wall was loving the show, with laughter and clapping at the spectacle.

"That was close." Braiden let out a pent up breath.

"That was on me, boys, I shouldn't have given you the order until I was sure it was safe," Jonesy apologized.

"Keep that one between us too?" Sam asked.

"I think that would be for the best or your Dad will throw me overboard. Let's go."

They rounded the corner with a greater appreciation for the attentiveness of the prison's defenders. Jonesy had made the mistake of assuming that because they were dumb enough to have been locked up in the first place, that they would not carry out their duty responsibly. Their vigilance would prove to be another obstacle when it came to breaching the facility. The moans of the dead gave way to the rush of flowing water as they came to the rear of the compound. The walls were broken by another heavily guarded entrance and tower, although this gate hadn't been breached as the main bulk of the dead were occupied elsewhere. The concrete ramp that led to it from the water's edge may have been used at one time for supplies. The fangs of thick, rotten timber that sprouted from the water marked out the shape of the old dock. The shrubbery came to an end and their hiding place with it; they would have to dash the last thirty feet in the open to reach the sloped bank and the angle of cover it provided.

"Where do we go?" Sam whispered, "If we make a run for the riverbank we could be seen."

"I agree, but if we go back they are already spooked and we could be spotted," Braiden said.

"Braiden's right, we go on," Jonesy nodded, "We wait for an opportunity and then make a break for it."

They watched the watchers, who watched the gathered corpses of Ford town. This far from the main road they were only three deep at the walls and the lookouts were less concerned about the danger. After fifteen minutes, cravings got the better of the group and they huddled in a circle to roll themselves a cigarette.

"Now!" Jonesy told the boys and they rushed across the untended field, diving over the edge and skidding down on the loose soil.

They lay in the earth, listening for the shouts that would signal their exposure. The easy chuckles that greeted an unheard joke told the trio that their cover wasn't blown, so they soldier crawled through the mud until they were out of sight.

"You did great, lads, like proper troopers," Jonesy said and the youngsters beamed with pride.

Time was against them and the methodical scouting mission had taken longer than Jonesy had planned for. They chose to call off collecting the fishing rods and tools until another day, it wasn't as if they were going anywhere. The final section of wall was the easiest to observe unseen. With a growing population, the small town had seen a growth in construction of both houses and commercial premises to cater for the burgeoning business opportunities. Each building was separated by an access alley that led to a steel fence which looked out onto the prison. The only thing of note on the western section was a small, recently erected compound.

"What's that for?" Sam asked.

"It's a contractor's yard, see the signs?" Jonesy pointed to the 'Morton Atkins' banners that had been cable tied to the mobile railings; the name of a well-known construction company.

"They must have been doing some building work inside the prison before the shit hit the fan," Braiden assumed.

"I think we have another way in," Sam said.

The site 'offices' consisted of converted shipping containers stacked atop one another. Windows and doors were cut into the thick, corrugated metal walls and temporary stairs had been constructed to reach the higher levels.

"They are taller than the wall," Jonesy was giving it some thought, "We could set up a zip wire and get across."

"The watchtowers are nowhere near that part of the wall either. In the dark they wouldn't even know," Braiden voiced Jonesy's observation.

"We have some good points of entry, not including any tunnels we can find with Jason's help. This mission was a success, now let's get back to a warm meal." Jonesy patted them both on the back.

CHAPTER SIXTEEN

"At least it isn't hopeless," nodded DB at the news. "Not at all. If anything I feel confident we may have a good chance of keeping innocent casualties to a minimum," Jonesy agreed.

"What are you up to, Dad?" Kurt asked as John fiddled with something.

"Just winding the radio up," he said, turning to them, "I want to see if there is any more news."

Gabrielle was in the middle of a recap speech, repeating the information that was unknown to any new listeners, but not the group who had picked her up from day one. Her tone of voice was tired and the constant repetition of the horrific events was obviously taking a toll. After a ten-minute coffee break, she tried to bring some life to the broadcast with the caffeine buzz.

"This is Gabrielle, your friendly zompoc shock jock. So the search for a cure has hit the buffers and the Daresford Institute has drawn a blank with decoding the pulse. We are assured they will keep working on it, but without the experiment notes from the Hadron Collider scientists it is nearly impossible."

"Damn," John grumbled, "I was hoping for more than that."

"We all were," admitted Gloria, sitting beside him and stroking his leg in support.

185

"Now for some good news, or bad news depending on your point of view. I am in direct contact with what remains of the government. The prime minister and most of the cabinet managed to reach safety before the Houses of Parliament fell and are now working on a plan to fight back."

"Typical politicians," Jonesy said, throwing his hands in the air, "They are like rats; impossible to get rid of."

"The command structure has been reestablished on HMS Dauntless, with the surviving heads of all three wings of the armed forces now safely aboard. Communication and agreement between the two parties is strained, with disagreements on the strategies with which to attempt to retake the British Isles. Estimates from Admiral Wright put the combined combat readiness at less than five percent, and he is unwilling to engage in open warfare with the hordes now in control of our country. The government feel that risks must be taken to secure a beachhead on the mainland, and that this will then allow the gradual reclamation of towns and cities over the coming months."

"What a fucking joke. How the hell can they try and make decisions hiding underground?" DB muttered.

"Maybe they should offer to lead from the front and show us how it is done," Jonesy replied, shaking his head.

"Can you imagine how afraid the zombies would be facing off against the might of Her Majesty's loyal government," John sneered.

"I will bring you more news on the coordinated response as I receive it, but don't hold your breath. In the meantime, the remnants of the armed forces have gathered on high ground in strategic positions which provide the best security. Parts of the Brecon Beacons, Chiltern Mountains, and the Pennines have all been fortified as much as possible, with their lack of accessibility aiding in their defensive potential. I'm sure anyone listening will join me in a prayer for their continued safety."

186

"At least there are survivors," offered Peter to the soldiers.

"I hope we can somehow join forces and help, but the logistics of supplying even a small force is incredible. With the dead around every corner and bases overrun, I can't see what they can do other than sit there," DB said.

"The first thing they should be doing is securing as much equipment and weaponry as possible, that way at least they are being proactive. You're right though, if the bases are zombie city then it is hopeless," Jonesy sighed.

"I am pleased to announce through the shit storm of unimaginable horror, that pockets of survivors have been identified by satellite imagery on the Dauntless. Groups numbering less than five and more than a hundred have managed to seal themselves off from the dead, we just have to hope they can survive the winter. In my brief conversations with the admiral, I have suggested supply drops for the plucky humans, though I have no idea if it will be agreed. With the temperatures plunging, the danger from freezing or starving is greater than that of the undead at this stage."

She signed off and the group looked at each other.

"At least we aren't completely alone," smiled Sarah.

187

CHAPTER SEVENTEEN

"This ends today," said Eldridge as they made their way back to the barracks from the execution.

"What the fuck are you talking about?" replied Harkiss who was following.

"I mean tonight we take this place back, winner takes all. I can't go through another one of that bastard's 'I'm killing this soldier for your own good' speeches," she explained and several of the other soldiers nodded.

"Quiet!" whispered Harkiss, "The walls have ears. Come on, get inside."

They arrived at the bunks and pulled the door closed. Seating themselves, they leaned in close to keep their voices low.

"How many do we know for certain are with Baxter?" Eldridge asked.

"About thirty, which means we have the advantage of numbers," replied Gladstone, a newer member of the mutinous group.

"And we know for sure that once we take out a few of the key players, the rest will fall into line to save their own hides."

"There is just one problem," Harkiss said, arms wide in frustration, "We don't have any fucking guns."

"It will be a bloodbath," said Gladstone honestly.

"No it won't, that is why we are here," Eldridge declared.

"Do you have weapons then?"

"No, but we will. Hague is with us," she told the gathering and they all started laughing.

"Are you shitting me? That fucking coward is going to help? Help get us killed more like," Harkiss grumbled. The plan was turning to shit already.

"Everyone has their limit. Growler has been riding him so hard he is either going to kill him or himself," Eldridge insisted.

Growler, real name Corporal Groll, was so named because he didn't breathe as much as rumble like an animal. Exercises were always a noisy affair, but the hilarity ended at his exhalations. He was a pure loyalist to Baxter, violent, and not shy in doling it out. Hague was always heavily bruised around the face these days and walked with a limp.

"I've seen the looks he gives that fucker," Derby affirmed, "He will do what's needed."

"We need to take the armory without raising the alarm or it will be near impossible. As soon as the claxons start, the guards will cut anyone down they see," Eldridge stressed.The tension had been building like a pressure cooker for weeks and everyone knew something would have to give. Baxter's soldiers such as Moseby and Filton would throw down their weapons and beg for mercy; the same couldn't be said for Rabson and Trimble, the communications room guards. They would die on their feet, taking as many of the mutinous soldiers as they could.

"There is also the matter of how we get up close and personal with the armory guards. They are under orders to shoot anyone that even approaches the lockup," Harkiss pointed out.

Eldridge smiled, "I have that covered."

Standing up, she lifted her mattress and pulled out a thick, wooden chopping block that she had stolen. It was covered in gouges and chunks were missing from the edges.

"What the hell is a chopping board meant to do?" Derby questioned, frowning.

"This," she answered and placed the board against the wall.

Taking out two small kitchen knives concealed within her pillowcase, she felt the weight of the blades. With a fluid motion, she launched one and it embedded, point first, into the wood.

"Beginners luck," Harkiss said.

Smiling, Eldridge took several paces back and repeated the throw. Once again, the tip stabbed deep within the grain of the wood and the men whistled their approval.

"When did you become a circus freak?" Derby laughed.

"It's taken me weeks of practice, but it was worth it. As long as Hague can cause a commotion or even take one out, I will finish the second. Even if Hague pussies out I should be able to get both before they shoot me. If I go down, you have to promise to finish this," Eldridge asserted and they all nodded.

"Let's hope it doesn't come to that," Harkiss said, "But you have my word, by the morning Baxter will be fucking dead. Or we will."

"If all goes well at the armory we need to take Communications and Baxter at the same time. If we can cut the head off the snake the rest will be more likely to toe the line," Derby offered.

"I think the new artillery commander will be an issue," Harkiss pondered.

"Then he dies too," Eldridge shrugged, "Meet in the mess hall at one am."

"Are we really doing this?"

"It's either this, or DB and Jonesy die along with more of our friends. Morrow is close to breaking point, it won't take much for him to give them up," Eldridge explained.

"Fuck it, what have we got to lose. Everyone we love is already dead," Derby declared and walked out of the room. In a world of unending horror and loss, life loses much of its value and survival without hope is pointless.

CHAPTER EIGHTEEN

"**I**'m not judging, but why kill all those people?" asked Winston as they hopped another fence.

"We needed a distraction," shrugged Mike, "They were it."

Winston nodded, unperturbed.

"What, no smart ass response?" Debbie said.

"Nope. You did what you had to do," he replied.

"But what about the children?" Mike asked, becoming irritated.

"Even with all this shit going on, they called me names," Winston said sadly, "Every day, I would catch them laughing behind my back."

"So you aren't in the least bit concerned that we killed everyone inside those walls?" Mike snapped, grabbing him by the lapels of his thick coat. The lack of recognition of the monstrous act was driving him to distraction. Mass murder deserved more respect and the lack of fear in their new companion was annoying them both.

"I didn't want them dead," he admitted, "But I won't lose sleep over it. The nuns were riding us all day long, telling us to repent our sins, asking what we had done to bring the wrath of God down on the world. The adults just ignored me the whole time. Surrounded by people, I was still alone."

"So you're not scared of us?" Debbie demanded. The first person to witness the ruthlessness of Mike and Debbie and here he was plodding along as if they had just walked through the complex waving at everyone.

"Everything is dead, or sort of, walking around instead of lying down. I could get eaten today," he explained, "I don't have time to be scared of you."

"You are an enigma," Mike said, shaking his head.

"I have never been used to wash out a bum hole, I'll have you know!"

"Enigma means a puzzle, you dumbass. You're thinking of an enema," Debbie sniggered.

"It was a play on words." Mike looked at Winston and threw his hands up, "You see what I have to put up with."

"No wonder you are murdering your way across Sussex," Winston acknowledged, patting him on the back in pity.

Debbie regarded them with confusion, "What are you talking about?"

"Winston agrees that you are not the sharpest knife in the drawer," Mike explained.

"Huh?" she scowled.

"More like the lights are on, but no one is home," Winston carried on.

"What fucking home?" Debbie was getting angry as she looked around.

"You can't tell me you have never heard those sayings," Mike said with suspicion. The blank look on her face made the two men laugh.

"It means you are deficient," Winston pointed a finger at his temple.

"You fat wanker!" she screamed when it finally clicked and started chasing him around the field.

In spite of his size, he managed to outpace her and this just added fuel to the expletive diatribe pouring from her mouth.

"I'll fucking kill you!"

"If you want my body, you have a funny way of showing it!" he shouted over his shoulder.

"I'm going to cut your balls off!" she gasped, finally slowing.

"I haven't tried anything kinky before, but I'm game if you are!" he laughed as she bent double, trying to catch her breath and was rewarded with the middle finger.

"She makes up for the lack of smarts in bed," Mike confided.

"Go… fuck… yourself…" she panted.

"No, that's what your holes are for," Mike stated. This got him the wanker hand motion.

"Plus, she is really beautiful, which helps," Winston added.

"Fuck off, lard ass," she snarled, able to breath properly again. They couldn't miss the slight upturn in her lips, a sure sign that even with the insult, she had loved the compliment.

"If you keep being mean to me, I won't sleep with you," Winston cautioned.

"Over my dead body," she snapped back.

"You would make a decent looking zombie," Winston agreed, "I would probably still sleep with you."

"What the fuck?" Mike looked amused and disgusted at the same time and Debbie screwed her face up in horror.

"Ok, a bit too much, sorry. I take it a bit far sometimes," Winston admitted.

"Freak," Debbie muttered.

After fifty feet Winston turned to Mike and whispered, "I'm right though, aren't I?"

"Freak," Mike chuckled.

CHAPTER NINETEEN

"**W**hy are you so fat?" Debbie asked after another mile, her aches making her irritable.

"More calories being consumed than being used by my daily bodily functions?" Winston offered.

"Ha fucking ha. I meant how can you still be this big with no junk food. I doubt the sisters were stocking much in the way of chocolate and snacks," Debbie sneered.

"Would you believe I am part Eskimo and the fat is just an extra layer of insulation against the cold?" he replied.

"No."

"Ooh, tough crowd," he said, holding a hand up for a high five from Mike that didn't come.

"It's a fair question, we don't have any food for you," Mike said.

"Well, you know that tree I climbed over the wall from?"

"How can we forget, it meant you could survive to drive me crazy," Debbie huffed.

"See!" Winston fist pumped, "I told you I would drive you crazy with desire."

"Jesus H Christ, do you have an off switch?" she complained.

"Sorry, I get carried away sometimes. Anyway, I have used that tree on several occasions to go... shopping," he admitted.

"Shopping?" Debbie looked at him quizzically.

"Mostly it was just breaking into houses to steal their sweets and potato chips. All the nuns had was vegetables for dinner, followed by vegetables for pudding," Winston explained, wrinkling his nose.

"You don't like vegetables?" Mike asked,

"Fuck no!" Winston declared, "I didn't earn the nickname Salad Dodger by eating healthy food."

"The nuns called you names?" Debbie asked.

"No. My parents," Winston replied, falling silent for the first time, his perpetual grin sliding away.

"Aww, mummy and daddy didn't love you?" Debbie mocked.

"Don't!" Mike growled.

"What? It's not my fault he is such a fucking loser," she laughed.

Mike rounded on her and grabbed her by the face, digging his fingers painfully into her cheeks, "I said… don't!" he snarled inches from her face.

"It's ok, Mike, she is right," Winston said quietly, "I am a fucking loser."

"You've made it this far on your own. You went out alone, through the zombies to find fucking snacks for Christ sake! I'd say that makes you a winner," Mike said, releasing her. It was a rare thing for him to throw out a compliment, and almost unheard of for it to happen after only a couple of hours. Winston was proving to be a resourceful teenager as well as quite fearless in the face of the dead.

"Hold up," Winston said, "Mike can I borrow your hatchet quickly? I want to see if there is any food in that home. I totally understand I can't take yours."

Through a break in the trees they could spy a small house; a simple two up, two down. It had likely been used as a farmworker's cottage in olden times, much smaller in stature than the sprawling farmhouses of the landed gentry.

A couple of undead were walking back and forth in the garden, possibly the owners who had returned home after falling to the plague.

"Have at it," Mike said, handing the small axe over.

His bulk was still an issue, but once that weight achieved momentum it would cause some damage. Mike watched him tackle both of the zombies, the power of his blows carrying on the cold wind. A further zombie ambled from the open doorway and it met the same fate, splashing green goo all over the entrance. Picking up the corpse, much the same way Mike had done with the doomed nun, he threw the body to one side and disappeared into the gloom.

"I hate him; why do we have to take him with us?" Debbie hissed.

"Why do you hate him? Because he made you look like a retard?" Mike fired back.

"Don't call me that!" Debbie sobbed, "It's a horrible word."

"Ok, sorry." Mike pulled her close, "I see some of myself in him, that's all. I was a big lad when I was younger and my parents never let up on me. Instead of just names, they would beat me too. Craig would try and protect me and take the punches sometimes, he is the only reason I am alive today."

Debbie regarded him with pity, understanding his earlier anger at her taunts towards the young man. "I'm sorry, what an awful way to grow up."

"In a way it has helped. It made me a survivor, the same as Craig. Without people like us, the dead would have already won," he replied.

"I never wanted for anything. Even though we lived in a deprived area, my parents paid for the best education, the best clothes, the best toys. Most of the time they had nothing for themselves."

"Yeah, we can tell," Mike laughed.

"What do you mean by that?" she sulked.

"It means you are a spoiled brat, but one with a fine ass," he said, playfully squeezing her firm bottom.

"I know I can be a bitch. In a way I wish I had had it tougher, like you."

"Don't ever wish for something like that," he said quietly, a shadow passing over his face. The memories of trying to hide when his father would come home drunk, looking for a reason to beat him.

Winston came jogging back through the trees with a merry smile and two backpacks. He came to a stop and looked at the pair, "Are you ok? Have I done something wrong?"

"Not you," Mike answered, "Memories, mate, bad memories."

Winston nodded, "I get them too."

"What the hell have you got there?" Debbie asked with curiosity, yet still unable to talk to him without an attitude.

"I have two gifts for you, M'lady," he declared, bowing at the waist, which wasn't easy.

"I don't want anything from you," she sneered and Mike squeezed her hand tightly enough to hurt.

"I'm not talking about my seed, or even my hand in marriage," Winston replied, back to his jovial self.

"As if you would have a chance you disgusting..." she started to say but Mike squeezed hard enough to grind finger bones together and she fell silent.

"All joking aside, I thought you might need this." Winston knelt down and showed her the contents of one of the bags. Within was a sleeping bag, assorted clean clothes, ration packs that soldiers used, which were highly nutritious, and water treatment tablets.

"Who leaves a perfectly packed rucksack in the apocalypse?" Mike asked, frowning.

"I think they might not have had much choice," Winston said with sorrow. Turning the pack, the dried bloodstains were evident, "There was a lot of blood in the hallway. I think they were caught just as they were going to run."

"Tough break," Mike laughed.

"Thanks, I guess," Debbie said with less venom than normal, "What was the other present then?"

"This," Winston pulled out a huge bar of chocolate and handed it to her.

"Don't you need it more than me? You wouldn't want to ruin that fine figure," she giggled and Mike's face darkened.

"It's ok," he said, to Mike more than Debbie. "I was going to hide it and eat it later, but I really need to get in shape. I can't rely on luck, good looks, and wit forever."

"Well, thanks," Debbie said with no mocking. Her mouth was watering at the thought of the sweet chocolate melting on her tongue.

"It's my pleasure," he smiled broadly, "And at least we won't be as cold in the night with the sleeping bags."

"You did good, buddy," Mike patted him on the back. "I would have ignored that place completely."

"I'm just glad I could help." He grinned and even Debbie returned the smile.

***

The snow was largely melted by midafternoon, leaving the fields like a quagmire. Their feet were caked with clods of dirt and if they hadn't been wearing the hiking boots, the suction of some of the terrain would have claimed their footwear long ago.

"What is that smell?" Winston asked, sniffing the air like a bloodhound.

"I don't smell anything," Debbie admitted.

"It smells like something has been burned," Mike replied, finally catching the scent.

"If somethings burning, shouldn't we avoid it?" she said fearfully.

"Not burning, burned," Winston whispered, "Listen."

"Zombies, and not just one or two," Mike said quietly, pointing to a crest in the hill they were climbing.

"Shall we take a look?" Winston asked and Debbie cringed at the thought.

"Fortune favors the brave," Mike agreed.

They kept low as the hill evened out and revealed the next valley. Before they reached a point where they would be visible to any waiting horde, it became clear they didn't need to worry. The fields were barren of crops, with only the hardiest weed's able to begin taking root. It wouldn't be long before nature took back what was rightfully hers, with civilization falling to decay no less than the dead which stalked the world. In the middle was a deep, blackened crater with remnants of a large home spread far and wide. The moaning was coming from the undead, who had been literally blown to pieces by the explosion. Body parts lay strewn across a diameter of three hundred feet; arms, legs, torsos, and heads writhed on the ground. Only a couple had escaped injury enough to drag themselves slowly in circles, gradually burying themselves in the furrows as if they wanted to return to the grave.

"Do you think the gas blew up?" Debbie asked, remembering the story of how Kurt had detonated the houses of the child murderers.

"I don't know," Mike admitted.

"A gas explosion would have just levelled the building," Winston explained, "That crater was from the impact of a missile or a shell. Something with a high explosive payload."

"How the fuck do you know?" Debbie was dubious.

"Despite my magnetism with the ladies, I find it easier to play computer games than break their hearts," Winston chuckled.

"Figures," she sneered, but it made sense.

"Why on earth would they be destroying homes?" Mike pondered.

"Beats me," Winston said.

"What's that over there?" Debbie was pointing to a large expanse of concrete covered land surrounded by chain link fence. An abandoned tower rose from the ground on one side, bushes growing through the broken windows and rusted antennae leaning awkwardly from the roof.

"It's Tangmere airfield. During World War II we needed as many runways as possible to launch bombing raids on the Nazis. These places were built to defend the south coast from the Luftwaffe but closed in the sixties when the cost got too great. It was used as a flying school and museum for a while too," Winston revealed. He loved the tales of bravery and brotherhood that came from one of the darkest periods of history. If he had been more physically gifted, he would have joined the armed forces.

"We can try those hangars, there may be somewhere to bed down for the night." Mike pointed to the colossal derelict buildings which once housed hundreds of combat aircraft.

Darkness was creeping across the horizon as they pushed under the rusty fence. The open expanse allowed them a good view of their surroundings and very few zombies had managed to trespass. Those that had were mostly specks in the distance and only two came to investigate the new arrivals.

"I've got these," Winston said, while taking Mike's axe again. "Get inside and take a look."

"Shout if you need help," Mike offered and watched the bulky figure jog towards the undead.

The massive doors stood open a few feet and wouldn't budge on the corroded runners. They would be out of sight but unable to restrict entry to any zombies that managed to get inside the grounds. Just as Mike was about to look for a better place to hide, a glint of paintwork caught his attention in the gloom. Shining a flashlight, a small charter plane was situated to the rear of the hangar.

"Hello!" Mike called out and it echoed in the vast chamber.

"I think we are alone," Debbie said after a few seconds of silence.

The aircraft had been cannibalized for parts, with the engines stripped bare and various sections of bodywork missing. It made Mike think of the zombies, the way they kept going even when torn and broken.

"What is it?" Debbie asked when she felt him shudder at the bizarre, macabre thought.

"Nothing, just giving myself the willies," he replied.

"The only person you should be giving the willy to is me," she teased and grabbed his crotch.

Heavy footfalls bounced from the walls as Winston returned. "We are all clear, none of the others saw me. Fuck me, it's a bit dark in here, Deb, can I hold your hand?"

"Get lost," she muttered.

"Can't blame a man for trying," he chuckled.

"What do you think about spending the night in that?" Mike pointed at the lone aircraft.

"It's either that or the abandoned control tower," Winston shrugged.

The door stood open, inviting them to step inside. When it was in service, the craft would have ferried businessmen and celebrities to various functions, ensuring a swift and private journey. Now only a faint smell of mildew permeated the air as Mike leaned inside and called out again. Nothing stirred, not even insects so he climbed aboard and the smell worsened.

"Eww, I can't stay in here!" Debbie complained, pinching her nostrils.

"It's safer than the alternative. Here," Winston held out a tiny metal jar.

"Do my lips look chapped, you imbecile?" Debbie scowled.

"That isn't the purpose, my obnoxious beauty. Smear some under your nose and it will mask the smell," he said, before liberally rubbing the shiny mixture on his own stubbly upper lip.

"Oh," was all she could muster. Her attention was taken by the luxurious looking seats that the torch beam illuminated.

"This would have been a high end model by the look of it," Mike nodded appreciatively. The interior was untouched apart from some cigarette ends and empty beer bottles which had been left behind. Whoever had slept in here previously was long gone, and probably dead.

"What do you think?" Winston asked, indicating the rubbish.

"The leftovers in the bottle are moldy, I don't think we will be getting any living visitors," Mike said, "And even if we do, I have this." He pulled the gun out.

"It will be warmer than the building without windows," Winston added and Debbie was convinced. Taking the lip balm, she dug a sizeable blob of the moisturizer out and put her finger up each nostril, twisting the digit to spread it out.

"No, not up…" Winston tried to stop her.

"Huh?" she asked, finger still buried to the first knuckle.

"Never mind."

"Do the doors shut?" Mike asked.

"Let's try," Winston said and pulled on the rope which had preceded the more modern mechanical closing devices. It rose without protest and latched as if it was brand new, a testament to the quality of the engineering.

"At least we are completely safe now, thanks, Winston," said Debbie and he nearly choked with surprise.

"She's tired," Mike explained. "Her mouth seems to run dry at the same time as her batteries."

"Fuck you!" she yawned and the men smiled.

"I will take the cockpit so that you can be alone in here, ok?" Winston offered.

Debbie was thinking of a clever response about him taking the cock, but her eyes were grainy and she was dead on her feet so she merely waved dismissively.

"Let's get some food inside us first," Mike offered, seating himself, "And you have got to tell us how the fuck you made it to the convent."

They settled into the soft leather seats and removed their meal of choice. Debbie was happy with the chocolate and savored each square as it met her moist tongue. Mike and Winston opted for the high energy ration packs, one with stew and the other with spicy noodles.

"Eight hundred calories per serving," Winston tutted, patting his belly.

"I have a feeling we will be using up each and every one of those when we fight our way to the prison tomorrow," said Mike between cold mouthfuls.

"Do you think the prison will have kept them out?" Winston asked.

"I know it!" Mike declared. "And if Craig hasn't already taken it for himself, he sure as hell will when I get there."

"Won't everyone inside be working together to survive?" Winston said naïvely.

"Things have changed, mate," Mike growled in the shadows. "The world is ours for the taking."

"Don't worry, you picked the right side," Debbie said cheerfully, a mixture of comfort and endorphins from the melting candy.

They both missed the look of uncertainty that played on his features. "Anyway, you want to know how I made it to the warm and welcoming arms of the nuns? It's an epic tale, no less wondrous than Frodo and Samwise in The Lord of the Rings as they battle to reach Mordor and the fires of Mount Doom."

"Are you going to get on with it or talk us to death?" Debbie yawned again.

"My thespian genius is wasted on you common wastrels," Winston tried to sound hurt, "It went like this."

CHAPTER TWENTY

*W**inston** watched the seconds ticking down until first break, click by agonizingly slow click. Why was it that when you craved something time seemed to slow down? His stomach was grumbling and only a bacon and egg baguette would silence the ravenous organ.*

"Soon, my pretty," he whispered downward.

"Did you just call me pretty?" asked Vanessa Porter with a look of disgust.

"What? No I was just thinking aloud," he mumbled back, looking at the desk and blushing.

"Did you wish to add something to the discussion, Winston?" asked their teacher.

"No, Miss. Morescu."

"Well perhaps you should spend more time listening than talking to Miss Porter, then you would have something constructive to say," she replied sternly.

"Sorry, miss." He wished the floor would open up and swallow him whole.

The lesson continued for two more minutes, but he didn't hear a word of the information. The others in the class were shooting him sly glances of ridicule and sniggering to each other. Maybe it would be best to go and hide in the library until his next period, that way the topic of conversation could have moved to other things.

"Ok, everybody remember the first homework task is due in no later than next Monday," Miss. Morescu called out, trying to be heard over the clatter of tables and chairs.

"Fat cunt," mocked one of Vanessa's friends.

"Thanks," Winston replied.

"As if she would ever be attracted to someone that looked like you," sneered another as they filed past.

"She's below my usual standard if I'm honest," he fired back.

"Yeah right," laughed Vanessa, *"Your standard starts and ends with your own hand."*

"That's quite enough of that, girls!" cautioned Miss. Morescu as the girls left the room.

Winston packed his textbooks and notepad before carefully placing his chair back under the table. Scarcely able to look his teacher in the eyes he tried to scurry out as fast as possible.

"Winston, if they are giving you a hard time you only need to let me know. We take bullying seriously in the college," she said with genuine concern.

"It's fine. They just need to get to know me and they will see I'm a stud," he replied, pushing through into the corridor.

Students dodged and jostled to get through the cramped space and Winston waited for a gap to join the flow of people. The corridor was awash with garish murals from the art department; a hideous mishmash of colors posing as 'art'. It wasn't that he didn't appreciate a good painting, but from overheard conversations, most of the members of the course were doing it for an easy ride. His father had shown him many different landscape paintings from legends such as Turner and Constable and the intricate brush strokes seemed to sing. The abstract splatter paintings by Pollock and other artists just looked like an angry toddler got into the paint pot. On a few occasions, his father had invited him along to try painting and they

207

had set the easels up in the middle of nowhere to ensure tranquility for the task. After an hour or two Winston would get bored and fidget, which only served to disturb the older man's concentration. After three attempts, all ending with a heated argument he was never offered again and the alienation grew insurmountable between he and his parents.

"Thanks a lot, dad," Winston mumbled, reaching the cross section of corridor which would take him left to the library, or onward to glorious sustenance.

"Out of the way, wide load," shouted an acne ridden youth who barged him to the side, much to the amusement of his group of friends.

"Sorry."

"Yeah, you better be sorry, gut," he hissed, poking Winston in the belly.

"I can lose weight, but you will always have a face like roadkill," Winston argued back.

The tension was rising and the students could sense something was in the offing. They gathered 'round, eager for the promised blood. Acne turned and his infected cheeks quivered with anger.

"What did you say, blubber belly?" he growled, standing so close that Winston could smell the noxious cigarette breath and body odor.

"Have you never heard of deodorant and mints?" Winston said, trying to avoid the vile fragrances.

The crowd laughed and the bully punched him in the cheek, a flailing blow without training or power. Instead of crying in pain as expected, Winston grabbed him and in one fluid motion, twisted and slammed his skinny body into the wall. Skull met brickwork with a dull thud and the crowd cheered.

"Get off me, you faggot," shouted acne and he threw more punches but they were weak from pain and embarrassment.

Winston pulled him away and body slammed him again, ending the assault. The bully was crying and reaching to feel the tender lump on the back of his head. Most of the crowd dispersed when it became apparent the violent altercation was over, losing interest at the lack of blood.

"You come near me again and I will pop your fucking head." Winston glared at the youth, before letting him go and walking away.

"You're going to get stabbed, bruv," called another skinny white kid, trying to sound like a London gangster as he helped his injured friend.

"You live in Sussex, stop making out you're a Cockney hard case," Winston shouted back.

Without even realizing, he found himself in the canteen, surrounded by smells and sounds that calmed his racing heart. The clatter of cutlery on china plates was a soothing din and he joined the queue with a smile. A seed of fear was planted by the threat of bodily harm, but he couldn't do anything about it now. The reputation of the small group of thugs was well known so he made the decision to sneak out after eating and miss the next lesson, just in case.

"Hi, Winston," said Marjorie, a cheerful canteen chef, "The usual?"

"Yes please. Can I get a couple of extra rashers of bacon?"

"Of course. Are you ok? Your cheek is really red," she asked, placing the crispy meat between the cut bread.

"Yeah, I was blocking fists with my face," he replied.

"Winston!" Marjorie scolded, "You are too smart to be getting in trouble."

"I didn't start it," he protested, taking the paper wrapped baguette.

"Well I'm glad to hear that," she smiled, "Hope you enjoy it."

209

"You know I will." He winked and looked for a quiet table.

Before he could settle into the chair the sounds of shouting carried through the open double doors that led to the main entrance. Teachers and students alike bundled towards the disruption, the former to stop whatever was happening and the latter to get as much footage as possible on their camera phones.

"Fight, fight, fight!" came the chanting.

Winston wasn't normally interested in the juvenile antics of the masses but after his earlier battle he wanted to make sure no one got really hurt. Where the teachers had to abide by a no touch rule, he could intervene and separate the combatants. Carefully stowing the breakfast treat in his bag he was only just standing when the chants turned to screams and the doors burst inward with the flood of fleeing youngsters.

"They're fucking eating people!" screamed one girl who went flying over the top of a table in her haste. Running to her aid, Winston helped her up.

"What are you talking about?" he shouted to be heard.

"I don't know, zombies or something!" she screeched and pulled loose, running out through the opposite side of the canteen.

As he neared the doors, the uninjured members of the college stopped and were replaced by torn and bloodied figures who stumbled through, clutching at their wounds. Shock was evident on their blank faces, as if their mind had closed down after seeing the nature of their assailants. Winston had been dubious of the fanciful claims of the girl, but the deep bite marks and missing flesh left little doubt.

"All of you, head towards the nurse's station," he tried to usher them past even as the first collapsed to the floor.

"I need my fingers to write," explained one of the students languidly as he held his damaged hand towards Winston, *"How can I do my work now?"*

"Dear God," Winston exclaimed as he looked at the spurting stumps. *"Wrap this around it to slow the blood."*

He offered a wad of napkins, but the vacant expression didn't change and the paper fluttered to the ground unclaimed. The student turned and walked away, unable to maintain focus on anything as the infection spread.

"All I wanted was a bacon fucking sandwich!" Winston yelled, fear taking hold.

The clear glass of the swing doors was smeared with red and he had to pick a small patch that was unsullied. In the reception area it was a slaughter house, with spilled blood coating every wall. Droplets fell from the ceiling, splashing into the growing pools of claret. The fallen staff and students were in varying stages of consumption and the horrors that kneeled by the dead were greedily forcing warm flesh into rotten mouths.

"I must be dreaming," Winston whispered.

Nothing could explain how the feeding monsters could be moving, most were riddled with maggots and worms. Their grey, sloughing flesh was wet with the moisture of death and the recent activity had left it hanging in dripping chunks. The first of the victims started to stir and the other zombies left them alone, sensing the undead kinship. Moaning from behind startled Winston and he turned slowly, dreading confirmation of what he knew was going to be waiting. The injured students had died and now turned their eyes toward him from the cold ground. Their new state of un-life was his saving grace and he dodged expertly as they started to stand up on unsteady legs.

"Winston, what is happening?" Marjorie asked, peering from the kitchen.

"Get out of here." He pulled her from the hiding place and guided her to the exit.

The image of the rack of knives on the counter was a temptation he couldn't ignore. Looking back, the undead were gaining confidence and pushed through the furniture

211

to reach the next meal. With a speed borne of fear and necessity, he darted into the kitchen, took the two biggest knives, and ran as fast as he was able from the canteen. The corridors had quickly become a scene of pandemonium, with the living and the dead fighting in an unequal battle. Single members of the faculty or lone students were set upon by growing numbers of the bloodied hordes. Feeling a pit of despair and guilt, he moved as quietly as possible around the feeding frenzy.

"Hey you, help us!" called Acne from a classroom. He and his small gang were trying to keep the zombies at bay but it was hopeless. The wannabe gangster was stabbing at their chests, wrongly assuming they could be stopped with a damaged heart.

"Get them in the head," he ordered and the boy took the advice.

"It's not working!" he screeched. Fear was causing him to stab wildly and he was inflicting grievous wounds on their faces, but no fatal blows.

"Shit!" Winston looked at the empty hallway, the inviting daylight and freedom.

"Don't leave us," begged Acne, "I'm sorry about earlier."

His innate goodness won and he charged into the room, using his bulk to send the dead flying. Tossing one of the kitchen knives to his nemesis, he put a heavy boot on the back of the zombie's neck and stabbed into the brain.

"Like that!"

They worked as a team and killed the remaining cadavers, but the screams from the college building left no doubt the battle was far from over. Acne nursed his arm, blood dripping from a bite wound that had been sustained in the melee.

"Thanks for coming back, we would be dead if it wasn't for you. I'm James," Acne nodded in gratitude.

"Winston," he replied with a look of regret. He knew what the bite meant.

"We have to get out of here," James said.

"Follow me, the corridor doesn't have any zombies." Winston led the group out and came to a stop, despair threatening to rob him of the last remnants of strength.

"I thought you said it was clear?" wailed one of the members as more arrivals stumbled up the previously empty hallway, cutting them off completely from escape.

"We need to get to the main entrance," James declared until Winston held him back.

"It's full of those things," Winston explained as the horde moved in for the kill, "We have to go up!"

"The library? You must be fucking joking, I'm not getting stuck up there," shouted one of the gang and he bolted towards the reception.

"I need to get my sister before she gets hurt," said another who followed in a blur of tracksuit.

"Maybe they will make it, should we try too?" James asked slowly, eyes rolling like a drunk.

"I'm not risking it, you didn't see what I saw," Winston said and moved up the wide staircase as fast as he could. An incline with his figure was difficult and he was huffing before he reached the top.

"What's wrong with him?" whined the last member of the group.

Looking around, James had sat down on the stairs, exhaustion from the infected bite finally defeating him. The zombies converged and bit into his face, making Winston gag as the pus burst from his pimpled cheek between the eager teeth. Death was so near that he didn't even struggle against the gnashing mob and Winston took advantage of the horrific distraction to pull the last boy through the doors of the library.

"Why did he let them eat him?" asked the ashen faced youth.

213

"I think it's like the movies; you get bitten and you become one of them," Winston said as he dragged the book trolley over to the door and tipped it over.

"Don't say that!" shrieked the boy, hiding his arm behind his back, "Why would you say that?"

Drops of blood led in a neat row from the doorway to where he stood and Winston could only mourn the inevitable. The pasty, sweaty face was only due in part to the fear and the telltale lethargy was already taking hold.

"Help me to pile the books on top of the trolley, it will buy us some time," Winston tried to take the dying boy's mind from the creeping darkness, "What's your name?"

"Toby," he slurred, tossing a single book as if it weighed more than anything he had ever lifted.

"Can we help?" called out a girl who had been hiding in the rows of literature. She was followed by a mixed group of international students who were on a study exchange. Tears flowed like rivers from some of the group and all looked utterly terrified.

"Do you know what's happening?" Winston asked, keeping a wary eye on Toby who was fading by the second.

"We saw them from the windows and tried to warn the teachers but they just shouted at us," said the girl quietly, "They ate everyone they came across."

"We need as much weight as possible to hold them off while I think," he said but the group were already working industriously, forming a human chain to pass the thick tomes.

"Is he ok?" she asked when Toby started to sway.

"No, he's not," Winston tried to convey what was happening, but her face didn't pick up the emphasis of the words. Unconsciousness beckoned and he fell to the ground in a faint.

"Oh my God, help him," she cried until Winston pulled her back. Taking the bitten arm, he held it aloft and she

held her hand to her mouth in horror, "Will he...?" she gasped and Winston could only nod.

Groans and dull thuds reverberated through the thick doors and the barricade team redoubled their efforts. Winston looked at the still form of Toby and then back to the pile of books which was being forced inwards. A cold, clammy hand grabbed at his wrist and he felt his chest clench with terror. The dead eyes stared up and the lips curled back in a grimace of inhuman hunger, revealing the white enameled plague bearing teeth.

"I'm sorry," Winston yelped and stabbed through the glazed eyeball.

"No, no, no," screamed one of the foreign students, raising his arms in surrender at the apparent murder.

"I had to, he had turned," Winston pleaded but their fear of him was greater than the unseen menace on the other side of the door.

"No," they all yelled as he walked toward them, bloodied knife still in hand.

Caught up in the hysterics, they fled between the bookshelves like cockroaches when the lights turn on. The incomplete book blockade tumbled as more undead pressed their weight to the task. James had fully turned and his ravaged face snarled at Winston, straining to clear the widening gap.

"What's your name?"

"Jessica," replied the girl, running from the monsters.

"We have to take the fire exit," Winston yelled, hoping the other pupils would forget their fear of him when faced with the rotting and shredded monsters who would soon be among them.

Nobody answered his call, but he could see eyes peering at him between the shelves. Pushing on the bar, the door opened and daylight bore into the room, blinding him for a moment. The sound of muffled footsteps warned him of the danger a split second before his eyes could adjust to

215

the glare. Stepping backwards, he tried to pull the door closed but a grotesque arm got trapped and prevented it from latching. More arms reached through the crack and even with his strength they pulled it wide open and poured in.

"Fuck!"

"What are we going to do?" sobbed Jessica.

Winston looked around, but both exits were spewing forth a torrent of dead. The floor was solid concrete and the only illumination was from stripped fluorescent tubes and high set windows around the perimeter of the building.

"We climb!" Winston shouted.

Praying the college had abided by basic safety standards and bolted the heavy bookshelves to the floor and wall, he picked a section on biology. He sighed at the irony of climbing past the thick texts and their lack of any possible explanation for the walking dead. The girl climbed by his side, concentrating on the task instead of the approaching monsters. Screams of sheer agony carried from one corner of the room and Winston ascended with increased urgency. The wooden top was covered in dust and the corpses of hundreds of desiccated insects.

"That's gross," complained Jessica, wiping at the surface to clear a patch.

With one final heave, Winston pulled his bulk up and sat down, facing the room from his high perch. What he saw would forever haunt his dreams.

"Oh my God, no," he whispered.

Desperate faces of the exchange students regarded them both across a chasm of death and they reached out imploringly for help. They had understood enough to follow his instruction, but not in the way he had intended. The three girls and one boy had chosen the closest racks to climb which stranded them in the center of the library, adrift in a sea of zombies. Undead flooded through the open doorways and filled any available gap to reach for the doomed youths.

"Helping, please," they begged in broken English.

"Think, you useless lump, think!" Winston berated himself.

"We have to help them," she reached out with her arm toward theirs, as if she could magically pull them over the void.

"That's not helping," Winston told her, scanning the room for a solution.

The library was busier than it had ever been, hundreds of patrons reached not for the books, but what was on top of the books. That was it! The shelves.

"Cover your face, I need to break the glass so I can balance properly," Winston ordered and drove his elbow through the window.

The safety glass crumbled into tiny fragments and rained to the ground below. Pulling the rubber seal on the double glazed unit free and throwing it aside, he shifted his weight further back. The shelf he was seated on was only about eighteen inches deep, and to reach his goal he needed to bend forward which would have only served to tip him into the waiting dead.

"What are you doing?"

"If I can pull the shelf loose, we can use it as a plank for them to walk across and reach us," he explained, tossing books down onto the agitated zombies.

Each side was mounted onto an upturned hook which stopped it being pulled forwards, but not upwards. Cheering with delight, the final books toppled and he claimed his prize.

"Is it long enough?"

"It has to be," Winston prayed and held it out as far as he could reach.

One of the exchange students took the offered end and sat it precariously on their shelf top. Two inches of support was all the wooden length allowed and if it moved at all during their passage, the dead would feast on their flesh.

"Quickly," the girl urged the frightened youngsters. It must have been unimaginable to be trapped in another country without knowing if this was localized or more widespread, worrying for the fate of loved ones a thousand miles away.

"No!" Winston yelled, "Slow down, watch the ends."

The first student was in such a blind panic the timber plank was shifting dangerously and came close to sliding from the top. With a deep, shaky breath she resumed the passage, taking time to crawl slowly until she reached the safety of the outer cases.

"Now you," Winston smiled at the next young girl who was as white as a ghost and trembling. Making a 'come to me' gesture, he tried to break her paralysis with soothing words.

"It's ok, I've got you," he tried to sound as friendly as possible but she only shook her head.

The zombies were hammering at the freestanding structure and with each blow, the frame weakened. What had stood tall and proud for five decades providing educational resources, now creaked as the wooden joints started to break under the fluctuating weight of the dead flesh. The male student was trying to push the girl onto the rickety platform but this only made her more reluctant to take her chance.

"Come on, you will be fine," tried Jessica, "You have to move or you will get hurt."

Patience exhausted and driven crazy with fear by the reaching arms, the boy pushed the girl from the bookcase. The suddenness of the act didn't give her an opportunity to scream as grateful teeth severed muscle from bone, tearing her to pieces in seconds.

"Why the fuck did you do that?" screamed Jessica in horror.

"It's too late anyway," Winston said in resignation as the bookshelf crumbled, pitching the remaining students into the thronging dead.

"Thank you, thank you," said the rescued Chinese girl over and over as the fresh bodies were dispersed across the library floor in gouts of blood.

"Don't thank me yet, we still have to get out of here." Winston squeezed her hand in support as he planned their next move.

Looking around the library, there was nowhere they could venture which wouldn't put them within reach of the zombies. Turning around, he placed his legs over the edge of the window sill and the ground fifty feet below seemed to pull at him.

"Whoa," he gasped as the bout of vertigo passed.

"Can we get down?" asked Jessica.

"No. It's a sheer drop straight onto concrete. We would be nicely tenderized for the waiting diners though," Winston remarked at the growing group below.

Jessica looked around frantically, "So we are trapped?"

"Maybe not," Winston pondered, carefully looking at the outside of the building from his awkward position.

The window ledge projected six inches from the main brickwork to help with rainwater dispersal. Above them was a recess set in the external insulated metal cladding which had been installed to minimize heating bills. If they could shimmy along the rim, they could reach the flat roof of the construction department. The plan was met with trepidation and he could only offer his opinion that they didn't have a choice. In the distance, screaming and crashing noises were coming from all directions as the plague spread.

"We need to get out of the area while we still can, you know how these things go," he said.

"How what things go? A fucking apocalypse?" Jessica shouted.

"We go," nodded the Chinese girl, "We go."

From being seated on a fairly safe surface, to leaning out into nothingness and grasping upwards for the metal lip was a feat of superhero bravery. Winston's legs quivered in fear and his throat was dry from looking down at the ground below.

"Don't look down, you moron," he whispered as the fingertips found purchase and he stood.

The wind was picking up and tugged at his clothing, like an evil spirit who wanted to see him fall. With his face pressed to the smooth metal covering, he moved away from the open window to allow the girls through. His figure would have ensured the task was impossible if it wasn't for the handhold, the portly belly pushing him away from the wall. Trying to focus only on the grey painted metal made his eyes ache so he looked to the side to check the progress of his companions.

"Ok?" he asked Jessica.

"No," she replied honestly.

"Take it slow, we have about thirty-five feet to cover before we can jump down to safety," Winston explained and started to shuffle sideways, inch by inch.

The multitude of sounds intensified as they risked life and limb to reach safety. Groans and screams were intermingled with explosions and rapid gunfire. Risking a glance, huge plumes of black smoke rose from burning cars which had crashed while trying to avoid the dead. Dozens of blue lights flashed their warning of the police firearms unit which had responded to the attack on the college campus. The buildings were emptying of their newly turned pupils who streamed toward the officers. It was a timely diversion and Winston had to avoid the urge to watch the firefight, concentrating on the promise of safety from the roof instead.

"The police are here, we should go back inside and wait until they regain control," said Jessica with relief. Their crazy stunt was at an end.

"Did you see how many zombies there are?" Winston explained, remembering the hundreds that were stumbling toward the officers.

"Must go on," said the Chinese girl sternly.

"But I think…" Jessica started to protest until a huge spider scurried from the gap in the metalwork and onto her hand.

With a shriek of disgust, she batted at the arachnid and lost her grip, arms flailing for purchase as gravity took over. In a moment of pure terror, she grabbed at the young Chinese girl to try and fight the inevitable. The sudden shift in weight was enough to pull them both free of the window sill and they plunged to the ground. Their screams were cut short by the hard concrete and blood spread around their broken skulls like a demonic red halo. The hellish symbolism held no fear for the reanimated dead who fed without complaint.

"No!" Winston cried, hot tears running down his cheeks.

Feeling the bile rise in his throat, Winston had to swallow several times to calm his churning stomach. He had failed those girls because of a fucking spider! Despair was spreading through his body and for a brief moment all the loneliness and sadness of his existence formed into a single thought, 'let go'. His grip loosened and the wind increased in speed, an eager accomplice to the suicide. A twang of metal on metal made him jump and he clutched the rim harder again, suicidal thoughts evaporating. The smoking, circular hole was only two feet from his head.

"What the fuck?" he questioned.

More shots rang out as the police line was overwhelmed, fingers going into agonized spasm as teeth ripped into their bodies.

"Shit, shit, shit," Winston channeled his inner wizard, willing an invisible shield into existence to provide protection as he sidestepped the last few feet.

Nothing hit him, which was probably more down to luck than his prowess as an undiscovered arcane mage. The zombies followed as if sensing he wasn't safe quite yet and the meal was still up for grabs. One small jump would take him to safety or death, and now he had reached the corner he could understand how awkward the angle would be. The construction department roof was set back ten inches when it had been constructed to allow for it to be properly tied in with the older library structure. The thin ledge ended and to make it down he would need to jump around the corner, which was nearly impossible with his size.

"I believe I can fly, I believe I can touch the sky," Winston sang shakily, trying to build up his nerve.

"What's the problem, you were going to jump a minute ago anyway," he closed his eyes and jumped.

Maintaining his grip on the cladding for as long as possible served to pull him around the corner just enough and he sprawled face down on the bitumen coated roof. After his chest stopped pounding with the adrenaline, he crossed himself despite being an atheist. Someone was watching over him, a guardian angel perhaps. The skylights gave views of the workshops and after one, Winston had seen enough. The grey painted, easy sweep floors were covered with huge pools of red liquid and the figures that moved below had no urgency, the fighting was done.

Taking out his phone, the screen had cracked but the touchpad could still be used. Dialing the number of his mother, she answered too early and he couldn't miss the deep sigh of frustration at the call, "What is it, Winston?"

"Something terrible is happening. I don't know if I am going to make it, I love you both," he said.

"Are you watching those awful movies again?" she sighed again after hearing the screams.

"No, I'm at college," he protested.

"I don't know why you insist on lying to me? We didn't ask to have you," she said spitefully.

"I love you, Mum," he repeated, "Mum?"

The phone was quiet; she had hung up.

***

"Jesus Christ, how did you get from the college to the nunnery?" Mike said, shaking his hand with newfound respect.

"I got over the motorway during the chaos," Winston whispered, sitting back down. The howls of dying children were always fresh in his mind, a constant companion during the darkness.

"So you think you're a tough guy?" Debbie asked.

"No," he replied, "If I was I could have saved people."

"Ignore her," Mike dismissed her with a wave, "You got out of the city, on foot! Shit, I hid inside the pub when the first zombie came knocking." It was the first time he had admitted to any kind of weakness.

"I'm going to hit the sack, and by sack I mean the captain's chair," Winston stood up straight, sucked in his belly and saluted.

"Who's going to keep watch?" Debbie asked, rubbing her grainy eyes.

"Not you I'm guessing, sleeping beauty?" he replied.

"Hell no, I need my eight hours," she yawned.

"You'll take your turn and like it," Mike glared at her, then turned back to Winston, "If you don't mind doing first shift, mate, wake me in a couple of hours and I will take over."

"No problem," Winston nodded, "Try not to dream about me while I'm gone."

Blowing a kiss at Debbie, she screwed her face up in disgust, "A nightmare more like."

"I'll take it," he chuckled and pressed his bulk through the thin door into the cockpit.

Sitting in the pilot's chair, he looked out at the vast, empty hangar and the last slivers of dying light. His cheerful smile faded and the images of the torn and bloodied children superimposed on the dark canvas of his mind. High pitched screams of the doomed infants of the clogged roads were joined by the more recent death wails of the convent. He shuddered with the knowledge that tomorrow they would reach the prison, and more people like Mike and Debbie.

CHAPTER TWENTY ONE

orporal Hague sat behind the cage, like an animal in captivity, there for the amusement of the two bullying guards. His swollen face was aching and the glasses perched on the bridge of his nose were broken beyond repair, held together only with crude tape. The butterflies in his stomach were going to burst from his mouth at any moment, exposing his part in the coming assault.

"I might take you home with me tonight," rasped Corporal Groll though the steel mesh, licking his lips.

"You a homo?" asked the other guard.

"Fuck no," Groll sounded disgusted, "I just want some fun, doesn't make me queer."

"Wouldn't you rather have Eldridge then?"

"She will get her turn after I am done with him," Groll rumbled, staring at the fearful soldier.

"She may have something to say about that," laughed the guard.

"I have work to do if you don't mind," Hague tried to be more assertive and attempted to straighten the twisted glasses, but his words came out as a croaky whisper.

"Oh you're going to work for it alright," Groll nodded.

The hour was just past one in the morning and with each tick of the exaggeratedly loud clock hanging from the wall, destiny approached. Taking out a packet of cigarettes, Groll lit one and inhaled deeply.

"I thought they were banned?"

"Not for me," Groll puffed out his chest, "Baxter has given me permission."

"What, on duty?"

"Well, no. But it's not like he is going to be up at this hour is it?" Groll replied, unsure of himself. The lieutenant was renowned for not needing much sleep and going hall to hall in stealthy silence to catch out the negligent.

"Can you move away with that thing, it stinks." Hague wrinkled his nose at the drifting tobacco smoke.

"You want me to move away?" Groll laughed and took a drag, blowing the smoke straight at the seated corporal through the bars.

"You are an animal," complained Hague who wafted at the acrid smell.

"You need to be careful when you talk to me, or I won't be gentle later," Groll holstered his pistol and leaned through the small opening, "You didn't like my fists the last time."

The other guard was laughing at his unease and missed the furtive movement from the end of the corridor. Eldridge had risked a swift peek after hearing the commotion and could see the brutal bullies tormenting Hague. She knew the moment was the best they could get and stepped into full view, an easy target had they been paying attention. Hague saw her and the two guards mistook his panic for fear of them, laughing even more. Groll flicked the half burnt cigarette at the terrified corporal and it was if the showering sparks ignited all the fear and hatred that had been bubbling for weeks.

"Fuck you," Hague screamed as he grabbed a fistful of lank, greasy hair, slamming his head into the desk with enough force to daze Groll.

Pulling out a sharpened dinner knife, he stabbed at the head and neck in a frenzy, the guard squealing in pain. Again and again the blade punctured skin and muscle, until a stray blow cut through part of his spinal cord and the body flopped to the floor. Groll's companion had been caught totally off guard by the brutality of the meek soldier and raised his gun too late. Eldridge's knife whistled down the hall as it cut the air, before burying itself to the hilt in his back. Twisting in spasms of pain and dropping the gun, he tried to reach behind until the second blade found his neck.

"Hague, are you ok?" called out Eldridge as she ran toward him, flanked by several male soldiers.

"Help me," begged the second guard, but Harkiss just pulled the knife from the blood soaked throat and stabbed into his heart, stilling him. Groll looked up at them as his vital organs shut down from the severed nerves, and Eldridge smiled until his eyes glazed over.

"Cunt," she spat.

"Hague?" Harkiss said quietly, seeing the pale man shaking and crying.

"Open the cage," said Eldridge, "It's all over."

"I hate cigarettes," he answered, then keyed the code into the lock.

"You did good buddy," Harkiss admitted, patting him on the back.

"Do we hide the bodies?" asked Derby.

"No," Eldridge said, "We don't have time to clean the blood anyway. Hague, you and Private Clarke are going to hold the cage in case we fuck up and they try and arm up."

Clarke got into position, rifle aimed down the shadowed hallway. Hague was looking at the corpse of Groll who was starting to awaken from death, eyes fluttering. Harkiss sighed, knelt down and stabbed the brains of the fallen.

"Snap out of it," Derby slapped him and the corporal came out of his daze.

"I'm good, I won't let them get in here," he declared, taking his own weapon from the rack.

"You and I will take Baxter," Eldridge ordered Derby, then turned to Harkiss, "And you two will take Comms."

"Silence?" Derby asked, lifting a suppressor.

"No, we want the rest of the barracks to hear the gunfire. Once the next four guards are dead, some of the loyalists will try take us out so I want everyone to know what is going down. If we can take out a few more here when they come for weapons our job will be that much easier. The rest may even give up without any more bloodshed," she replied, strapping on a Virtus combat vest.

"If you get killed, can I have your moisturizer?" Harkiss joked.

"You need it for that flaky complexion," she laughed.

Arriving at the fork, they wished each other well and moved off as quietly as possible. It was agreed that Baxter was the priority and hence she and Derby would open fire first, which would cost Harkiss the element of surprise. It didn't matter, events had been set into motion that could have only one conclusion; death or freedom.

"Ready?" Eldridge whispered as she neared the officer's quarters. Derby checked his safety was off and nodded.

Knowing Baxter's men would be fully alert, she rounded the corner with the trigger already pressed. The muzzle flashed and the line of impacts streaked towards the two guards in slow motion. Expertly trained, even they couldn't draw fast enough to return fire and the slugs punched through their bodies, puffs of red mist bursting from the exit wounds. Slumping to the floor, the blood smeared the walls as the two soldiers rushed forward to cover Baxter's room. More chattering fire came from the barracks, but this was met with gunshots fired back. She prayed they would be safe.

"Baxter, come out with your hands up!" shouted Eldridge from the safety of the side of the door.

"I'm afraid that you will have to come in and get me Private Eldridge," he sounded remarkably calm, "Are my men dead?"

"Almost," she answered and put a bullet though each skull to prevent their reanimation.

"That's a shame, they were real soldiers, unlike your ragtag band of misfits and criminals," Baxter said with regret.

"If you give yourself up, I promise a fair hearing," she explained.

Faces appeared from the corner, trying to gauge what was happening. They were enemies of Baxter so Derby slid his pistol along the floor to their waiting hands.

"Keep us covered," he said, pointing to his eyes.

"I see you have brought friends," Baxter laughed, "I am going to enjoy punishing you."

"I don't think you understand how this works. You are finished Baxter; your men are dead or being rounded up as we speak. Why don't you save us a lot of shit and just come quietly?"

"I have gathered a sizeable number of explosives and they are all wired to blow if you so much as touch that handle," Baxter seemed to be enjoying the whole thing, "It seems we have a stalemate."

"Not really. We can starve you out, use tear gas, any one of a number of things," Eldridge replied.

"But not before I destroy most of this building."

"What do you suggest?" she asked.

Harkiss joined them, nursing a wound to his cheek. The shallow furrow had cauterized itself as the bullet passed and if it had been an inch or two to the right, half of his face would be missing.

"We have communications. Holbeck didn't make it though," he explained.

"Get word out to command that we have the base," she directed, "Tell them we have a situation and ask for orders."

"You got it," Harkiss nodded and ran off to pass along the message.

"So Baxter, what is it going to be?" she asked again.

"I guess he is thinking through his options?" Derby wondered but something seemed... off.

"Baxter?"

No answer.

"Fuck it, I am going in, get everyone back," Eldridge whispered and Derby ran down the corridor, ushering people clear. Knowing she was in mortal danger and bullets could tear through the door at any moment, she yelled and kicked at the lock. The flimsy door burst inward and the frigid air bit into her skin from the open window.

"Mother fucker!" she screamed, running to the opening and looking out, "It was a bluff, get everyone out on the grounds and flush that prick out."

"On it," came Derby's reply.

The darkness provided a thousand places to hide and if they didn't find him before dawn, the chances are he would be long gone. Even without the light, by the time enough soldiers were dressed, armed and carrying torches to scan the perimeter he could have escaped.

"Fuck!" Eldridge shouted into the night.

CHAPTER TWENTY TWO

"This is Admiral Wright, to whom am I speaking, over," squawked the radio.

"Private Eldridge, sir. Did Corporal Graff bring you up to speed? Over," she answered.

"Yes he did, Private and I must say I am deeply troubled by what has gone on there. Do you have Lieutenant Baxter in custody? Over."

"I am sorry to say he has currently eluded us, sir. We have everyone at our disposal scouring the grounds for any sign of him, over."

"That is unfortunate. I am sending someone to take command at first light, I trust they will receive a warmer welcome than my previous reconnaissance party? Over," came the Admirals reply.

"You can count on it, sir, over."

"Eldridge?" he asked, ignoring protocol.

"Sir?"

"You did remarkable work there against an armed force. I want a full briefing when you join me on Dauntless. Until then, you are in command, do what you can to apprehend that rabid dog, but don't put any more lives in danger, do you understand? Over."

"Yes, sir. Thank you, sir. Over and out."

Addressing the emaciated and sick communication engineers, she said, "Go and get a shower, some food, and a good night's rest."

"What about the radio?" Graff wondered.

"I will station Jackson here to maintain contact. If anything urgent arises, he can come and get you. After weeks of being ignored, a few hours won't hurt anyone."

Harkiss almost knocked the two men over as they were leaving, "There is no sign of him. A hole has been cut in the fence, but unless he swam in the freezing water I don't see how he can have escaped."

"He's a slippery bastard," she agreed, "Have we secured the choppers and flight crew?"

"As soon as we retook the place," Harkiss confirmed.

"Then he is either hiding somewhere, drowned, or on foot, soaked and cold with millions of zombies on the loose," she said, shrugging.

"We will keep looking all night. What do you want done with the prisoners?"

"Lock them up until the new commander arrives. They can decide on their fate, because right now I would shoot every last one of them."

Saluting, he nodded and made off to follow the order.

"Make sure you get that cheek looked at too!" she called out.

"Yes, ma'am."

Leaving the communication room, she walked among the jubilant soldiers. Free of the repression of Baxter, they could finally be part of something bigger again and begin the fight back against the zombie legions. Whoops and cheers greeted her passage through the mess hall and dormitories. She protested, trying to deflect their admiration on the whole team, but it didn't work. Word had spread like wildfire of the knife throwing heroics and even Hague was being hoisted on the shoulders of troops who had once mocked him. The broken glasses were lost in the huddle but he had never been happier or felt more included.

"Where's Morrow?" she asked the men.

"He's still on patrol," said one who had been stood down after the lack of available torches hindered the search.

"Can you go and find him for me?"

"At once," he saluted.

Minutes later, Morrow returned with the man, disappointment evident on his features.

"Still no sign I'm afraid," he explained.

"Don't worry about that, he will turn up sooner or later. I want you to make sure the bird is ready to fly; I need your eyes in the sky to find our missing brothers."

"I can get her airborne now if you want and use thermal imaging?"

"Idiot!" Eldridge slapped her own forehead, "Can you do a scout of the local area first? Concentrate on the marina and Emsworth Village. If he has made it off the base, we will nail the bastard."

The preparations were made and his subordinate gave the signal that the Watchkeeper drone was ready for reconnaissance. With expert care, the monitor showed the green tinged, night vision image of the runway as Morrow took flight.

"Switching to thermal imaging," Morrow said and switched the camera mode.

The screen changed to varying hues of black, blue and green showing a total lack of heat. As the drone passed over the mass of zombies at the main gate, the red bodies of the guards paled in comparison to the thousands of cold, dead blue signatures of the walking corpses.

"I guess we know for sure they really are dead," Eldridge whispered, horrified by the movement of the massed bodies.

"We will have a problem as we get closer to the site of the helicopter crash," Morrow explained.

"You mean the shot down helicopter?" Eldridge said, gritting her teeth as a fresh wave of hatred flowed through her veins.

"Of course, sorry. I just hate even thinking about the poor bastards he's killed, and the one's I helped him kill…" He fell silent.

"You didn't have a choice, you know that," she said sincerely.

"Still doesn't stop me dreaming about them."

"I think if we can put an end to Baxter, you may sleep a little easier." She rubbed his shoulder.

The fire of the burning fuel had raged through parts of the village and the glow could still be seen in the distance from the barracks. As the drone moved away from the zombies, everything was dark and lifeless beneath. The ocean was freezing and the black waves crashed onto the beach.

"Marina clear," Morrow informed her.

"Do a fly past of the shops and then double back to the road leading to the barracks."

"You got it," he answered.

The village was abandoned, but the camera started to register the heat from the still smoldering remnants of the missile attack on the doomed troops. It was throwing the images off and some areas seemed to be moving, but it was just the angle of the drone. A patch of red and orange was backlit by a much fainter yellow and Eldridge pointed.

"Go back, quickly!"

Turning the Watchkeeper around, he performed another pass of the spot and it was only yellow.

"I don't see anything," Morrow admitted.

"Keep circling that area, I know I saw something. Zoom in a bit," she said, leaning forward, willing to see his heat signature.

For five minutes they circled and nothing else seemed out of place. The proximity of the radiated heat was casting a dull pall of amber across the scene.

"Stay on it, I want to go and check in with the search parties."

"I'll call if I see anything else. How long do you want me to keep looking before I change mission to go and look for DB and Jonesy again?" he asked over his shoulder as she was leaving.

"Thirty minutes," she stepped through the door, then had a thought, "Do the drones have a maximum altitude?"

"Yeah, about eighteen thousand feet. Why?"

"Take the bird as high as you can, then have another look. I want to see if the sound is a factor or whether I am just seeing ghosts," she ordered and he nodded, beginning the ascent.

In the corridor the guards were dejected about their lack of success.

"Sorry, we have searched as much as possible for the conditions. No sign of Baxter around the outer perimeter from the hole in the chain link."

"Don't sweat it, he was always a slippery fucker." She saluted and they hurried off to continue the fruitless exploration.

Ten minutes later, Private Eldridge was looking out into the night from the central watchtower. The beams of flashlights cut through the darkness and she was proud to see their absolute determination to find the murdering psychopath. The radio came to life in her hand.

"I think I have him, over," shouted Morrow with excitement from the handset.

"Slow down," Eldridge cautioned, nerves of anticipation fluttering in her stomach, "What did you see? Over."

"The fire is still burning, but I swear I saw someone moving amongst the buildings. I think he is trying to use the heat to throw us off. Over."

"How certain are you? Over," she asked breathlessly.

"Eighty percent," he replied, "No, ninety. Over."

"And it is just one person? It couldn't be a group trying to use the heat to survive?"

"Impossible. If it was survivors, they wouldn't be moving from cover to cover. Besides, who the hell could survive in the middle of the village for this long anyway? Over."

"I was just trying to think of every possibility…" she pondered.

"Eldridge, are you still there? What do you want me to do? Over."

"I'm here. Proceed with your next mission. I have a surprise for our friend," she smiled.

"Roger. Over and out."

She thought for a few minutes, weighing the possibilities of the course of action she was planning. The fire could merely be playing tricks as more debris ignited from the heat, but Morrow was almost certain.

Pressing the transmit button on the radio, she said, "Someone bring me Dodson, I need a little chat. Over."

Minutes later, the prisoner was pushed through into the room and Eldridge turned to him.

"Dodson, I am afraid to say that Admiral Wright has sentenced you and the rest of the collaborators to death. You will be executed in the morning," she lied.

"You brought me up all those stairs to tell me I am a dead man? Bullshit, what's your game?" The artillery commander stood tall, refusing to be intimidated by a woman.

"Oh I am deadly serious. You will be tied to the post one at a time, along with the rest of your sick friends, then shot through the head." She glared at him, continuing the bluff, "I was just thinking that you might want to try and earn a favor from me, where I may be convinced to speak up on your behalf to the Admiral?"

"Go fuck yourself, I was just following orders," he argued.

"Fair enough, take him away." Eldridge waved a hand and the guards seized his arms. "Try and get some rest, it's sunup in a few hours and you have a busy morning."

"Wait!" he cried out, "What favor?"

Turning to him, her eyes blazed with anger, "I want you to level Emsworth, beginning with the site of the downed helo. Drop enough explosives so that it looks like Hiroshima."

"But why?" Dodson asked, then it clicked, "You don't have Baxter yet, do you?"

"We will with your help," she said, holding his gaze, "Think quickly, I need to get airborne if you won't assist me."

"And you promise that I won't be executed?"

"I promise that I will try. Refuse me and you will be the first to be tied to the post," she vowed. Time was running out and if Baxter managed to slip through to the outskirts of the village, he could escape completely.

Dodson stood for a moment, thinking. A pent up breath escaped, "Very well, untie me and I will get my men together. We will raze Emsworth to the ground," he agreed.

"That's good. Don't think of it as murder, think of it as exterminating a rat. A very big, evil, psychotic, murdering rat."

Word had spread of the possible sighting and the search parties gathered at the four Vikings to watch the show. Eldridge watched from above as the night sky lit up with the howitzer barrels' flash, followed by the deafening boom of the unleashed shell. In the distance the explosion could be seen rising into the air, a mixture of fire, mud and building material. For thirty minutes the howitzer coughed the death dealing ordinance, gradually levelling every square inch of the village in righteous vengeance. The night receded as more fires burned and after the artillery fell silent, the whole base was lit up by the glowing conflagration.

Satisfied they had certainly killed Baxter and nothing, alive or dead, could survive in the fires, she spoke into her radio, "Ceasefire. Dodson, you have my gratitude, and I will speak to command right now on your behalf. To all search parties, use the light to carry out one final sweep and then call it a night. Tomorrow, we begin to take back our country, over."

At the guarded bridge, cheers rung out and shots were fired into the air in celebration.

"Please be alive," Eldridge muttered to herself, meaning DB and Jonesy. They would rejoice that the cause of much of their pain had been dealt with.

CHAPTER TWENTY
THREE

"**R**ise and shine," Mike called through the plane. Winston awoke with a start, pulled from a nightmare of a high ledge that stretched on forever with spiders pouring from the cracks in the metalwork. Their thick bodies scurrying over his skin, trying to get inside his mouth to lay eggs in his stomach.

"I'm up," he finally answered.

"Lazy cunt," muttered Debbie, loud enough to carry through to him.

"And a good morning to you, princess," he called back smiling.

They breakfasted and packed up their belongings, ready to make the final leg of their journey. In the hangar, nothing stirred in the shadows so they exited and made for the eastern fence line of the airfield. Zombies that caught sight of the fresh prey were disappointed when they discovered the chain link in their way and the survivors disappearing into the distance, middle fingers raised.

"How do you think we will get inside the prison if the dead are around?" Winston asked, his sense of unease growing with each step.

"Worst case scenario is we have to try and get over the walls on our own," Mike explained, "With a rope and some bolt croppers, the razor wire won't be an issue."

"I hate to even ask, but what if the prison has fallen?"

"It won't have," Mike glowered, "It can't have."

"Hey," Winston smiled, "If your brother is half as ruthless as you are, I'm sure it will be fine."

"He is," Mike grinned back, taking the strange compliment.

"If you two are done sucking each other's dicks, we are nearly there," Debbie said, "Keep the noise down."

"Ok, boss," Winston replied.

They came upon the town from the open fields. Homes and gardens stretched into the distance from the estate which Jonesy, Sam, and Braiden had scouted the prison from. Jumping the low, wooden fence, they cautiously approached the road, expecting the streets to be teeming with the dead.

"Where is everybody?" Debbie asked, feeling the same sense of loneliness that had taken over in the middle of the dead city days earlier.

"Can't you hear them?" Winston whispered.

A steady drone broke the silence as they stood there, more noticeable without the crunching footsteps.

"That sounds like quite a welcoming party," Debbie said with growing apprehension.

"Zombies mean people," Mike declared and jogged down the road, heedless of the danger from the dark houses.

"Mike, wait up," Debbie called, trying to keep pace.

Reaching the same corner that Jonesy had peered around days earlier, Mike nearly shouted with glee at the gathered dead and the guards who watched cautiously from the walls.

"I told you he would be ok," Mike said, "And it looks like the prisoners have already taken over the place."

Winston looked at the surly looking men that patrolled the perimeter and his concern bloomed into full-fledged panic. Heavily tattooed and muscled, the men didn't look like they would welcome him with open arms. It was more likely they would use him for sport or as a sex toy, even with Mike as a potential friend.

"How do we get their attention?" Debbie wondered, seeing the hundreds of undead. They hadn't been sighted by the zombies because their attention was riveted on the prison building, but the prisoners started to gesticulate.

"We may as well go up and knock," Mike laughed, throwing caution to the wind and running towards danger.

"What the hell are you doing?" Debbie hissed in fear, following in spite of her terror.

The dead were unaware of the newcomers until Mike started to communicate with the laughing guards.

"How do we get inside? Is there another entrance?" he shouted and rotting faces turned in unison.

"You don't get inside, you prick," replied one of the men, then shouted down to the crowd, "Feeding time you dead fucks!"

"When I get inside I'm going to kill you first," Mike smiled back at the man, ignoring the dead who shambled towards them.

"Good luck with that. You'd better start running."

"Lucky for me you can't run," Mike answered, standing firm, "You will be right there waiting when Craig and I decide how to kill you slow."

The grin died on his face, "You know Craig?"

"He's my big brother, and by the look on your face you know what he is going to do to you," Mike confirmed.

"Shit, I'm sorry, man," the man started to babble in fear, "Listen, head in that direction and look for a flare. We have tunnels which can get you inside safely."

As the trio fled from their growing undead following, Mike was relieved to hear barked orders to wake his brother. Adrenaline gave them energy and the growing optimism of Mike and Debbie was not shared by Winston. They reached the fields once more and watched the sky for several minutes, the moans of the zombies approaching by the second.

"There!" Debbie cried out at the red hissing flare as it rose to the heavens.

"Quickly, we are nearly home and dry," Mike shouted and they dodged between buildings until they found the source of the blazing beacon.

A group of armed men had pushed a sheet of plywood clear of a tunnel entrance and stood looking around for the survivors.

"There they are!" shouted the previously laughing guard, trying to ingratiate himself.

"No thanks to you," Mike growled as he approached, before turning to his brother.

"Mike, how the hell did you make it? I am so glad to see you," Craig Arater asked, tears of joy in his eyes as he bear-hugged his brother.

"It's a long story, buddy," Mike said, then pointed to Debbie and Winston, "It's partly down to these two crazy fuckers."

"My house is your house, you saved my brother and I won't forget that," Craig said sincerely and then hugged them both too.

"I'm Debbie," she blushed like a teenage girl at the handsome thug.

"Winston," he nodded and caught the smirks of the other prisoners.

"Well we have warm beds, warm food, and warm pussy, you can have them in whatever order you want." Craig clapped Winston on the back and laughed.

"Do you think we should get moving?" Debbie asked as the first of the dead skirted the building and spotted them.

"All things in good time," Craig replied and turned to the laughing guard, "Did you really put my brother in danger?"

The others moved back and the man looked about ready to cry, "Sorry, Craig, I didn't know he was your brother."

"You could have killed my family!" Craig screamed, his face going dark red with rage.

Taking hold of the terrified man, he punched him repeatedly in the face, skin splitting and teeth falling from the broken mouth. Head rocking on his neck, he fell in a heap to the floor, unconscious. The men gathered 'round and Winston saw no pity in their eyes, just deadpan expressions that spoke of a lack of empathy for his plight.

"You weren't kidding when you said he was a hard man," Debbie husked to Mike, aroused by the violence.

"I told you, we are going to rule this world," he replied.

"Drag him to the wall, I'm going to peel him for the dead to feed on," Craig ordered and the prisoners pushed him down the hole, then followed.

"After you," Mike graciously offered and Debbie and Craig climbed down the makeshift ladder.

"I can't go with you," Winston said quietly to Mike.

"What are you talking about?" Mike said with surprise.

"I don't belong here, I will get murdered in my sleep." Winston started to back away, aware of the firearm lurking in his belt.

"You don't have to be afraid, you are with me. I won't let any of them touch you."

"I'm sorry, I really am. You should get to safety before they eat us both." Winston pointed out the dead who were only thirty feet away.

Mike stepped forward and Winston flinched, expecting a punch. He looked heartbroken as he pulled the large youth in for a hug, "I wasn't going to hit you for fuck sake. You look after yourself, you fat bastard. If you ever change your mind, you know where we are, ok?"

243

"I will," Winston smiled, "Get your ass in that tunnel and keep Debbie warm for me."

"I'll tell her you will come back to claim her," Mike laughed as he descended the ladder.

"Don't scare the poor girl," Winston chuckled, "Goodbye, Mike."

"See you around," he answered and slammed the wooden panel down over the opening.

Looking upon the hundreds of prison dead, Winston remarked, "Can we talk about this?"

Their raised arms and snapping jaws told him they were in no mood to discuss the merits of a vegetarian diet, so he turned and started to jog away. Some had fallen onto the thick wood, scratching in desperation to get inside. Most followed, eager for him to tire and provide their first meal in weeks.

CHAPTER TWENTY FOUR

The time had come. The weather was proving to be elusive in predicting from one day to the next, the temperatures had gone back and forth like a fiddler's elbow. Periods of harsh cold had given way to unseasonable sunshine, and the group had opted to make their attempt on the castle with warmth on their side. The cold had proven a useful ally, but was temperamental and could lull them into a false sense of security at just the wrong moment. DB was fully recovered, the wound consisting of a long scar and a lump of tissue that had formed which Christina said may shrink with time. The survivors had carried out more raids into the shops and housing estates to gather as much as they could for the winter. The fishing rods had also been collected and, with some small success, Jonesy had rekindled his love for the hobby.

"Mmm, this is so good," said Sam between mouthfuls of cooked trout.

"Indeed, my compliments to the chef," added Gloria.

Jonesy doffed an imaginary cap as he finished grilling the last of the fish in the oven. The family had been sat around discussing the plan for days, even before DB was on his feet and able to add another expert point of view.

"We have seen all we can see of the prison and its vulnerabilities. I think we stand a good chance of retaking it with minimal loss of life," DB noted, before the conversation moved onto the upcoming battle.

"I hope so, buddy, I really do," Kurt said. He had forced himself to avoid the subsequent reconnaissance missions, where ropes and other items had been secreted for the eventual breach. The boys had taken to the training like a duck to water, Jonesy had remarked on their diligence.

"All things in good time," John cautioned, "We need the boys to show us the layout of the castle."

Sam and Braiden had used some blank paper to draw the perimeter of the castle as best they could remember from the school tour of the previous year. They had loved the opportunity to get away from the classroom for differing reasons; Braiden so he could try his luck with one of the girls in the hidden rooms of the building, Sam so he could study the ancient architecture. Braiden's trespass would be useful when they got inside the mazy hallways of the fortress.

"There are four main entrances," Sam pointed to the crude sketch, "The main gatehouse and courtyard with the drawbridge and portcullis, a second and third gatehouse that used to be the entrance for the markets that took place within the grounds, and lastly a modern entrance for the vehicles to reach the garages set in the north east wall."

Sam pointed at the three sites and their position in relation to the river which ran around the grounds in a southerly direction before veering west, skirting the town before resuming its flow south again. The safest entry points were the main gate and the newly added car gateway, as they lay closest to the fallback of the narrowboat in case they ran into insurmountable danger.

"The most secluded is the vehicle gate, it sits on a track that is hidden by trees. The Duke and Duchess of Norfolk prefer their privacy," Sam continued.

"And the main drawbridge faces the town?" DB asked and Sam nodded.

"It means they are probably swarming around which puts us in a precarious position," Gloria added.

"So it will be safer to take the rear passage," Sarah said.

"Is that an offer?" Kurt couldn't help himself and most of the group burst out laughing, even Gloria covered a sly grin with her hand.

Sarah finally understood the double entendre and slapped his arm, "Here we are planning to lay siege to a castle and all you can think about is sex."

"Sorry," Kurt bowed his head.

"You get me into that place safely," Sarah smiled and winked at him, "Then we can talk."

"What the actual fuck?" Sam spluttered.

"Oh my," Sarah flushed a deep shade of crimson, "Wait! How would you even know what we were talking about?"

"It is twenty sixteen," shrugged Braiden, "We get porn on our phones."

"Well... you shouldn't," she blustered, "You are both banned from porn until you are at least eighteen."

"I don't think they can get it anymore anyway," explained Peter, "The apocalypse has knocked out the power."

"Yeah, I guess you are right," Sarah shook her head at her absurd restriction, "I am so embarrassed."

"Anyway, you were telling us about the entrances," Jonesy deflected the conversation.

"Yes," Sam continued, refusing to meet the eyes of the group, "If I was invading, I would go through the... erm... rear gate."

"That way we can take the main gatehouse from the inside. If we can get to the upper chamber, we can dismantle the mechanisms that have been installed to keep the portcullis raised. As soon as that is sealed, we go wing by wing until the place is ours," Braiden added and Jonesy nodded proudly at Kurt; they were already showing solid tactical decision making.

"It takes us into the north eastern part of the grounds. From there we are out in the open as the main buildings sit to the south. In some ways it helps as we can retreat easily, but we will be totally exposed until we get into the main complex," DB leaned on the table, finger pointing and triceps straining at the sleeves of his combat fatigues.

Peter caught the appreciative glance of the doctor and nudged Kurt, who looked and smiled. Love had been stolen, but now it looked like a new relationship could be blossoming. The level of care she had given the unconscious soldier had gone above and beyond, not simply because of the apocalypse and the need for fighting men.

"If we disembark, how far is it on foot?" Jonesy asked the boys.

"The surrounding areas have public paths for tourists to use, it gives a full tour of the outer perimeter. We are looking at about a quarter of a mile to reach the gate itself," Braiden explained. They had taken the walk as a group before the main visit and he remembered the sense of awe as he regarded the towering battlements.

"It's a straight shot, with good views between the trees. We won't be caught unawares," Sam declared.

"Does anyone have any other ideas, let's hear them?" DB asked.

"I think it is the best option," agreed John, "Worst case scenario is we are forced back to the boat and need to make another plan."

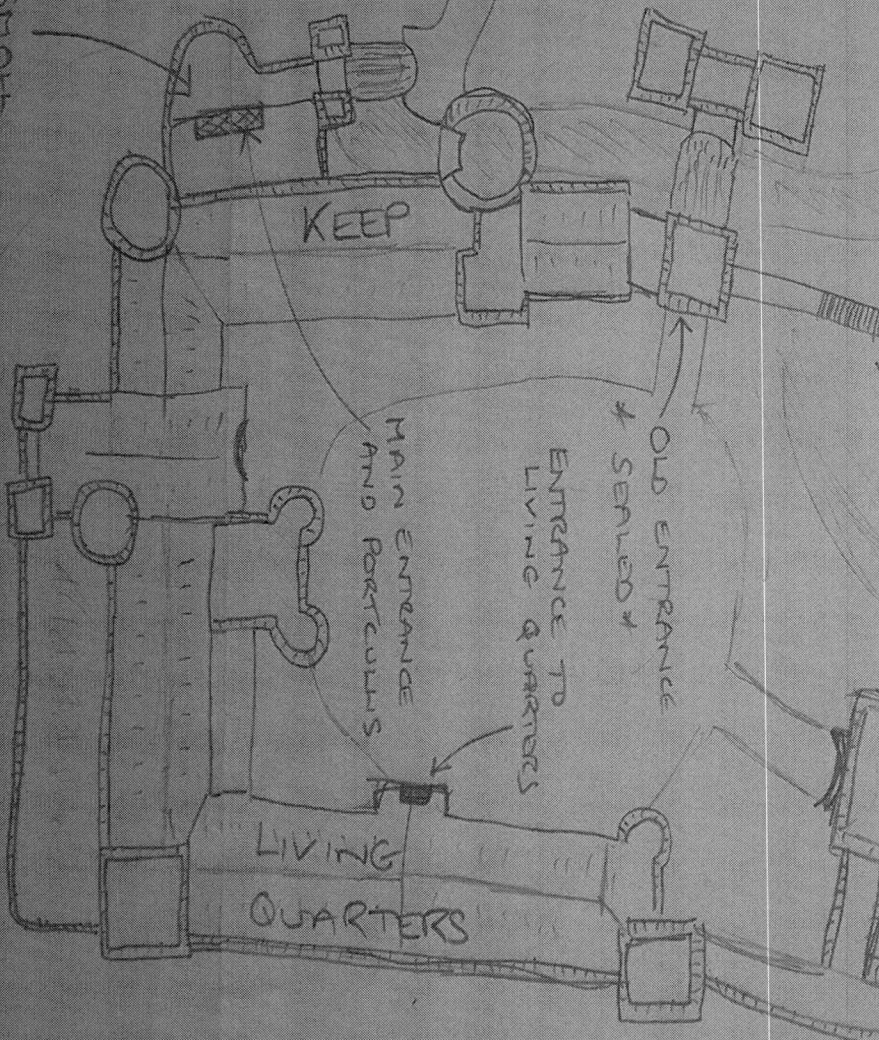

SMALL
COURTYARD

KEEP

MAIN ENTRANCE
AND PORTCULLIS

ENTRANCE TO
LIVING QUARTERS

OLD ENTRANCE
↓ SEALED ↓

LIVING

QUARTERS

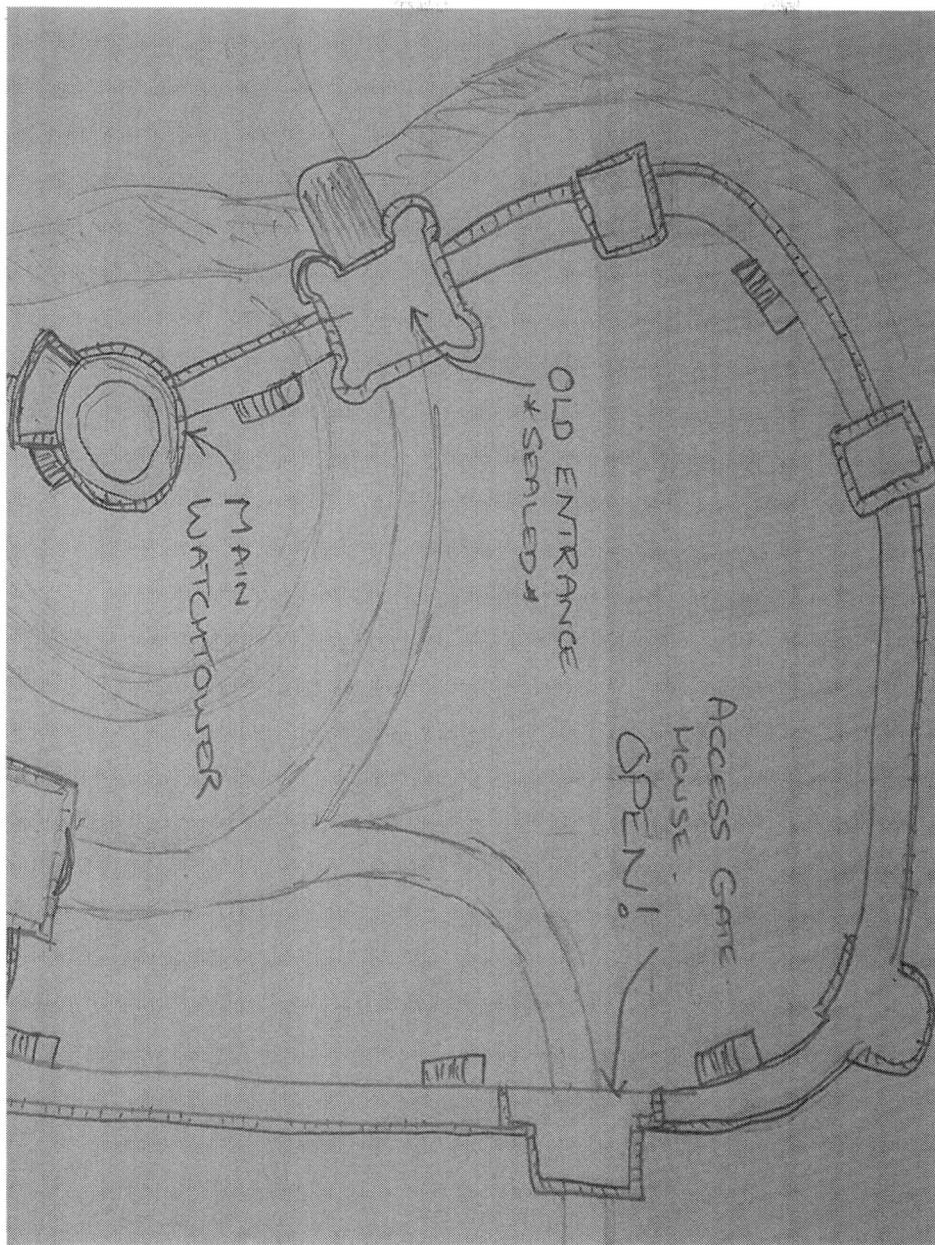

OLD ENTRANCE
★ SEALED ★

MAIN
WATCHTOWER

ACCESS GATE
HOUSE -
OPEN!

CHAPTER TWENTY FIVE

A nervous tension started to manifest in the group as they made their preparations. Christina was charged with piloting the vessel as she had navigated the canal ways and rivers before. The firearms were cleaned again and the handheld weapons were sharpened by a whet stone that had been found with the tools of one home. The blades glinted wickedly in the sunlight that bored through the circular windows into the vessel's lounge.

"It's all yours, Captain," saluted DB and Christina blushed.

The boat was untied and the quiet engine started to propel the craft upriver, against the current. The day was gorgeous, with a cloudless sky. Where once white exhaust trails followed the distant airplanes as they carried excited holiday makers to exotic destinations, now only a couple of birds circled, looking for prey.

"Spooky," Peter grumbled as they floated beneath the burned out train carriage; an empty, metallic corpse.

The charred shell was left in the distance and the panorama opened up into the open fields of the sprawling Sussex farmlands. In any other circumstance, the voyage would have been thoroughly enjoyable, with breathtaking views and a calming lull with every gentle bob on the water. Knowing what lay at the end of this trip left them unable to appreciate anything, and the faint figures that wandered aimlessly in the open lands reminded them of the reality of their situation.

"Heads up," Jonesy called out.

The first homes came into view on the horizon. Construction spanning centuries had grown from the mud as the town had grown, houses of ancient style melding with modern apartments. One thousand years ago, the first stones had been laid for the monolith that now rose above the homes like a cold, grey sentinel. The huge round tower inside the grounds that was raised even higher than the castle keep had acted as a watchtower in the days of knights and squires. The guards would have been able to see for miles around, giving advanced warning so the villagers could seek sanctuary within from any invader. Now they were the invaders, and no guard stood anywhere on the crenellated walls to sound the alarm.

"Stay quiet. Everyone except Christina get out of sight," Jonesy ordered.

The town had two bridges that spanned the rushing water and the dead were in abundance. Lacking the ability to reason, any that caught sight of the slow moving craft could only lean against the protective barrier and groan. The near silent engine purred within its insulated compartment and the sound of lapping waves was insufficient to get the attention of more than a token number of zombies. They were lucky that the stealthy craft could move largely unheard or they would have gathered a sizeable following.

"There are so many, I hope we can seal the castle before they wander in for a visit," whispered Sam to Braiden as they crouched inside the boat, looking out of the windows.

"Wow, look at that," Braiden answered, ignoring Sam's fears.

Backlit by the sun was Arundel Cathedral; a stunning structure in a French Gothic style. Gargoyles looked down on the surrounding houses, acting as sentries and chutes for the rain water that would cascade from the roof. The lead lined windows rose to evenly spaced smaller spires which continued like the tines of a fork around the building. Above the entrance was the main spire, a slate tiled belfry with a golden cross mounted atop to be closer to God. A fantastically intricate rose window had been built facing the castle, the twelve spokes each glazed with colored glass depicting one of Jesus's apostles.

"I can see why people would be drawn to worship in a place like that," Sarah commented.

"Sadly, I think people have been fooled," Gloria added glumly. Her faith used to soar at the sight of the magnificent houses of God. Now they filled her with a sense of mockery, as if the money she donated was used to aid some heinous fraud against the weak minded.

Christina guided the boat around the gradual northerly curve in the river and the town disappeared, concealed by the colossal towers and living quarters of the castle. Trees sprung up and lined the banks as human habitation gave way to nature. She stamped on the deck to indicate they could return topside and the others made their way up the stairs.

"We are going to have to drop anchor and use the portable ramp to get on and off as there is no dock on this stretch of river," Christina informed them all. Even Honey sat down and stared at her, waiting for more instructions.

"Can we be sure it won't float away if we need to retreat?" Peter asked.

"The anchor will hold the old girl steady." Christina patted the steering console.

"That stretch would be ideal." DB pointed to a further bend in the river's course that took them to a point as close as they could get to the castle.

With expertise, Christina guided the canal boat to a safe distance, ensuring it didn't run aground and beach itself.

"We have gone a bit too far, Doc," DB mocked lightheartedly.

She smiled at him and walked casually to the edge, before throwing the anchor overboard. Reversing the throttle, the boat followed the current slowly until finally stopping as the chain pulled taut. The boat was perfectly lined up where he had asked for it to be.

"Happy now?" she asked.

"Well I'll be damned," DB nodded with admiration.

"Not today I…" Gloria had almost said pray, "Hope."

"What can you see?" DB asked Jonesy who was surveying the area between them and the castle with binoculars.

"The gate is wide open, which is good and bad," Jonesy said.

"Bad how?" Peter asked, "It means we don't have to break in or climb over."

"It also means *they* don't need to break in or climb over. From this angle there could be ten thousand waiting for us on the other side of that wall."

Peter visibly blanched at the thought. Jonesy kept staring as if the power of his mind would transform the binoculars into x-ray specs that would give them the answer.

"What about between us and the gate?" DB continued, unfazed by the thought of destroying a few more hundred before the day was over.

"There are about thirty, some of which will need to be taken out on the way. I can't see behind every tree but I think Sam chose wisely on the infiltration point," Jonesy complimented the youngster.

"Ok, we travel light as discussed. Until the portcullis is dropped and that place is ours, the bulk of our goods stays put on the boat." Jonesy was hoping for the best outcome.

The castle was awe inspiring and every second that passed reinforced his belief that it would be a fearsome base. They could house hundreds within the high walls and have no fear of the dead. Food would be another issue entirely, but they were so close to safety he would give it more thought if they lived. The group were ready and stood facing him, weapons ready. Armed and dangerous, he thought, chuckling at the scowls of determination.

"Let's take this mother fucker," growled DB.

CHAPTER TWENTY SIX

The huge soldier dropped the boarding ramp over the edge where it embedded into the soft soil. Securing it to the boat with the inset catches, they disembarked and some of the confidence immediately disappeared. On foot, with no water to keep them safe, it was just them and the herculean task of securing a castle built a millennium ago against the reanimated dead. Peter let out a sick groan and Braiden patted him on the back in support.

"We got this, mate, just like the mine," Braiden said and Peter felt a little better.

"Sorry, just a bit scary. I mean look at that thing!" Peter whispered.

He wasn't wrong. Every step took them closer and, except the dog who was loving the freedom of the fields, the group felt pitiful in its presence. How the hell had medieval soldiers felt, drums banging in time with their march as they advanced on the fortress beneath a rain of arrows?

"Sam, take point with me. Use the slingshot to take out those." Jonesy indicated a group of three zombies who would block their path in seconds.

They all paused while he took careful aim and scored one kill for each bearing, brains bursting from the ruptured skulls. The suppressors had started to fail so Jonesy and DB were reluctant to use them. The near silent coughs were fast becoming more like the full cracks of regular shells. Once

257

separated from the festering zombies by the thick walls, they could fire without being overly concerned about what it summoned.

"Sarah, Jodi, watch our flank," DB ordered and they fell into position.

They had reached the tree lined public paths which would have been heaving with nature ramblers before the horror, even in the cold winter. The wide trunks of the old yew trees offered concealment for waiting monsters, aided by the thick cover of the evergreen branches which cast a dark shadow below. An older zombie staggered towards them, leaving fluids in its wake which burst from bloated pustules. Sarah didn't blink as she ducked below the clutching arms and drove the machete up through the chin and out of the top of its head. DB and Jonesy exchanged glances, proud of their decision to join forces with such resilient and brave individuals. In minutes, the arched gateway loomed high above them and the daylight shone through, revealing nothing in the fifteen-foot-long passageway. A doorway was cut into the stone to the left and right, serving as a means to climb to reach the wall walks.

"We need to get these gates shut," Peter stated, looking at the hollows in the ground for the heavy bolts to drop in.

"Wait, not yet. I want to kill the stragglers so if we need to head back to the boat, we don't have a welcoming committee waiting here for us on the other side," DB explained. "Sam, you're up!"

On their journey, a dozen had caught sight of the group and staggered across the open fields, seeking prey no less eagerly than the buzzards which circled overhead. Sam picked most of them off and those that got too close were hacked apart by the members hiding in the pitch black doorways.

"Get the bodies out of the way," Jonesy whispered, dragging a zombie outside of the grounds.

The rest followed the direction and they piled them at the foot of the walls. It reminded Sam of a painting he had seen of the siege of Constantinople, but he couldn't remember the name of the artist. Soldiers had lain dead in their hundreds as the defenders successfully repelled the attack, ladders had been knocked down and arrows rose from the ground and corpses like feathered decorations.

"Keep to the shadows, I don't want us to be seen," DB slowly leaned around the corner.

The upper bailey portion of the northern castle grounds were roughly four acres of open land, surrounded by the ten-foot-thick, forty-foot-high walls which would hopefully be their salvation. At every hundred feet, a tower rose from the structure to give a better firing angle to archers of the past. To their left stood the main watch tower; a hill mounted circular defensive construction that rose above even the golden cathedral cross. Beyond this was the main Keep and the L shaped living quarters which had been built many years later, in the thirteenth century. It resembled a loose figure-eight which tapered in the center to cut off the upper and lower grounds with the watchtower as cover. A swimming pool was buried in the ground, used by the Duke and Duchess before the world died, no doubt. Now it was dark and murky with algae blooms floating on the surface from lack of chemical treatment.

"We have some sightseers," said DB.

"How many?" asked Jonesy, dreading an answer that would mean a potential suicide mission.

"A few hundred, give or take," DB grinned, "Who's up for a turkey shoot?"

"Peter, seal the gates," Jonesy gave the command, "We take this place now."

The hinges groaned and creaked as the gate was closed to the outside world for the first time in months. The bolts dropped into the ground and Peter slid two more heavy duty latches across, reinforcing the barrier.

RICKY FLEET

"When we have cleared the grounds and gathered our belongings from the boat it would be a good idea to block this entrance with some vehicles. I doubt they could get through, but why take the chance?" John added.

They already felt safer despite the fact they were sealed with hundreds of rotting cannibals, and those were the ones in the open. Who knew how many lurked in the cold and windy corridors of the castle itself.

"We fucking made it!" Kurt punched the air and they all hugged and congratulated themselves in near silence. Honey ran back and forth, sensing the mood of the group and receiving as much attention as she could manage; there were so many hands reaching to stroke her she thought she was in dog heaven.

"I saw the perfect firing position, follow me," DB said and ducked through the northern doorway.

The steps were wet and the stone was cold as they climbed. The passageway was narrow, designed to make any attacks up and onto the battlements as difficult as possible.

"Look at that!" Sam announced, pointing at the wall.

"What? I don't see anything," complained John with a snippy tone.

Sam ignored him and ran his fingers along the furrows gouged into the stone, "Swords have been used in here," he said with awe, the sounds of clashing steel and grunts of exertion created in his mind.

John huffed and carried on, shaking his head. Sam looked hurt as Kurt followed and said, "I see them, mate, can you imagine what it would have been like fighting for your life in here?"

"I know, it's awesome. I'm sorry I annoyed grandad, I thought he might be interested," Sam replied.

"Don't worry about him, he is just on edge. We are so close, but things could still go wrong," Kurt explained and Sam nodded with understanding.

260

DB stopped them at the top of the staircase to give them a warning, "Things are going to get dangerous. Once we start firing, every single one of them will be coming for us until they are fully dead, or we are. Me and Jonesy will provide covering fire, but our main focus will be on dropping as many of those fuckers as possible before they can reach the steps to get up here. Any that make it past will need you to take them out by hand. If anyone has any doubts, now is the time and we can still bail."

Each of them looked from face to resolute face. They had suffered unimaginable hardship to reach this point and to turn back now would be unthinkable, regardless of the coming battle.

"Our family needs this place," Sarah answered for them all and she made sure the two soldiers knew they fell within that category.

"Ok, stay low," Jonesy cautioned as they got into position.

CHAPTER TWENTY SEVEN

The two soldiers laid themselves on the stone, facing south towards the figures which had sensed the new arrivals. The clotted gurgling and groans rebounded within the high walls, seeming to come from all directions. Removing the suppressors, they got as comfortable as possible on the cold, hard wall and pulled their rifles in tight at the shoulder. Sam split the fully loaded magazines and placed them to the side of the soldiers within easy reach for reloading. The others separated themselves evenly to cover both sides of the walkway, blades at the ready and Kurt with his ever faithful hammer.

"On my mark. Three, two, one, NOW!" DB cried out and the assault rifles sang their chattering song of leaden death.

The horde of undead turned as one and began their advance on the survivors. Used to the life and death pressure, the soldiers remained calm as they pulled the trigger and most shots found their mark. The newer turned were gaining faster so they focused their fire on those corpses, heads bursting with the impact of each slug. Kurt and John were competent enough with the grenades to use them as cover, and the small egg shaped lumps bounced at the feet of the approaching dead before detonating. Bodies were ripped asunder but the separate parts kept coming regardless. The group knew the grenades would be near useless at killing and were only hoping to slow the zombies down by a few more seconds for the soldiers to finish off.

"They are gaining ground, this is going to become a real fight," Jonesy shouted. The undead were closing the distance faster than the soldiers could kill them and some were breaking off for the steps which gave access to the walls.

"Do we meet them as they reach the top of the stairs?" Kurt called out over the sharp cracks of the guns.

"No, stay tight. We don't want to split up," DB replied without breaking his firing pattern.

"Dad, throw the last grenades at the steps," Kurt yelled and two more were lobbed.

Several of the dead were already coming up the steps and the proximity of the blast threw them clear, falling in a heap to the ground below. The foam padded box was empty and now it was going to be hand to hand. Sam and Gloria didn't have the luxury of quick reloads like the soldiers and would only delay the assault by a few moments. Bearings whistled and the shotgun bucked, coughing out fire and lead pellets at the monsters.

"They are on the wall!" Peter called out unnecessarily.

"Don't panic, remember the way. Jump forward, strike quick and true, then get back," John ordered.

The first cadavers to take advantage of the lull in gunfire reached the gathered survivors. Slashing quickly, they were cut down and either slumped to the stone or fell from the wall to join the gathering mass below.

"We are going to be overwhelmed!" shouted Jodi as she swung her bat with enough force to lift the zombie over the crenulations. It fell to the outer walkway and splashed green blood up the wall from the impact.

Jonesy and DB had switched to full auto and were spraying the horde indiscriminately. The hundreds they had seen were closer to a thousand, and more were filing up the stone staircases. The walls were awash with the truly dead and dozens more were converging on the group. It was nearly hopeless.

"Brother, I fucked up on the numbers, sorry," DB reached across and patted Jonesy in commiseration. The writing was on the wall.

"Don't give up just yet, if we can hold we may just break them up here," Jonesy snarled and leapt to his feet, "Take the right side!"

It was like a scene from The Lord of the Rings; blades lashing out and rending heads and limbs, the metal clashing with the stonework at times. This is what it must have felt like to be under attack in ancient times, Sam thought to himself as he picked off as many as the slingshot would allow. DB and Jonesy pushed through and let off shot after shot, buying the melee fighters a chance to catch their breath. The clustered zombies below had started to break away and follow their compatriots towards the stone steps.

"It's hopeless, there are too many," Peter complained, starting to panic.

"Fuck!" screamed Kurt furiously, "We were so close!"

"I'm so sorry, everyone, I didn't think there were this many. John and Christina, get the ropes tied off around the merlons, we rappel down and retreat," DB called out.

The group were distraught at coming so close to safety only to have it snatched away by the sheer number of dead. They did as instructed and the ropes dropped to the ground below.

"We won't all make it down before they swarm us," Sarah said, tears flowing freely.

"And how will Honey get down?" cried Braiden.

"We have to leave her, mate, there is no other way." Kurt pulled him close.

"You go; we will hold them back!" Jonesy shouted.

"We aren't leaving you behind!" Christina ran to DB.

"This is on me, sweetheart," DB smiled, "It's my duty."

The bullets ran dry and the guns were useless. Looking at each other the soldiers let out a fierce war cry and surged forward with a machete in each hand, swinging wildly. The group wept for the brave soldier's last stand and with heavy hearts reached for the ropes that would carry them to safety.

"I'm staying," shouted Christina, "If they die, I die."

"But we need you," said Sarah, "You are more valuable than gold in this world."

"I'm sorry." She shook her head and joined the madly flailing troops.

"Shit, what do we do?" Kurt asked the rest of the survivors, torn between fleeing and staying until the bitter end.

"I don't want to be running anymore," Gloria said honestly.

"I won't leave Honey," declared Braiden.

"Jesus Christ," Kurt was more terrified than he had ever been, "Let's do what we can. I love you all so much!"

The group left the ropes and split themselves evenly, joining the soldiers who were enraged they weren't retreating. Their faces left no doubt this was to be all or nothing, they would live or they would die in this battle.

"What the hell?" Peter shouted as the sound of a racing engine caught their attention.

From the lower end of the castle a Jeep was speeding along the road towards them, horn blaring. With a shriek of rubber and a juddering stop, the doors were flung open and six people jumped out, four women and two men. They carried what looked to be swords of varying sizes, from short swords to double handed claymores. If truth be told, most looked even more terrified than Kurt and his family who were fighting on the walls.

"We thought you folks could use some help," shouted a blonde lady in an American accent. She was in her mid-forties and had a look of determination on her face, but no fear.

"You're not wrong," shouted Kurt, a mixture of laughter and crying with relief.

"Get down and look to the sky, we have incoming!" she barked the order in a tone that brooked no argument.

The wall defenders closed back together into a tight group and wondered what she was up to. From the watchtower they heard a voice cry out more commands.

"Draw," came the yell, "Loose!"

In the distance a stream of arrows rose from the circular tower, before streaking down and embedding themselves into the tightly packed dead. They pierced flesh and bone, though not many brains. They were just too inaccurate, but the combined arrival of the Jeep and the hail of missiles was providing a much needed distraction. Dozens of the horde broke away towards the blonde lady and her companions as more arrows fell from the sky. A couple of the sharp projectiles landed very close to the survivors and they pressed together even further to minimize the target.

"Ceasefire!" shouted the stranger after five volleys, and the six rushed forward to meet the zombies head on.

"We have a chance, split up again," said Jonesy and they parted to do battle once more.

On the ground, the newcomers were obviously untried in facing the crumbling monsters. Seeing the advancing horrors, one man shrieked and fled back to the Jeep, stealing the vehicle and driving back towards the safety of the Keep.

"Clive, you fucking asshole," shouted the American woman in disgust as she cleaved another head open with her sword. The remaining man brandished the claymore with relish, swinging wildly and carving the dead. Such was the weight and the power, it slashed effortlessly through the monsters, leaving separate parts at his feet. Raising it above his head, the next zombie was cut neatly in two from the top of its head to the groin.

"Maura, get back here," called another blonde lady amidst the chaos. She was younger by a few years than the leader and tried to reach her companion who had moved off, hacking at the dead.

"They killed my children!" she screamed back, driven insane by repressed grief.

In moments she was surrounded by the horde. With sword in hand the zombies paid a heavy toll as they converged on her. Heads were split open in her frenzy and even as they bit into her flesh, the pain drove her to even greater feats of destruction. Shrieking in rage, she slashed at her killers and more fell to her blade before blood loss took over. With a final surge the zombies overwhelmed her and she collapsed, screaming as they fed.

"Goddamn it!" shouted the leader.

"We have to pull back, there are too many," cried one of the other women as the claymore wielding man was devoured by eager teeth.

"We will retreat back to the forecourt and take some with us, it's all we can do," the leader shouted apologetically.

"Get clear, you have given us a chance. Thank you, whoever you are," yelled Kurt.

"Denise Kinsella." She gave a thumbs up and her group turned and jogged away, covered in the green gore of a battle well fought. As they passed the imposing watchtower she shouted, "Cover our asses."

The hidden archers resumed their barrage and the arrows rained down, affording some protection to their escape.

"Stay tight, use the bodies to slow them down," Jodi said while crushing the head of a female zombie. The bone crumbled with a dull crunch and brain matter splattered over the grey stone.

They followed her advice and DB used his strength to rearrange some of the bodies into a barricade to funnel the zombies. One got within biting distance of his arm and Honey came from nowhere, jumping and hitting the horror in the chest, sending it plummeting from the wall.

"Thanks, girl, you saved my ass," said DB while grabbing at another zombie and effortlessly throwing the skeletal body from the parapet.

"We are going to win!" Kurt shouted with glee.

Their saviors had pulled nearly half of the remaining number back towards the main structure and the relentless march of the dead on the walls was slowing down. Hundreds lay slain below and the walkways were thick with the slumped corpses of the hand to hand fighting. Hope was an infectious emotion and the family could see victory within their sights.

"We aren't out of the woods yet," rebuked John, turning to his son, "Stay focused."

An arm reached from the pile and pulled at John's leg, sending him sprawling. The force had hauled the still living upper half of the zombie free and it bit down, through the trousers and into his thigh. Bellowing in pain, he drove the machete through its eye and into the brain.

"Oh my God," cried Kurt, rushing forward.

Blood flowed freely, covering the pants leg and the stonework. John pulled himself backwards and leaned against the cold embrasure, sighing at his stupid mistake. Kurt ripped off his sleeve and held it to the wound, trying to stem the flow as Christina came to help.

"What can we do? We have to stop the bleeding. Christina, please help him!" Kurt was frantic, but John was calm.

"Son, I'm so proud of you. Your mother will be too," John said, holding a hand to his face, caressing the tear streaked skin.

"Just hold on, we will get you patched up," Kurt sobbed. Christina was tending the wound, but it wouldn't make any difference.

"You carry on protecting our family," John continued, "That is your only concern, do you understand?"

Everyone was crying, even as they carried on the fight with the final zombies. The tears of anguish heralded a fresh burst of energy at the unfairness of the world and the zombies were hacked apart. The punishment meted out was personal, each blow was delivered with a shout of denial and rage.

"Tell Sam I am sorry for the way I spoke to him earlier," John said softly, unable to see his grandson standing only a few feet away as the infection closed down his body in preparation for his rebirth.

"Dad, don't leave me!" Kurt cried out.

"I'm going to see your Mum now, I've missed her these past years," John whispered as the blood slowed to a trickle.

"But I need you!"

"I love you, Kurt," sighed John.

"I love you too, don't go," Kurt pleaded.

John breathed his last, a final exhalation and his eyes rolled, head slumping to his shoulder. Sarah rushed over and held Kurt tight, gently pulling him away from the body of his father.

"Can someone...?" Sarah gasped through the tears, unable to fully articulate the request to destroy the brain of the beloved man.

"I will," offered Gloria who was no less distraught. She crouched down by the body, taking the head and kissing John's forehead, "Goodbye, my love," she whispered, feeling the first stirrings of un-life in him. Using a small knife that DB had handed to her solemnly, she pushed it through his temple with as much tenderness and compassion as was possible. The spasms ceased at once and John was at peace, no longer at risk of stalking the world for the living.

"Grandad!" Sam and Braiden wailed, breaking down.

Heaving sobs shook Kurt as he grieved at the loss of his father, and Sarah pulled the boys in for mutual support through the heartache.

"Kurt, I'm so sorry," Christina said, head bowed in sorrow. The loss was more keenly felt because of the unknown fate of her own parents.

DB, Jonesy, Jodi, and Peter had covered the two sides as the agony of the bereavement took hold.

"Kurt, we need to move. I promise we will honor him later, but until then we have a castle to secure," Jonesy said quietly, squeezing his shoulder in support.

Pulling away from Sarah's tear soaked shoulder, he wiped at his cheeks and a look of pure hatred replaced the sadness in his eyes. Sarah knew the look and held his face tight, locking eyes.

"Don't you go all crazy, do you hear me?" she said sternly. "I can't lose you too."

Some of the fire in his eyes cooled down and he could only nod, his stricken heart still crushed by the death.

"I don't want to chance climbing the bodies on the wall," DB started to explain, but then realized how callous it sounded with John laying only feet away, still warm.

"We will have to use the ropes," Jodi finished and pulled them both up from the outer wall, before tossing them down into the grounds.

Braiden and Sam shimmied down them first, watching the bodies warily. Spaced apart, instead of piled high on the walls, it was much easier to keep an eye out for movement. The wounds were fresh and brains lay dripping on the ground. Sam gave a tearful thumbs- up when it was clear they were safe and Braiden hugged him tight.

"He was a brave man, I was so proud when he called me his grandson," Braiden said.

"I'm going to kill every last one of these Godless mother fuckers!" Sam growled and Braiden nodded in agreement.

"Together we will help retake this world," declared Braiden.

The rest took their turns and the soldiers waited until last, covering the descent. Honey was about to be tied onto the rope to be lowered, but dodged clear of DB and ran the gauntlet of the heaped bodies instead to go down the steps.

"Bad girl!" Sarah shouted with fear as the yellow furred beast guiltily approached, tail between her legs.

"You mustn't go running off like that," Sam said, stroking her head and cooing, using the canine as a form of catharsis.

"Listen, we go first and you stay close. Shout out any target we miss," explained DB when they reached the ground. They had reloaded two magazines for their side arms and stepped carefully over the littered bodies. Most were already dead from the expert marksmanship and any that still moved were dispatched with a double tap, just to be certain.

"Hold your fire!" shouted Jonesy as they neared the watchtower.

A face appeared above, leaning over the edge and made tiny by their distance, "Ok, just yell if you need us."

Jonesy thanked them and the group moved further down towards the courtyard. A circular garden had been totally trampled by the careless wandering dead, and the gravel road circled the once beautiful flower patch to allow visiting dignitaries easier access to the banquet halls. The colorful fletching protruded from the ground as they passed, with a few zombies interspersed with the arrows embedded in the brain.

"They didn't do too bad all things considered," DB acknowledged the skill of the archers.

More than fifty had survived the arrows to follow Denise back to the living quarters. As with all castles, the windows were set high enough to be out of reach and the door was practically impenetrable. The dull thuds of the zombies as they tried to break down the barricade echoed within the walls. The Jeep had been abandoned with the engine still idling by the coward, Clive.

Kurt painfully recalled one of his father's last ideas and asked, "Peter, would you mind taking the Jeep and backing it against the gate?"

"No problem," he answered and climbed aboard.

"I'll go with him, just in case," offered Jodi and they set off.

Peter drove slowly and didn't give it too much gas, ensuring the festering crowd was unaware of the maneuver.

"Do we take them down while they are occupied?" Gloria whispered and Kurt nodded, the hatred burning again.

Spreading out, they butchered the remaining zombies before they could turn around, so intent were they on the people inside. As Peter and Jodi came jogging back, the inches thick door groaned open on old hinges and Denise rushed out to greet them all. More people hovered in the background, worried faces peering out on the savage looking strangers. The younger blonde pushed through, pouring scorn on the scared occupants.

"No thanks to you we made it and helped to save these people," she glowered at them as she passed.

"We can't thank you enough for putting yourselves in harm's way." Jonesy shook hands with Denise who waved away the praise.

272

"We couldn't just sit by and watch while you took them on," she replied.

"Some of us did though," sneered the younger woman who held out her hand, "I'm Louise Kelly."

"It really is a pleasure to meet you both. We are sorry for your loss," Gloria said, knowing how much it hurt.

"They were great people," Louise said thoughtfully, "Maura Butler was the lady and Greg Austin was the guy with the massive sword; we became good friends. Clive is going to pay for what he did."

"None of us have gone against them before though, he just panicked," Denise tried to explain.

"Then he should have stayed behind!" Louise argued. It was clear it wouldn't be the last they heard of this.

"Who was watching out for us from above?" asked Jonesy, looking up at the watchtower.

"That was some of the members of the school who were visiting when this all happened," Denise said and ushered them inside.

"Wait," Kurt stopped them, "Before we relax, have you dropped the portcullis?"

"No, we have sealed off the main Keep and areas that are open to the public," Louise answered.

"We have been hiding in the private wing of the castle. They flooded in over the drawbridge and nothing was going to hold them back," Denise added, shuddering at the memory of trying to save as many as she could from the hungry dead.

"What are you thinking, Kurt?" DB wondered.

"I think now is as good a time as any to bring our supplies in. I would be happier taking the Keep with you guys fully armed," he said, "We can set up fallback positions too with the light machine guns."

Jonesy looked at DB and nodded, "I agree, we can use the Jeep and load it up. It will take a fraction of the time that it would on foot."

"Wait just one minute!" whined a nasal voice from inside and a man in a crumpled suit pushed through. "What makes you think you are going to be staying? This is private land and belongs to the Duke and Duchess of Norfolk. There are quite enough commoners traipsing around where they shouldn't be, you will be leaving right now!"

The scared looking people lowered their heads in guilt at the implication they were a burden, but Kurt had had quite enough of being told what he could and couldn't do. Grabbing him by the throat, he drove him back against the stonework with enough power to knock his spectacles loose.

"I have killed hundreds of the zombies, and enough of the living to haunt my dreams until the day I die. My dad is lying dead on the walls of this fucking place. If you think you have what it takes to kick me out, give it your best shot," Kurt growled, holding the green coated head of the hammer to the man's throat.

"But the castle is owned by the Duke and Duchess, you can't be here," he protested in spite of the danger.

Kurt's lips smiled but his eyes were ice, "I think you will find it belongs to us now. While you have been hiding, we have travelled from Emsworth through this undead wasteland. When your Duke and Duchess come home, they can fight their way through a thousand decaying carnivores and I will consider sharing it."

Kurt released him and the man blustered back into the castle, "You haven't heard the last of this!"

Kurt needed a release that would prevent him killing the obnoxious little man, and he saw the fallen glasses. With a feeling of satisfaction, he ground the lenses beneath his boot heel and they crunched into pieces.

"You are nothing more than a common ruffian!" squealed the man who had returned to reclaim the spectacles. "Scum like you should have been the first to die."

"Now you've done it," cautioned Louise who stepped out of Kurt's way.

"Please, allow me," Denise said and jabbed the man in the throat. It was a snappy punch with enough power to incapacitate, but not enough to crush the trachea and kill him. Eyes bugging, he fell to the floor, hacking and coughing through his damaged airway.

"Denise just saved your life," Kurt growled and picked up the broken and twisted frames, before placing them on his reddened face, "Get out of my sight, you rancid little prick, or I will end you."

Another man hurried forward to help, and they retreated into the darkness. Some of the group inside were grinning at the rough justice and Kurt couldn't begin to imagine what it must have been like to be trapped with him. A change of leadership was long overdue.

A young girl came running from the doorway, "Miss. Lunsford wanted me to tell you that the noise has attracted more of those things, she can see them in the distance," she detailed breathlessly, then smiled at Sam. "I'm glad you made it, I'm Holly."

"There's no time to waste then. Thanks, Holly," said Jonesy.

"Yeah. Thanks, Holly," said Sam, cheeks flushing.

"Come on, Casanova," chuckled DB.

"Who's Miss. Lunsford?" Kurt asked Denise.

"Stephanie is their teacher," Denise replied, "She is a lover of history and archery. The longbows are still in good working order from all the reenactments that are held here apparently."

The narrowboat was cleared without incident and they said a farewell to the sturdy vessel. If circumstances allowed they would try and maintain it but with the dead swarming, it was unlikely. Medicines, weapons, ammunition, food, and farming equipment were brought into the castle. As they had been informed, hundreds more zombies were making their way across the fields, attracted by the gunfire and explosions. Their sanctuary would render them harmless and Kurt allowed himself a melancholy smile; they had made it.

"Baby, we need to get inside now," Sarah said, leading him away the boat.

Driving through the gateway, Peter jumped out and locked the gates before Kurt backed the Jeep against them. They walked out into the light and Kurt looked around at the death, then found himself looking at the slumped body of John in the distance.

"We will give him a proper ceremony tomorrow, I promise," Gloria offered.

A group of young people came running up from the entrance, plucking the arrows from the ground and placing them in baskets. The girl smiled at Sam again and Braiden elbowed him in the ribs playfully.

"Who's your girlfriend?" he teased.

"Shut up," Sam protested, blushing again.

"Sorry, mate. She's a fine one for sure, keep an eye out and see if she has a pretty friend." Braiden winked and laughed, then fell silent as the recent loss reasserted itself.

"Dad, can we go and help, there are a lot of arrows," Sam asked, eager to have any activity to take his mind off the death of his grandfather.

"Ok, but be careful. Watch for movement and warn them to do the same, they are running around thinking the zombies are guaranteed to be dead," Kurt pointed out and the boys rushed off to be with kids their own age.

"Boys, we will meet you inside," Sarah shouted and they both waved an acknowledgement.

"We can always recharge our batteries and take the Keep tomorrow if you want," Jonesy offered Kurt, but he shook his head.

"I won't sleep until that metal barrier is in place."

"You won't be any use to us if your minds elsewhere," DB added, his huge hand rubbing Kurt's back in support.

"I know what you are saying, guys, but I can lock it down. After this I will need some time to myself to grieve, but right now I need to fight," he said with conviction and the soldiers understood the feeling all too well.

CHAPTER TWENTY EIGHT

The fighters gathered their wits in one of the reception rooms. The high ceilings were molded with beautiful plaster diamonds, and the walls were adorned with carved mahogany paneling and bookshelves. The first edition hardbacks were priceless and the glass frontages were firmly locked to keep the nosy interlopers at bay. An old fireplace with soot streaked stone lay set back from a stunningly patterned iron mantel, lions roaring fiercely with paws raised.

"How many of you are there?" asked Kurt as he reclined on the comfortable sofa, staring at the ceiling. The patterns calmed him as he traced their intricate design.

"About fifty, roughly half and half of staff and public. I was just visiting with my friend Patricia Statham when the shit hit the fan," Denise answered and a dark haired lady from across the room waved a greeting.

"How have you survived?" DB asked, "I mean I know you have barricaded yourself in here, but that's a lot of food and water."

"There were a ton of food supplies when we took cover. The delivery driver had only just left according to the chef so the larders are full. Not that it stops that righteous asshole Mr. Vincent from complaining every time we have a meal," Denise replied, scowling at the doorway which led to his office.

"Mr. Vincent?" Kurt wondered, "My new best friend?"

"You got it, babes," laughed Patricia as she joined them, "He can go to hell if he thinks he is taking my glasses to replace his though."

"I think Denise would probably just throat punch him again," Sarah smiled.

"It felt so good," she admitted, mimicking the jab again.

"Where do you sleep?" Gloria asked.

"There is an old storeroom on the ground floor," Patricia explained, "They cleared some space and we use the old mattresses. I swear we had to kick the rats out before we could move in."

"Are there no bedrooms in this wing then?" Kurt asked, looking around the room at the tired faces.

"Yeah, but we aren't allowed in them. Mr. Vincent has them all locked and the keys hidden," Denise said.

"I swear I'm going to toss that vile little cunt from the walls," Kurt growled.

"Kurt, language!" Sarah gasped, "There are ladies present."

"I ain't no lady," Denise laughed, "I can swear with the best of them. I was a Buffalo police officer before retiring."

"Sorry," sighed Kurt, "Sarah's right. It's been a tough day, please accept my apologies."

"None needed, honey," Patricia said, "Y'all have been through the mill today."

"Did I hear you say you were in the police department?" asked Jonesy and Denise nodded.

"So you are proficient with firearms?" DB added.

"We both are," Patricia acknowledged.

"That will make the demonstrations so much easier when it comes to teaching the rest of the folks about maintenance and shooting," DB grinned.

"That's if you don't mind helping us?" Jonesy asked.

"Of course not, sweetie," she clapped her hands in excitement, "I have been bored to tears just sitting here. I want to come with you when you retake the main Keep too."

"The more guns the merrier," Kurt agreed, "But I was thinking about trying to retake it as quietly as possible."

"The suppressors are finished, mate, we don't have any spares," DB explained.

"I wasn't thinking about guns," he said cryptically, "Where is the teacher, Miss. Lunsford?"

"I think I saw her putting the last of the arrows and bows back into storage. Why?" Patricia wondered.

"If what the guides say is true, which I don't doubt as Braiden has confirmed it too, is that there are three long corridors until the portcullis room. If we go out all guns blazing, then the whole town could come for a visit," Kurt explained.

"And the alternative is?" Gloria wondered.

"We get the students to come with us armed with the bows and arrows and line up, one row kneeling and one behind standing. We know they have skills and if they can take out the zombies quietly, we can drop the portcullis without drawing in any more to deal with."

"And as soon as that gate is in place, we can go all shock and awe on their asses," whooped Denise.

"Exactly," Kurt slammed his palm down on the arm of the chair.

"Holly?" Sarah called as the young girl returned with Sam and Braiden, their recovery mission over.

"Yes, Miss?" she answered, walking over.

"Call me Sarah. Now don't feel under any pressure or obligation, but Kurt wanted to ask you a question," she said and Kurt stood up to face her.

"How confident do you feel with those bows, Holly?"

"Pretty good I guess, why?" she asked cautiously.

"And the rest of the class?"

"We have all been practicing, even though that awful Mr. Vincent complains every time we use the equipment," Holly replied.

"You have heard we plan to take the Keep today, and by dropping the portcullis we will be totally sealed in and safe from the zombies," Kurt started to explain, "I would like you and some of your class to cover us in the hallways so we can destroy them in silence."

"I'm not sure," she sounded afraid, "Miss. Lunsford won't like it and it won't be like shooting them from up high where we were safe."

"I understand, sweetheart, it was only an idea." Kurt smiled and sat back down.

"I'm not saying I won't do it," she rushed forward after looking at Sam, "Will you all be there to protect us?"

"Absolutely," Kurt responded, "We will be between you and the dead, but to the side obviously. We wouldn't want to become pin cushions."

Holly giggled, "So we won't really be in any danger?"

"Not if I am there as well," said Sam.

"None at all. DB, Jonesy, and Denise will be fully armed with the guns," Kurt pointed out.

"Don't forget me," called out Patricia.

"And Patricia," Kurt smiled, "If it looks at all like the plan won't work, you will fall back and we protect you with bullets and axes."

"Don't forget deadeye with his slingshot," Braiden added, pointing at Sam.

"Are you really that good with it?" Holly sounded impressed.

"Better," confirmed Braiden as Sam started to blush again.

"Would you mind running off and finding the rest of your class and Miss. Lunsford? See if they are prepared to risk it and then bring them back if they are," Kurt said and the girl hurried away.

"Do you really think it's a good idea taking the children with us?" asked Jodi.

"Possibly not, but you saw the faces of the people when we arrived, they were terrified. If the kids can take the lead and have a hand in the fighting, we may be able to get the rest of them on board. I'd rather have fifty seasoned fighters than just the ten of us," Kurt's logic was undeniable.

"Ladies, are you familiar with the Glock Seventeen?" DB handed over the two pistols for perusal.

"I would be happier with my trusty three-fifty-seven Smith and Wesson, but this will do," said Denise, snapping the magazine home and chambering a round.

Holly came running back into the room smiling, "They all want to help, but Miss. Lunsford says she has to come too."

"Thank you, Holly," came a new voice from the hallway and a lady with short, red hair and pink framed glasses walked in.

"Miss. Lunsford, I presume?" Kurt said, offering his hand which she shook with a firm grip.

"Yes, you must be Kurt," she replied with a warm smile.

"I wanted to thank you for saving us earlier, it was a brave thing to do."

"You are most welcome, I'm just sorry we couldn't save all of you," she said with a look of sorrow.

"Dad will be watching us, happy that we made it I'm sure," he answered, emotions bubbling below the surface until he shook himself.

"You need our help again?" she asked, seeing his discomfort and changing the subject.

"Did Holly explain what I would like to do?"

"Yes, and as long as I go, I think it is probably the best way to secure the castle. I have been training them as much as possible in case we ever took the chance, but we lacked the firepower that you bring," Stephanie told them.

Ten minutes later the students were ready. Peter had offered to be the arrow carrier as well as hand to hand back up with his machete. DB, Jonesy, Denise, and Patricia were locked and loaded and the rest of Kurt's group was tooled up with axes, machetes and a couple of swords. The long shanked blades were not the cheaply produced store bought imitations, carrying the nicks and dents of ancient battles embedded in the time worn steel.

"The most important thing to remember is don't panic," Jonesy explained to the rapt youngsters, "Take your time, pick your target carefully. If any get too close, the melee fighters will take them down. If it looks like there may be too many, we retreat under our covering fire." He indicated DB, Patricia, and Denise.

"Brother, as soon as we get through that door we could use the light machine guns as a fallback," DB added as the others gathered behind the group.

"That's actually not a bad idea," Jonesy agreed, "Has anyone here served in the military?"

One of the elderly groundskeepers stepped forward, "I was in the Army from sixty-two to seventy-eight."

"Do you feel confident enough to cover the doorway with one of the LMG's?" DB asked.

He turned the gun over and looked at the feeding mechanism and trigger, "I think I can do that."

"Good man," Jonesy said, "The rest of you, could we have some volunteers to carry these tables through to place the guns on."

Several people stepped forward, eager to help in any way that didn't involve actually fighting the undead. Even Mr. Vincent was lurking in the shadows and Gloria had been instructed to ensure he didn't try to sabotage the attempt.

The students nocked their arrows and kept the bows lowered, sweating in fear at the door as the barricade was removed. No moans or thuds could be heard which might mean the hallway would be deserted, but they wouldn't take any chances. Twisting the heavy metal key, the lock disengaged and the door was pulled open, revealing the long expanse. The nearest zombie was twenty feet away and heard the creaking hinges. It turned and the students shrank back, the pitted and festering visage ghastly in the morning light.

"Just like you trained, straight lines are your friend," Sam stated and stepped forward. The slingshot pinged and one of the last of his bearings ripped cleanly through the skull, staining the expensive rug.

Sam's bravery served to embolden them; if he could do it, so could they and they raised their bows. The arrows whistled down the corridor, more lethal at range than the rounded balls. The first volley missed totally, mistimed releases and shaky hands throwing the shots off. Braiden and Sam went between them, providing encouragement and advice about controlling their fear. The second volley was more precise and the arrows stuck out from the bodies of the dead, one even falling from a shaft through the eye.

"Way to go," Sam whispered quietly, patting them all on the back.

Peter leaned in and they each took a fresh arrow, the protection of the soldiers and the fearsome looking newcomers filling them with more confidence.

"Again," Braiden ordered and Kurt couldn't help but smile at the maturity he was showing. Jonesy winked and looked every inch like a proud father.

More arrows whined and the first section of the castle corridor was cleared. Members of the rear guard made up of the castle staff lifted two tables through and placed them to the sides, before lifting the machine guns into place. The Army veteran took up position and gave a brisk salute to the others as they moved down the poorly lit hall. Dust motes drifted in the beams of weak sunlight, disturbed by the deadly activity.

"Are those doors locked?" DB asked from their fortified position, indicating the archways which gave access to various function rooms, dining rooms and activity suites for the paying public.

"We didn't have time," explained Denise.

"Ok, one at a time," Kurt moved forward and cautiously tapped the hammer on the stonework, luring any hidden threat out and taking cover to avoid the missiles. A few more undead joined the fray and were laid low by the increasing skill of the archers.

"We move down the corridor one doorway at a time. Sarah, would you mind taking the keys and locking the rooms behind us so we don't have any nasty surprises?" Kurt asked and she took the large bunch, holding them tightly to prevent any unnecessary jangling.

The group moved slowly, leaving nothing to chance and neared the first corner to the next hallway. Sarah sealed the rooms, but not before marveling at the antiques, paintings and general beauty of the decor. In the back of her mind she knew that it was a sign of a turning point in their fortunes, the castle would be their sanctuary while decisions were made on the next steps of survival.

"Wait here," Peter whispered and went from body to body, pulling any loose arrows free and putting them in the basket. Some were buried deeply in bone and would need to be carefully pried out after the fighting was done.

Kurt put a finger to his lips and peered around the bend. More awaited, but in manageable numbers so the group moved as one and set up position again. The bows twanged, arrows sailed through the air and zombies fell dead to the floor as the steel tipped heads shattered through skulls at short range. The tapestries that hung from the walls depicted ancient battles, from Agincourt to Hastings, and he wondered if some day images of their bravery would be preserved for posterity. The armies of the living against the armies of the dead captured with intricate weaving. An hour had passed, the progress less than a foot a minute, but they reached the destination safely and with the students filled with hope for the first time in weeks. The fates of their loved ones were unknown, though not hard to imagine, so the chance to fight back was a remedy, albeit a violent one, to their feelings of helplessness.

"Can you cover the entrances?" Kurt asked the group and the students split into three four people sections, bows raised at the ready.

From the main gate guard room, the sides led left to the upper Keep and right out onto the upper walls. All would need to be cleared at some point, but for now the end was within reach.

"So how does this work?" DB asked, looking at the chains and pulleys.

"Those lumps of steel to the side are the counterweights," Sam indicated three blocks of metal joined to the thick chains, "As soon as we work out how to free them, we can then lower the portcullis."

Kurt pulled on them and nothing happened as expected. The public had access to this room and the last thing the owners needed was an accident with someone messing around with the massive iron frame. The chain links fed downward and they could see daylight from their position, hundreds of the dead milling around in the courtyard after being drawn in by gunfire that had now ceased.

"There!" Jonesy pointed and three heavy bolts had been drilled into the stonework, securing the chains in place.

Kurt tried to pry them out with the claw of his hammer but they were too thick. Shrugging he told the group, "Get ready, this is going to be noisy."

Swinging the hammer, the chains rattled with each blow and the noise echoed down every cold hallway of the Keep. It took nearly twenty strikes before the stone crumbled and the bolt dropped onto the fevered zombies below.

"We are going to have company, I can hear them coming," warned Stephanie, "Students, get ready."

"Fuck the noise, we don't have the element of surprise anymore," DB called out over the jangle of beaten chains.

"Two down!" Kurt shouted as the next chain fell free.

Zombies had answered the clarion call and filed through the arched openings, only to be met by a barrage of ammunition spanning thousands of years. Arrows joined the high velocity bullets and by the time Kurt had broken the third bolt, the doorways were filled with so many corpses, any freshly arrived undead struggled to get through the meaty barricade.

"Sam, Braiden, on me," Kurt said and the three pulled hand over hand, the counterweights rising as the protective barrier of cross hatched steel fell.

The sharp points of the iron crushed down through the gathered dead, pinning them to the ground in a welter of green fluid. The noise of the metal meeting the stony ground was a sound filled with such relief that Kurt would have swooned and fell to the floor if they weren't still under attack. Finally, all the hurt, the danger, the horror, had culminated in the securing of the fortress for the living. Once the grounds had been washed clean of the taint of death, the family could relax and enjoy a brief respite as the winter set in.

"Fall back to the living quarters, we will finish the sweep tomorrow," Jonesy yelled, "Students first, GO!"

The youngsters gladly made a break and dodged between the fallen carcasses on the floor. Denise and Patricia were proving invaluable, picking their targets and scoring one clean headshot for each bullet.

"Now you, ladies," DB said, moving to cover them.

"Hell no, sweetie, we got your back," Patricia grinned, loving the action.

"Y'all get back and man the machine guns, we got these fuckers for now," Denise ordered with authority and the rest of the group complied, running back to the protection of the old soldier.

DB passed his rifle through to Gloria and manned the second gun. Jonesy knew what was coming and handed out three packs of ear plugs. The veteran just smiled and shook his head.

"Son, I'm deaf as a post already, a few more gunshots won't make any difference."

Squeezing them in tight, the sounds of their surroundings faded away into silence.

"Get back through the door, you don't want to hear this," DB said, the words muffled and odd sounding.

Everyone moved back reluctantly, then pushed the door until it was nearly closed. The two women came jogging around the bend sporting wide grins as if they were having a blast.

"We brought you some friends," Denise remarked as she fell in behind the waiting troops and ducked through into the reception room.

In seconds a steady line of corpses who had pressed though their fallen comrades staggered around the corner only to be met by a hail of white hot lead. The machine guns chattered in small bursts and the undead would have fared better being fed into a meat grinder. Unable to understand the need to take cover, they came on undaunted and were chewed up by the fragmenting bullets. The work of two short minutes had piled the bodies high, with holes riddling the walls and ceiling. A torrent of flesh slowed to a trickle and the machine guns were laid gently down in favor of the assault rifles.

"Thank you, son," remarked the old man with a quick salute, "Brought back some fond memories."

Jonesy couldn't hear a word of it and just smiled, before taking aim and letting off single rounds. The zombies that were able to pinpoint the raucous disturbance had all been destroyed, and the murky green ooze was slowly spreading down the hallway from the torn bodies, running into the cracks in the stone floor.

"That's the last of them for now," Jonesy said, joining the others.

"I'll get the LMG's," Sam offered and Braiden followed, lifting the spent weapons.

"The barrels will be red hot, be careful," cautioned DB and they rolled their eyes as if to say 'we aren't that dumb'.

"We can't know how many are left waiting for us, but for now I need to lay down and sleep for a month," Kurt said as Sarah locked the door.

"Shall we build the barricade again?" asked one of the adults who had stayed behind.

"Yes please," Sarah replied, "We can move it when we make our final sweep."

Cheers of jubilation erupted from the room as people introduced themselves to the brave strangers. The family watched as Kurt made directly for Mr. Vincent who was the only one with a scowl on his face.

"Keys to the bedrooms," Kurt held out a blood soaked hand, "Now."

The weasel eyes flicked from the hand to Kurt's face through his broken glasses, weighing whether to press the issue.

"I said *now*," Kurt growled, taking the hammer from his belt.

"I'll go and fetch them," said Mr. Vincent, conceding defeat. Not that there was much of a battle of wills anyway, Kurt would have simply locked him in the corridor for any new arrivals to devour.

"Aren't you going to join in the celebration?" Sarah asked as she joined him.

"Not right now, love. I want to be alone for a while," he replied with a weary smile.

Embracing him, she noticed the rapid onset of greying hair, a sign of the mental weight he had carried for the past weeks of their living hell. The hated curator returned and handed over the keys with a haughty disdain, almost throwing them at Kurt. Breaking contact with Sarah, she mussed his hair and returned to her sons and their new friends.

"Your attitude had better change by the time I wake up, or you will be leaving *my* castle," Kurt said as he walked past.

"Your castle," he snorted with derision until Kurt turned and handed him an axe. Looking at the hatchet, Mr. Vincent didn't immediately understand the implication of the gesture.

Taking out his hammer, Kurt got into a fighting stance, ready to take on the sneering nobody in a fight to the death. With a shriek of fear, the man threw the tool on the ground and held his hands high, submitting.

"Yeah, my castle," Kurt walked away, ignoring the small puddle of urine spreading around the feet of the coward.

A NOTE FROM THE AUTHOR

I hope that you continue to enjoy the thrill ride that is the Hellspawn series. I have met some really wonderful people throughout this process and am grateful for the new friendships. The story continues and book four will be started in the near future. In the meantime I'm finishing starting the beta reading process for my first book in a demon series (nope, still don't have a title yet!) which will be released early 2017.

For upcoming news about future books, info about contests and prizes, or if you just want to stalk and harass me, please follow me on my Facebook page at

www.facebook.com/Author-Ricky-Fleet

And on my publisher's page at

www.facebook.com/OptimusMaximusPublishing/

www.optimusmaximuspublishing.com

AUTHOR BIO

Ricky Fleet has been a lifelong horror fan ever since he was (almost) old enough to watch the original Romero trilogy. Those shambling horrors gave birth to an insatiable appetite that has yet to be sated. After spending years in the plumbing trade, he then decided to start teaching, passing on his knowledge to the next generation of engineers.

Born and raised in the UK, cups of tea are a non-negotiable staple of the English life and serve as brain fuel for his first love, writing.

Today he shares his time between his real life students and the students of the zombie apocalypse in his first series: Hellspawn. At least the fictional students do as they're told. Most of the time anyway.

CHECK OUT THE OMP WEBSITE FOR
A COMPLETE LIST OF OUR TITLES

WWW.OPTIMUSMAXIMUSPUBLISHING.COM

BOOKS ARE AVAILABLE IN BOTH PRINT
AND ELECTRONIC FORMATS

RICKY FLEET

HELLSPAWN

SERIES

10.35 AM, September 14th 2015. Portsmouth, England.

A global particle physics experiment releases a pulse of unknown energy with catastrophic results. The sanctity of the grave has been sundered and a million graveyards expel their tenants from eternal slumber.

The world is unaware of the impending apocalypse, Governments crumble and armies are scattered to the wind under the onslaught of the dead.

Kurt Taylor, a self-employed plumber, witnesses the start of the horrifying outbreak. Desperate to reach his family before they fall victim to the ever growing horde of shambling corruption, he flees the scene.

In a society with few guns, how can people hope to survive the endless waves of zombies that seek to consume every living thing? With ingenuity, planning and everyday materials, the group forge their way and strike back at the Hellspawn legions.

Rescues are mounted, but not all survivors are benevolent, the evil that is in all men has been given free rein in this new, dead world. With both the living and dead to contend with, the Taylor family's battle for survival is just beginning.

Book 1 in the Hellspawn series.

Kurt Taylor and his family have battled the living and the dead and now find themselves on the run, their home reduced to ashes. With unimaginable horror lying in wait around every corner, the onset of winter and the plunging temperatures only add more danger to their precarious existence. They decide to forge ahead and try to reach the protection of others who have hopefully survived the zombie apocalypse. If this fails, their only choice would be to try and reach an impregnable fortress, a sanctuary that has stood for a thousand years.

Standing between them and salvation are the villages and cities of the damned, a path that will test their spirit and resilience unlike anything they have faced before. More companions are rescued from the jaws of death and join them in their perilous journey. Mysterious attacks befall the group and it becomes clear the dead aren't the only things that lurk in the darkness.

Tempers fray and personalities clash. The group starts to fracture and Kurt is forced to commit acts that cause him to question his own morality. Can they survive the horror of their new existence? Will they want to?

The Hellspawn saga continues.

BALLYMOOR, IRELAND, 1891

Patrick Conroy, a young American student of medicine in Dublin, decides to take a break from the hustle and bustle of the big city and spend a month in the quietude of the wild and beautiful Glencree valley, County Wicklow. However, surrounded by local legends and myths, he is soon dragged into an ancient mystery that has haunted the village of Ballymoor for centuries. Set on the background of the tumultuous years preceding the War of Independence, and colored by Irish folklore, the Haunter of the Moor is a ghost story written in the style of Victorian Gothic novels.

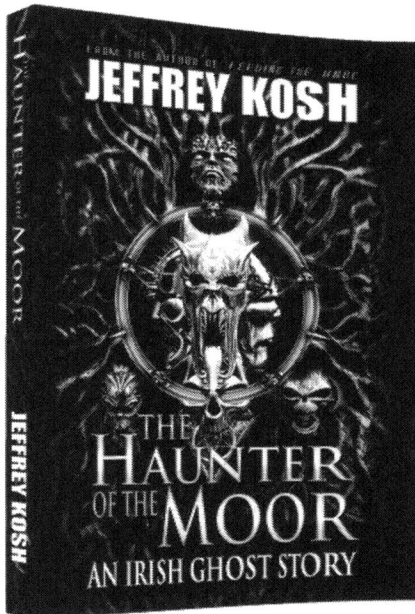

To Fight Evil with Evil

England, 1392.
As the Black Death quickly spreads through the kingdom, the little hamlet of Blythe's Hollow suffers under the yoke of a sadistic Lord. Desperate, the villagers decide to seek out the magical help of a local witch, causing the wrath of the Church. Torture and murder befall on those accused of being in league with the Devil, adding more sorrow to the beset folk of Blythe's Hollow. Yet, one man will rise against the tyranny; a man willing to learn Black Magick to fight back.

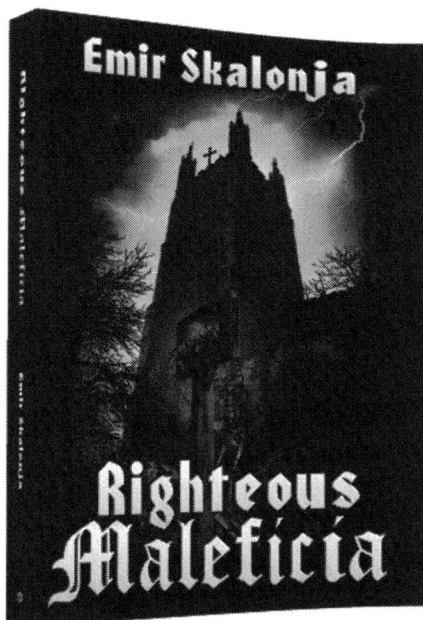

A modern dark urban fantasy, telling of two powerful families who uphold a secret duty to protect humanity from a threat it doesn't know exists.

Though sharing a common enemy, the two families form a long-standing rivalry due to their methods and ultimate goals.

Forces are coalescing in a prominent Central European city criminal sex-trafficking, a serial murderer with a savage bent, and other, less tangible influences.

Within a prestigious, private university, Lilja, a young librarian charged with protecting a very special book, finds herself suddenly ensconced in this dark, strange world. Originally from Finland, she has her own reason for why she left her home, but she finds the city to be anything but a haven from dangers and secrets.

Book One in a planned series.

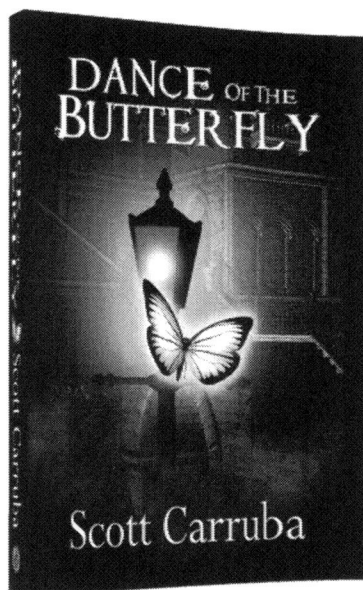

DANCE OF THE BUTTERFLY

Scott Carruba

Meet Mason Ezekiel Barnes, former NFL tackle turned successful author of the naughty ninja adventure series Mia Killjoy. Mason is obsessed with winning a Pulitzer and is thwarted by his fellow author and nemesis, the twerpy little gnome Conrad Bancroft.

Perk Noir is full of comedic relief, pop culture, NFL, jazz, a little touch of romance, and flashbacks of Lightning and his family during both the first half of the 20th century and later during the Civil Rights movement. Mason and Shelly and their adventures is a fun filled thrill ride that will appeal to all readers, there is something for everyone at the Perk.

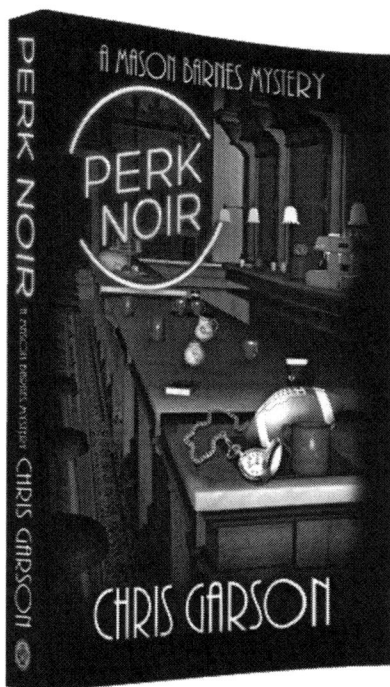

Two hunters pursue the same prey.

Fate has forged the slayer, Trey Thomas and the Sandrian vampire, Adalius, two natural enemies, into an uneasy alliance against an evil more powerful than either have ever faced. Only together do they stand a chance of defeating Anna; if they don't destroy each other first.

As they pursue Anna, the apprehensive Lycan watch as a confrontation looms on the horizon between vampires, the New Bloods and the Old Guard, which threatens to plunge the vampire world into civil war and trigger an all-out supernatural conflict which in the end could destroy them all.